DATE DUE

Dragonfly
Song

Dragonfly Song

WENDY ORR

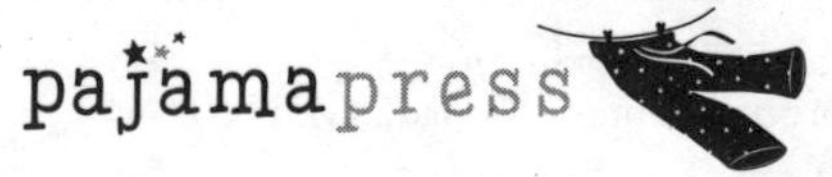

First published in Canada and the United States in 2017

Originally published by Allen & Unwin: Crow's Nest, New South Wales, Australia, 2016

10 9 8 7 6 5 4 3 2 1

www.pajamapress.ca info@pajamapress.ca

Canada Council for the Arts Conseil des arts du Canada

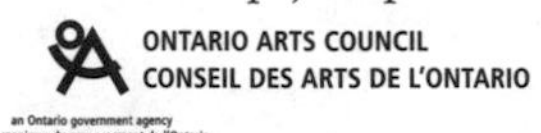

Canada

The publisher gratefully acknowledges the support of the Canada Council for the Arts and the Ontario Arts Council for its publishing program. We acknowledge the financial support of the Government of Canada through the Canada Book Fund (CBF) for our publishing activities.

Library and Archives Canada Cataloguing in Publication

Orr, Wendy, 1953-, author
Dragonfly song / Wendy Orr.
Previously published: Crow's Nest, New South Wales, Australia: Allen & Unwin, 2016.
ISBN 978-1-77278-037-6 (hardcover)
I. Title.
PS8579.R77D73 2017 jC813'.54 C2017-902606-2

Publisher Cataloging-in-Publication Data (U.S.)

Names: Orr, Wendy, 1953-, author.
Title: Dragonfly Song / Wendy Orr.
Description: Toronto, Ontario Canada : Pajama Press, 2017. | Originally published by Allen & Unwin Australia, 2016. | Summary: "Mute since the traumatic raider attack that took her foster family, Aissa struggles for survival in a mythical imagining of Bronze-Age Crete. Although she is forced into the lowliest position among the servants of her island's priestess, Aissa's mysterious bond with animals and the scars on her wrists are clues to her true identity as the priestess' firstborn daughter"— Provided by publisher.
Identifiers: ISBN 978-1-77278-037-6 (hardcover)
Subjects: LCSH: Bronze age -- Greece – Juvenile fiction. | Mutism -- Juvenile fiction. | Fantasy fiction. | BISAC: JUVENILE FICTION / Fantasy & Magic. | JUVENILE FICTION / Action & Adventure / Survival Stories.
Classification: LCC PZ7.O77Dr |DDC [F] – dc23

Cover and text: based on original design by Design by Committee
Map Illustration: Sarfaraaz Alladin, www.sarfaraaz.com

Manufactured by Friesens
Printed in Canada

Pajama Press Inc.
181 Carlaw Ave. Suite 207 Toronto, Ontario Canada, M4M 2S1

Distributed in Canada by UTP Distribution
5201 Dufferin Street Toronto, Ontario Canada, M3H 5T8

Distributed in the U.S. by Ingram Publisher Services
1 Ingram Blvd. La Vergne, TN 37086, USA

For my parents, who encouraged my love of mythology and archaeology as well as literature; my children and siblings, who cheer me on; and Tom, who listens with patience and love.

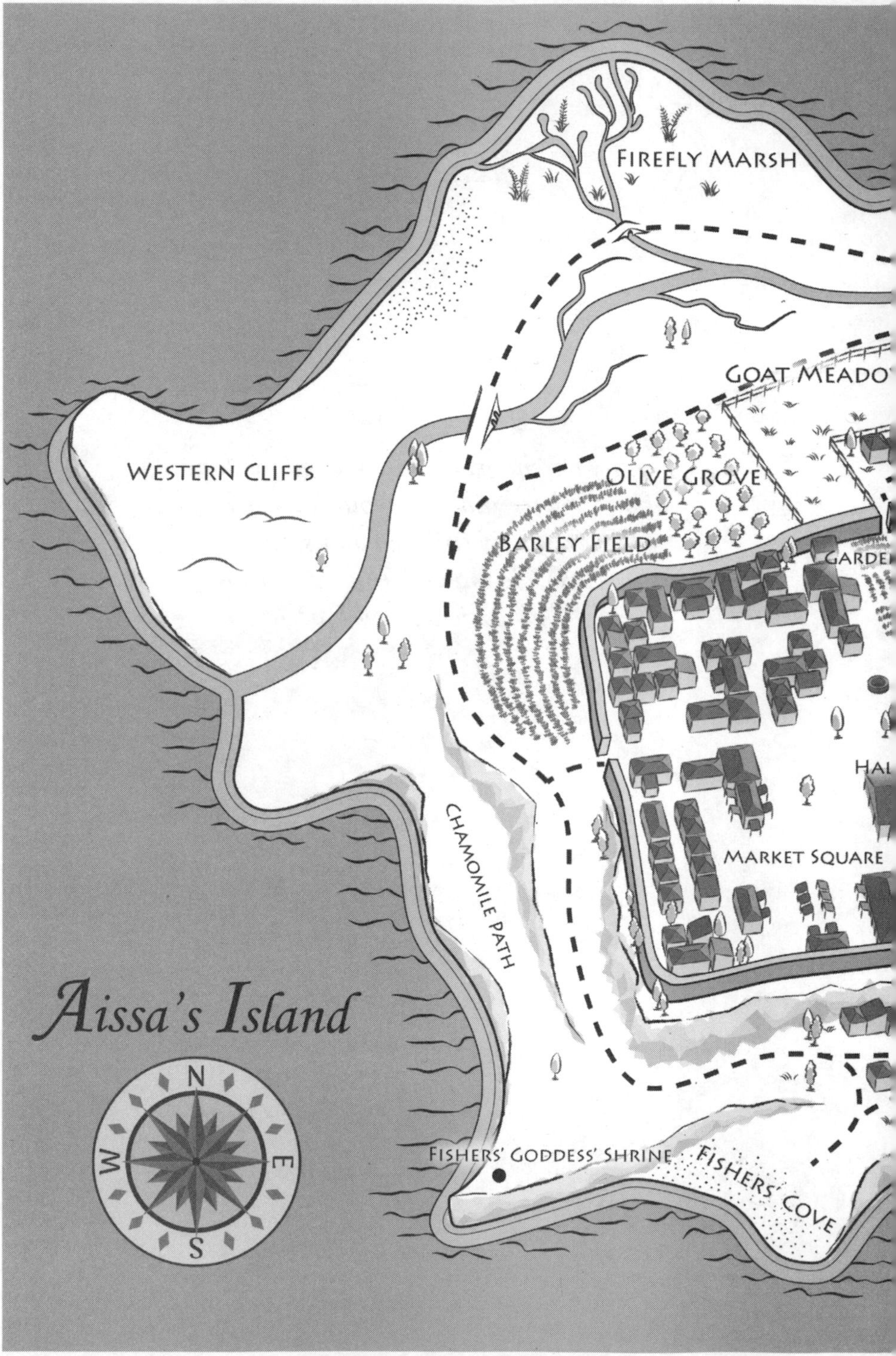

Aissa's Island

FIREFLY MARSH

WESTERN CLIFFS

GOAT MEADO

OLIVE GROVE

BARLEY FIELD

GARDE

HAL

CHAMOMILE PATH

MARKET SQUARE

FISHERS' GODDESS' SHRINE

FISHERS' COVE

N

E

S

W

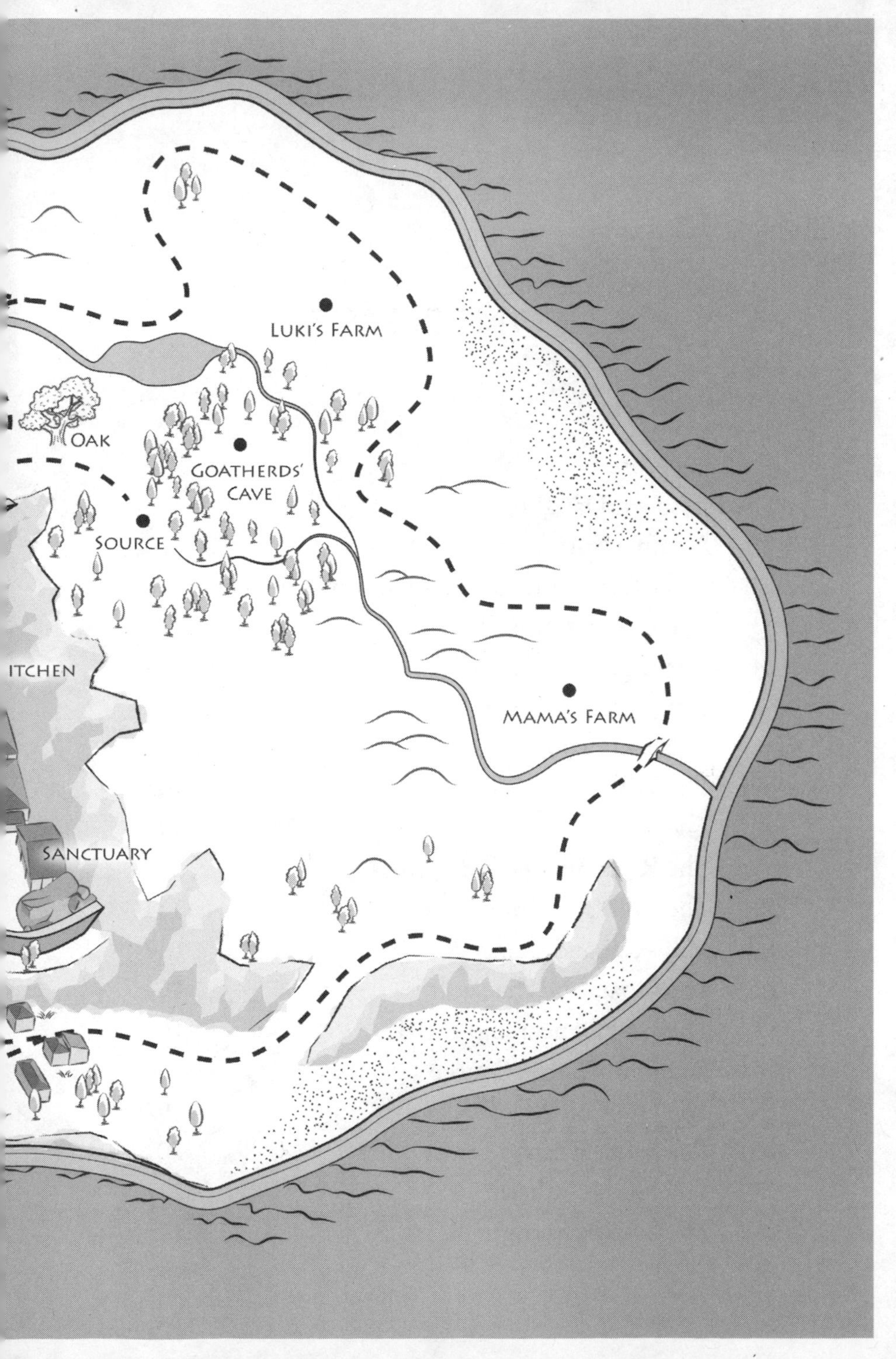

Luki's Farm
Oak
Goatherds' Cave
Source
ITCHEN
Mama's Farm
Sanctuary

CONTENTS

AUTHOR'S NOTE

Around four thousand years ago, on the Mediterranean island of Crete, a great Bronze Age civilization grew up. Its palaces had grand courtyards and stairways, flushing toilets, lightwells, and painted frescoes on walls, ceilings, and floors. They were filled with beautiful art, gold, and jewelry; images of priestesses holding snakes and of young men and women leaping over the backs of giant bulls. Archaeologists call it the Minoan civilization, in honor of the legends of King Minos of Crete.

One of the most famous legends is of the half-man, half-bull Minotaur that lived in Minos's palace. This monster ate human flesh, and every nine years—or every year, depending on who's telling the story—the town of Athens was forced to send seven youths and seven maidens for the Minotaur to catch and devour.

But do those bull-leaping paintings tell us how the legend truly began? What if the youths weren't sent to be eaten by a monster, but to gamble with their lives in a thrilling, dangerous spectacle? And perhaps tributes didn't come only from Athens, but from anywhere that the powerful Minoan navy could threaten. Maybe even from a small, distant island where a snake priestess still ruled...

THE FIRSTBORN DAUGHTER

In her dreams, Aissa feels
memory before memory,
before thought or words,
when she is still soft and small
and warm in her mother's arms.
A dada face leans,
squeezing her arms tight.
A flash of silver—
pain,
blood dripping from her hands
and the dada face dripping tears.

Slippery as snakes, the whispers slide from the Hall to the town and across the island, up hills and through valleys, from the fishers' cove to the furthest mountain farm.

The whispers say it's not true that the Lady's firstborn died at birth. They say it's worse—the baby was born with an extra thumb dangling from each wrist.

If she's not perfect, she can never follow in her mother's footsteps.

The whispers grow: "Is the Lady fit to rule us, if she can't have a perfect child?"

But the chief looks down at his newborn daughter and thinks she is the loveliest thing he's ever seen. "What does it matter if she's got an extra thumb? They're barely thumbs anyway, just wiggly lumps."

"Wiggly lumps!" shrieks the Lady, as if he's said "boar's tusks". "Whatever you call them—she shouldn't have them, and I shouldn't have *her*."

"What do you mean?" asks the chief.

The Lady cries, and doesn't answer.

And so, in a moment of madness, the chief defies the Lady, and the gods. He will make his daughter perfect himself. First left, then right: he holds the tiny arms and with his sharp bronze knife, slices away the useless thumbs. He pinches the wounds shut till the bleeding stops and rocks his baby till her crying stops, too.

The very next day, as he fishes on a peaceful sea, a high, curling wave comes from nowhere. It swerves and chases him; it towers over his boat, swamps, and sinks it. In seconds, the chief—the baby's father, the Lady's husband, leader of the guards, hunters, and fishers, ruler over land disputes and village squabbles—is gone. The gods have spoken: the baby's fate can't be changed with the cut of a knife.

Her mother wailing
  louder than baby Aissa,
  more weeping all around
  as if the walls have tongues and tears.
Aissa, too young for words,
  old enough for nightmares.
In the dark of almost-morning
  lifted from her mother's bed,
  cradled on a bony chest—
  smelling kindness
  and fear,
  but no milk—
  the baby sleeps again
  rocking, jolting
  through cool night air,
  up the hill
  and across a mountain.

Kelya is the wise-woman who takes the baby from the Lady's bed. Cradling her in a sling across her chest, she wraps her cloak around them both. It's too early for even the lowliest servants to be up; no one sees her slip through the darkened Hall and across the square to the kitchen gate.

The mountain lane is steep and narrow, but Kelya's feet know it well. She hurries as fast as she can in the darkness. She is old and stiff; she's carrying a heavy basket of gifts as well as the baby, and she has a long way to go. If she could have asked for help she would, but she can't burden even the other wise-women with this knowledge. Not when she's keeping the truth from the Lady herself.

She's happy to see the sky lightening by the time she reaches the Source.

The cave sheltering the spring is white, and so are the pebbles leading down to its shore, but the pool itself is bottomless and blue, bubbling up from the heart of the earth. Steam rises from it, mixing and swirling with the cool morning mist.

Kelya leaves her cloak and basket at the start of the rocky slope. There are flowers on top of the gifts: white and yellow daisies, bluebells, and blood-red anemones; clutching them in one hand, she picks her way carefully down to the edge of the water.

"Great Mother, accept my offering!" she calls, and throws the flowers into the pool.

They drift on the surface, twirling and bobbing. Kelya stands with her hand on her heart, watching and praying.

As the bluebells start to sink, a dragonfly hovers over them, iridescent blue in the dawn light. The wise-woman sighs with relief. Her gift is acceptable. She's betraying the Lady, but not the goddess.

She lifts the baby from the sling and unwraps her swaddling blanket.

No one knows all the secrets of the Source, but Kelya knows more than most. Hoisting her tunic up over her knees, she squats on the pebbles at the edge of a small, shallow inlet where the water is cooler. Farther in, the pool is hot enough to boil pork.

She dips the baby in the water.

"Keep this little one safe," Kelya begs. Once, twice, three times, dunking the tiny body under the warm blue surface. The child doesn't cry until she's lifted out and dried.

Kelya tucks her back into the sling, scrambles up the slope, and picks up her cloak and basket again. It's not far from here to the steep western cliffs, the final jumping spot of those who offend the gods—the place the Lady expects her imperfect baby to be taken.

But the sun is rising, birds are singing of new life, and the goddess has accepted the wise-woman's prayer. Turning the other way, Kelya follows the stream that winds down the mountain from the Source, carrying the baby through wildflowered hills to a farm on the rocky east coast.

Because whispers can work their way up from the island to the Hall, as well as down. It is Kelya's business to know who's had babies, and who has lost them. She knows a baby girl was born on this lonely farm the night that this child was born to the Lady. She also knows that the farm's baby died the same day the sea god took the chief. So she hopes the grieving parents will have room in their hearts for this rejected girl.

She's right. It's a small family: the woman who owns the farm, her parents and sister, her husband and seven-year-old son. No one else will know that Aissa wasn't born here. After all, there are few mountain goatherds without scars of one sort or another—no one is ever going to notice a girl with a small half-moon mark at each wrist.

The only thing Kelya forgets, as she starts on the long trail back to the town, is to remove the amulet the Lady had placed around her daughter's neck the day she was born.

The baby hungry,
    fretful and crying,
    delivered to new arms,
    to rough-skinned hands
    gentle with love,
    rubbing the wise-woman's salve
    onto the wounds
    where floppy thumbs used to be.
Waking to a new home:
    a goat smell,
    a hearth-smoke smell,
    but a smell of milk
    and comfort.
The arms are Mama's,
    and the home is her home,
    but in nightmare dreams
    they are new
    and strange.

BOOK ONE

I

ANOTHER SPRING, FOUR YEARS LATER

Night is warmth of Mama
  snores of Dada
  goat-rug softness
  hearth-smoke smell
  glowing coals.
Now night is screaming
  Zufi bursting through the door
  gasping, "Raiders!"
  Aissa waking,
  and the nightmare staying.
Brave Zufi out watching the goats,
  guarding against wolves
  and lions
  with his slingshot and rocks,
  all by himself, the very first time.
When Aissa is big
  she can do that too,
  brave like Zufi.

Now Zufi has left goats to run,
has forgotten wolves waiting
to eat young kids.
"I heard a noise, up from the sea
and the moon showed me:
a band of men
climbing the cliffs."
"Hide!" cries Mama, fear-eyes staring
at her home,
her family,
her Aissa.
"Fight!" says Dada. "They'll not take what's ours."
"Fight!" says Gaggie. "I'm too old to run."
Poppa grabs his wood-cutting ax
with the heavy stone head
and Tattie picks up her knife,
the sharp shining blade
that Aissa mustn't touch.
But Mama wraps Aissa tight in her rug
and runs,
panting up the hill
far from the house
to tuck Aissa in a hollow
under the sharp-scented, gray-green bush
where Spot Goat's kid
was born yesterday.
"Don't make a sound," says Mama,
brushing her fingers over Aissa's lips.
"No matter what you see,
no matter what you hear,

you stay quiet,
still as stone till I come back."
Mama makes her sign that keeps Aissa safe
and runs
back down to home.
Aissa sees her
because the moon is shining
bright and round
and Aissa's eyes are open—
a tiny seeing slit—
even though Mama said, "Close them."
Then the screaming starts.
Aissa wiggles farther
under the sharp-scented bush,
curls tight as a finger-poked bug,
squeezes her eyes good-girl shut
and tries not to hear.
Still as stone while the goats bleat and run
up the mountain, in the night
away from fire,
away from screams.
Flames lighting the sky,
higher than home;
screams tearing the night,
screams in Aissa's head.
Aissa's legs want to run with the goats
but Mama's sleeping spell
holds them tight to the ground
through the long red night,
Aissa cold
and all, all alone.

When the screaming stops
    Aissa's heart cries loud for Mama
    though her voice stays quiet, still as stone.
    Mama doesn't come
    but Spot Goat does.
Spot Goat bleats and nuzzles
    at cold toes in morning dew
    till Aissa wriggles, snake-silent,
    drinks from Spot Goat like a baby kid
    because Spot Goat's kid is gone,
    like Mama.
Morning, not morning, with no warm Mama bed
    smoke in the sky
    stinking stronger than the gray-green bush
    and her rug piss-wet and cold.
Waiting through that long fear-morning,
    waiting quiet and still as stone.
    Spot Goat waits too—
    but Spot Goat doesn't know what Mama said
    so she bleats
    till the man finds them.

It's the third time this year that raiders have attacked the island. When the flames of the burning homestead light the sky, distant goatherds call the alarm. Twelve men gather from the farms, but long before they get there, the silence tells them that they're too late.

They trudge on, dreading what they might find. It's as bad as they could have imagined.

The house and farm buildings were made of stone, but their roofs were thatched straw. The thatch flamed quickly when the raiders lit it, and the burning roofs collapsed, destroying everything underneath. The rock walls stand like chimneys, smoke pouring from the smoldering mess inside. The husband, grandparents, and dog lie dead in front of the door.

There's no sign of the two women or children.

The men search hopelessly. All they find is a pool of blood at the gate.

"Let's hope that's a raider's," one man says viciously.

It probably is, because a bronze dagger is lying under a bush nearby. The owner wouldn't have left it unless he was too wounded to notice.

It's a small sort of payment for the dead, and the women and children taken into slavery.

The dagger is a murdering weapon and it needs to be cleaned of blood and cleansed of evil, but the boy who picks it up can't help coveting it. Metal is expensive. His grandmother loves reminding the family that she'd paid six kids and a vat of olives for their one short and plain bronze knife. This one is very fine. Its blade is engraved, and the hilt is carved with the head of a horned beast.

"It's the sign of the Bull King," says the oldest man. "If he's behind these raids, the island is in big trouble."

"I'll take the dagger to the Lady," the boy decides. If he can't keep it, at least he can be first with the news. He whistles his dog and starts across the hills to town.

Three men stay to sing the dead to peace before their burial; the others go out with their own dogs and whistle to round up the straying flock. Which is how one man discovers Aissa, cold, wet, and terrified, sheltering under a nanny goat.

"What's your name, little one?" he asks.

She doesn't answer.

He calls the others; they're so relieved to find one survivor that for a moment they're almost happy. The man who finds her is a hero.

Except that now he has to go to the orphaned child's aunt, the husband's sister, and tell her that her brother is dead, and that she has a new child to care for.

The man with a crying face
    carries Aissa off the mountain
    past home,
    because home has fire and no roof,
    no Mama or Dada
    or Gaggie or Poppa
    or doves or Brown Dog
    or Zufi or Tattie.
Turning Aissa's face against his shoulder,
    so she can't see
    what's there
    and what's not.
    But her eyes peek
    and screams stay in her head,
    going down the mountain
    with Spot Goat bleating behind.
Staying quiet, quiet,
    small, small

waiting still for Mama
when the man leaves her far away
with Fox Lady.
Fox Lady has a sharp pointed face,
sharp pointed voice;
she asks questions
that Aissa can't answer.
Fox Lady doesn't know that Mama said
"Stay quiet, still as stone, till I come back."
And Mama's not back.
Fox Lady calls her ill-luck child,
cursed child, child that brings evil,
no child of my brother, that's for sure.
Aissa doesn't know all the words
but she knows what they mean
and she is quieter, stiller, smaller.
Fox Lady's eyes are hard like rock
and her voice sharp as a knife.
So dark early morning,
silent as a secret
Fox Lady carries Aissa
out and away from the sleeping house.
Spot Goat bleats and Aissa holds out her arms,
calling with her mind.
Spot Goat comes,
trot, trot, trot,
her nose reaching for Aissa's hand.
But Fox Lady slaps
Spot Goat's soft nose,
Aissa's waiting arms,

and hurries out the gate
leaving Spot Goat behind.
"Walk!" says Fox Lady, dumping Aissa down,
grabbing her hand to pull her along,
Aissa's feet stumbling,
loose rocks hitting toes.
But the hand tugs and her feet hurry.
Up the path, climb another hill,
another path,
wide and smooth under Aissa's feet,
the sky glimmering wake-up time;
a gray shimmering below
like the pond at home
but going on forever.
Fox Lady's hand snakes out
while Aissa stares.
Fingers grab the mama stone—
the stone that's hung from Aissa's neck
always and forever
with the sign of her name—
but the cord doesn't break
and Aissa bites the hand.
Slap go the fingers on Aissa's cheek.
"Keep it then," says Fox Lady.
"They'll still not bring you back to me."
She grabs Aissa's hand again,
tugging hard, tugging hurt,
climbing the road
winding farther up the hill.
Darker shapes in the gray,
houses jumbled up the slope,

side by side like sleeping pups;
the mountain above them,
and a giant's wall
like a goat pen for gods.
Now people, people all around.
Aissa smaller, silent as stone
but she can't be still
because Fox Lady tugs her
through the darkness of nearly morning
through the people:
the mamas and dadas,
the gaggies and poppas,
Zufies and tatties—
none of them are hers.
The sky turns pink over the mountain.
The people stop, like goats in a pen.
Fox Lady lets go of Aissa's hand.
"Let the little one see," says a gaggie
and hands push her through the forest of legs
till Aissa stands with more Aissas and Zufies
pressing faces to a gate,
wooden bars against her cheek
as the sun rises over the mountain
and out of the darkness
a lady comes singing.
The Lady is dark but her voice is bright,
singing not-songs—
not mama songs or sleeping songs
or weaving songs or goat songs—
but a sound that lifts Aissa tall,

lifts her high from small still stone;
lifts, "Oh!" from the people
and "Praise!" and "Thank you, Mother!"
From a pot at the Lady's feet
the song lifts a snake,
coiling up, standing high.
The Lady bends, reaching out
like Aissa to Spot Goat
and the snake slides up her arm,
up to her neck, and down again,
till the new sun is in the sky
and the snake back in its pot.
Bright and golden,
the Lady stands in front
of the dark cave door,
while all around Aissa,
the mamas and dadas,
gaggies and poppas,
put hands on hearts
like Mama talking to little fat goddess
by the hearth where the house snake hides.
Aissa does too,
because if Aissa is good, Mama will come back.
Aissa closes eyes to see Mama better,
to call louder in her quiet still head,
so Mama will be there
when she opens her eyes.
Eyes tiny-crack-open
like watching home from bed
when Mama says sleep.

Mama's not there.
Eyes open wide and still no Mama.
No singing Lady.
No legs all around.
No Fox Lady.
But a tall man, opening the gate,
pries Aissa's fingers off wooden bars.
"Where's your mama?"
But Aissa stays quiet, still as stone,
as he carries her inside
the singing Lady's walls.
"Kelya!" calls Tall Man.
A gaggie comes, crooked like Poppa,
wart on her chin
kindness in her eyes,
takes Aissa from his arms.
"Alone?" she says.
"Maybe lost," says the man.
Kelya lady carries Aissa
on her hip just like Mama
away from Tall Man,
to the wall of the Lady's house,
puts her down on a low stone bench
squats in front of her,
holding Aissa's hands,
rubbing thumbs over Aissa's wrists,
finding white moon scars that are Aissa's own.
And she looks at the mama stone
but doesn't touch.
"Little one!" says Kelya, kissing the scars,
looking around fast,

then squeezing Aissa tight,
arms like Gaggie's
but not Gaggie.
"No one must know!" says Kelya
and Aissa stays quiet,
still as stone.

It's a small island: even people who've lived all their lives inside the walled town, under the shelter of the chief's hall and the Lady's sanctuary, know someone from outside who knows someone else, till in the end everyone is connected to everywhere. They all know that the little girl has come from the raided farm.

People who've met her aunt aren't surprised that she's dumped the child at the gates. The girl is not the first orphan to be left there. She'll be raised in the Hall with the other unfortunates and the servants' children: a space on the kitchen floor to sleep, food to eat when everyone else is done, and chores as soon as she's old enough to do them.

"She'll talk when she's ready," says Kelya. "She just needs time and kindness."

But it's a busy place. There's not much time or kindness for a child who would rather hide than play with the other children, who bites if anyone tries to read the name-sign on her amulet.

And though the last thing Kelya wants is for Aissa to say her name out loud, where the Lady could hear, she does want her to be accepted. She sits on the stone bench with Aissa on her knees, smoothing olive oil into the black curls to comb out the twigs and tangles. Sharp tugs bring tears to the child's eyes but she never cries, not the tiniest squeak.

If I hadn't seen her tongue myself, Kelya thinks, *I'd swear the raiders had cut it out*. She finishes combing, and plaits Aissa's hair into two long tails. "Lovely!" she says, kissing the girl on the tip of her nose.

Just for a moment, she sees another face looking back at her, because Kelya is old enough to remember before the Lady was the Lady, all the way back to when she was a four-year-old girl.

Quickly, she undoes the careful plaits, rumpling the little girl's hair into its own messy curls. People see only what they expect: no one will look closely enough to see the Lady in a cast-off child with tangled hair.

Later she sees Aissa squatting outside the kitchen garden with the potter's daughter, making careful patterns in the dust: a ring of flowers in a circle of stones.

Kelya smiles to herself. The girl will be all right, she thinks: she'll make her own way.

Aissa at the gates
    waiting all the morning
    watching for Mama who never comes,
    but seeing through the bars
    butterflies,
    red wings on the sea
    dancing in the dawn.
No one else sees,
    busy, busy all around.

Guards pace,
singing Lady gone inside
with her snakes
and her crimson robe.
Watching through the gate,
as red wings sail closer,
and turn into a boat.
Guards run, singing Lady comes
no snakes or songs;
her man comes too,
the new chief in his lion cloak.
Flowing robe brushes Aissa
but the Lady doesn't feel,
doesn't see Aissa
trembling at her touch.
Bread lady, milk boy, washing girls, fish man,
pot lady, grain grinder,
woodchopper, hunter,
garden boy, and cheese girl,
like ants rushing
from a kicked-over anthill,
screaming to the road
pushing past Aissa,
small, still-as-stone Aissa
waiting by the gate.
Even Kelya,
with her warty chin and Aissa-watching eyes
hobble-runs past
and doesn't see Aissa.
Small Aissa tumbling
when the water boy knocks her

blood on her knee,
red and sticky pain.
Biting her stone so she doesn't cry—
the mama stone around her neck
because Mama said,
"Don't make a noise,
no matter what you hear, not the tiniest peep,
stay quiet, still as stone till I come back."
And the smell from the running people,
the rushing, shouting,
sweating people,
is the same smell as Zufi
when he shouted, "Raiders!"—
the sharp and sour
stink of fear.
So Aissa crouches
in a nook in the wall
a hole too small for anyone else,
and she watches and listens,
staying quiet, still as stone.

The Bull King's ship sails into the fishers' cove. It's the biggest ship that's ever landed here, because the cove isn't sheltered enough for big trading ships, but the Bull King's men don't care. They row straight in, and when the hull crunches on the pebbles, some jump off to haul the ship up onto the beach. The others stand on their rowing benches with spears raised over their shoulders, or on the front deck, bows drawn with arrows ready to fly.

There are nearly sixty of them, wearing leather

war helmets, with battle-axes or daggers at their belts as well as the spears and bows in their hands—the islanders know there's no point in fighting.

The captain and half the crew cross the beach to greet the Lady and the chief, leaving the rest to guard the ship. And although the captain uses a strange, barbaric language that the tall guard has to translate, the words stick in every islander's head.

"The Bull King, king of the sea, priest of the Bull God, hears that your island is troubled by slaving raids and pirates. He promises that these will end from today. In return for his protection, each year you will pay twelve barrels of olive oil, twelve goat kids, twelve jugs of wine, twelve baskets of grain, twelve baskets of dried fish, twelve lengths of woven cloth—and a boy and a girl of thirteen summers to honor the god."

"Your god requires children as sacrifice?" demands the Lady.

"Honor and glory, not sacrifice. They will join in the bull dances that the god loves. If they survive the year, they may return home and your island will be free of further tributes."

"Have any ever done so?"

The captain shrugs.

"And if we refuse?" the Lady asks, though she knows the answer.

"Then it will not be two youths, living and dying with glory. It will be your island and all its people, and there will be no honor in their deaths and enslavements."

2

After Eight Springs in the Servants' Kitchen

The Hall and inner town are on a small plateau against the east side of the mountain. They're protected on three sides by a great rock wall, but the fourth side is the cliff—higher, steeper, and more impossible to climb than any wall. The backs of the Hall and the goddess's sanctuary nestle into its hollows; the kitchen's cool room and the snakes' home are almost caves.

Between the sanctuary and the south wall, a giant boulder is wedged tight. It balances on an angle, as if the goddess has stopped it mid-bounce to protect her home. Its front is so shiny and smooth only a gecko could climb it, and it slopes out to shelter worshippers waiting to lay their offerings on the table at the sanctuary door. The top, as far as anyone can tell, slopes down to the cliff at its back. There is no way through.

No way for an adult, that is, or even a well-fed child. But if a thin-as-a-reed girl drops to the ground when no one is looking, she can slither like a snake under the gap where the edge of the boulder doesn't quite meet the bottom of the wall.

When she was four or five or six she could huddle there as long as she liked, safely alone with her thoughts and fears. At seven the space started getting tight, but when she was eight she saw that if she squeezed along a little way farther, under the bump that's jammed against the sanctuary, there was another gap where she could stand up straight.

Now that she's twelve, she's an expert in shinning up that gap to the top of the boulder. As long as she's careful to slide on her stomach once she's up there, no one can see her from the market square. And Aissa is always careful. It's the only way she knows how to be.

"Aissa is always hiding," the other servants say, "Always spying," as if they hate her sharp eyes even more than her silent tongue. But when you're the cursed child, hiding is the safest thing to do. And when you're hiding, you spy.

The top of the boulder has two spying places.

The first is a chink in the south wall. If she presses her face to it she can see out to the wide world, over the hills and the shadows of distant islands far across the sea. Mama is out there somewhere.

Remembering Mama
  hurts
  because Aissa doesn't know
  when they'll find

each other again,
though Aissa's done
what Mama said,
not made a sound—
and if she hasn't been
still as stone
she's been as quiet.
But thinking of Dada
is worse
because Aissa knows
that she will never
see him again.
And all that is left
is the memory
of his tickling beard.

She checks the chink in the wall in case there's a sign of Mama, but when she's watched for a while, and can see nothing on the hills except the brown dots of goats and nothing on the sea except the gray smudges of fishing boats, she wriggles on farther.

Halfway along the boulder, on the side next to the sanctuary, is a hollow about as long as Aissa. Once she slides into that, not even an eagle could see her.

It needs to be safe, because this is where she is truly, dangerously, spying. From here, she can see straight into the sanctuary.

The goddess likes her home dark, so there are no windows, just a slit under the eaves. Aissa is not only the first person to ever look in through it; she's the first person who's wanted to. The gods of this island are tricky beings—it's best not to make them angry by peering into forbidden places. But this is the one place where Aissa has never felt afraid, and because no one except Kelya has ever really talked to her, she doesn't know that she should. She just knows that she loves to stare into the darkness of the sanctuary, and the darker cave at the back where the snakes live. And since the only safe time to slip into her hiding place is before everyone else is awake and busy in the square, what she loves best is to watch the dawn ceremony as if she was in it herself.

By the flickering light of the torches on the walls, she can see the Lady select a pot from the snakes' cave, and drop in an offering: a frog maybe, or a lizard. As the chosen asp eats its meal, the Lady begins to sing, quietly, so that no one can hear beyond the closed sanctuary door. No one except the snakes and Aissa. Sometimes, as she lies on the cold rock listening to the strange, high notes, Aissa imagines that the Lady is singing for her.

But at the last new moon, Fila began her initiation into the mysteries. Aissa should have been struck deaf already for listening.

In the eight years since Fox Lady abandoned her at the gates, Aissa has grown from a shy four year old to sharp-faced twelve. The Lady's daughter Fila, two years younger than Aissa but half a head taller, has grown from sweet-faced toddler to sweet-faced girl.

That's just one of the differences between them. Aissa sees Fila every day, but Fila has never seen Aissa, not actually seen her, not looked in her eyes and wondered who is behind them. She doesn't need to. Aissa will always scurry out of her way if she is sweeping or scrubbing or cleaning the privies when Fila passes.

After all, Fila is the Lady's firstborn daughter, despite the stories of an earlier one that died, and one day Fila will become the Lady. She is loved by all.

Aissa, as far as she knows, is loved by no one. Kelya has gone blind and knows that if she can't protect the child, favoring her will make things worse. So Aissa has sunk to the bottom of the heap; spoken to only in anger, the last to eat, the coldest bed place in winter, the stuffiest in summer, the lowest, filthiest, stinkiest chores. She doesn't even have a nickname like the other servants: "No-Name," they call her. "Cursed child; the girl even the raiders didn't want."

Fila's only problem is that she has a voice to scare toads. The snakes do not come to her; they are agitated and hiss, and if the Lady didn't sing them away, her treasured daughter would die a swollen, painful death twenty times over.

Aissa still has no voice at all and has never been near enough to the snakes to bother them.

Luckily, Fila doesn't have to sing this morning: her only task is to take a cricket from a small wicker cage and drop it into a pot for the chosen snake. She can just about manage a cricket without crying, though Aissa can see her cringe. A few days ago, Fila cried so much that she dropped a wriggling mouse onto the floor. The mouse quickly disappeared. The Lady replaced the snake's pot in the cave and brought out the one she'd used the day before. She didn't say anything, but Aissa could hear the sharp anger in her song.

Aissa doesn't enjoy seeing the mice being dropped to their death, but she doesn't feel sorry for them. The snakes have to eat, and it's a mouse's fate to be eaten. The same with the crickets—besides, she likes eating crickets herself, crispy and fried and swiped off a market stall.

When the Lady steps outside, Aissa inches forward till she can look right out through the open sanctuary doors. Watching from behind the scenes, she can't see the crowds staring in through the gate, but she can imagine what they're seeing. She knows how they'll be blinded by the rising sun and how tall and dark and magnificent the Lady will seem against it. When the song begins again, calling the snake up to the Lady's arms and the sun to the skies, the sound lifts Aissa right up out of her body so that it is worth all the risks to be hidden on a rock and hear it, secret and alone. And when she goes back into her body, the song goes with her, so that sometimes, when she needs it, she can hear it again.

The song ends. The square will soon start filling up with people; Aissa needs to leave now—she can't risk someone seeing her sliding out from under the boulder. That could be worse than the beating Squint-Eye has promised her if she doesn't sweep up the dog droppings.

But something is different this morning. After the Lady steps back into the sanctuary and releases the snake to its cave, she turns to the altar. It is crowded with small statues in wood, stone, and bronze, amber beads and gold jewelry. The Lady picks them up and rearranges them into a new pattern, talking softly all the while, reminding the goddess of what they've given her. Finally she places the raiders' bronze dagger right in the center, surrounded by all the other riches.

"Use this symbol of the Bull King's power to strengthen your people," she says, loud enough for Aissa to hear.

Then she adds something that makes no sense at all. "I gave you my own. Will you let the bull take more?"

The goddess doesn't answer, but the secret door from the Lady's rooms opens. Fila leads Kelya in.

"What are the signs?" the Lady asks abruptly.

"My wise-women have seen two," says blind Kelya. "A skylark escaping from an eagle to rise again singing. Later they found an eagle's feather woven into its nest. And on the same day, a dragonfly such as they had never seen, wondrously large and blue, hovering above the Source."

"A dragonfly?" the Lady repeats.

Dragonfly? Aissa echoes in her mind, the word nudging at her from some long-ago memory.

"That's what they saw," says Kelya.

"That was the name of my mother's grandmother.

Could it be her spirit returning to save us from the bull?"

"Only the goddess knows," says Kelya.

So the Lady sprinkles white barley meal on the floor of the snakes' cave, calls the great house snake out with an offering of milk, and tries to find the goddess's answer in the pattern that he draws.

There are two ways of looking at Aissa's story. The searcher who found her under the bush still believes that she's the miracle girl who escaped the raiders. Everyone else thinks she's the cursed child who called the Bull King's ship to the island.

Spit the bad luck away when you see her; pinch or slap her to make her understand. Why bother talking to a girl who doesn't speak?

The worst time is the spring, when wobbly-legged kids are born to the goats in the warming air and the hills are fragrant with flowers. Now it's not only swallows and herons that return, but the Bull King's ship.

So that afternoon, when a sweet south wind blows and a smudge of color glows on the waves, Aissa knows exactly what it is, long before she can see the red sails or great black horns on the bow.

She presses herself against a nook in the wall, trying to be invisible as the market square erupts, people crowding in through the gates for protection or out for news, running, jostling and breathless down the road, the fisherfolk joining them as their little boats sail in too.

The ship nears the cove, below the town. The red sails drop and twenty-seven rows of oars flash from the black hull. Aissa can see the bronze glint of the battle-axes and spears of the men standing in the bow. The oars lift; some of the rowers jump in and tow the ship toward the shore.

But the beach is out of view from here, and now the ship is too. The square hushes: the traders stop their bustle. No children run or dogs bark. For an instant even the air seems to stand still.

Then the wailing starts, rising from the beach to the Hall, gathering volume as it picks up mourners on its way.

Last year's bull dancers have not returned.

Grief and fear all around
    but fear can turn to anger
    and slaps for Aissa
    because what can't be fixed
    must be her fault.
The hollow in the wall
    too small to hide her now
    but Aissa so quiet and still
    barely a breath to betray her,
    invisible as a lizard
    while the wailing swirls
    and the fear-snake
    curls in her belly.
Wailing people see only what they need.

No one wants to see
the privy-cleaner now
though some run to privies
with terror in their guts.
The new bull dancers race
out the gate to their homes,
a last visit and goodbye.
No time to spit
at the girl who will never dance,
and part of Aissa would be happy
to see them panicked always.
She hates the spitting,
wet on her face
muck on her hair,
her clothes, her feet.
She hates the spitting
and sometimes the spitters
but if she hates them all
she has no one.
So another part of Aissa
is wailing too
in chorus with her people,
echoing fears of long ago
of Zufi shouting,
Mama running,
of screams and fires in the night,
smoke stench and sadness in the morning.
The fear is a dark deep pit—
heart warns, "Keep away! Don't look!"

But the Mama longing is sharp
and her heart calls loud
till Milli-Cat comes running
from the Lady's rooms
out through the Hall
across the square to Aissa.
Milli-Cat is white as the snow
on winter mountains
and she can't hear.
"Deaf as a rock," people say.
So Milli-Cat doesn't care that Aissa
is quiet as stone.
Milli-Cat belongs to the Lady
and to Fila
so Aissa mustn't touch her,
but they stand together against the wall
as sorrow swirls around them.

The wailing rises in waves. People are sobbing, wandering aimlessly or dropping to their knees, pounding their foreheads on the ground. The potter has torn out a great hank of her own hair; a baker has slashed the sleeves of his tunic. The grief is for the boy and girl who haven't returned; the fear is for the ones who will take their places. Every year it's harder to hope that the bull dancers will survive and return, covered in glory.

The chief strides out from the Hall. His hair is oiled and his beard trimmed square, his lion-skin cloak is flung over his shoulders, and a dagger gleams at his belt.

"Close the gates!" he orders.

"What's the point?" a guard mutters. "It's not as if we're going to fight."

No one cares what they say in front of the girl who doesn't speak. Aissa learns a lot that way.

The gates' bronze latch clangs shut. The guard bangs his spear on the ground.

"Listen to your chief!" he bellows.

The chief waits until every eye is focused on him. "The Lady has read the oracle, and the signs are clear: the skylark that escapes the eagle will rise again singing. Rebirth is a greater strength than force."

Rebirth? thinks Aissa. The word dances in her mind. It's never easy to understand exactly what the oracle means.

"Don't let them think they've beaten us!" a guard shouts. The chief nods.

"They've taken our children," the potter sobs. "Of course they've beaten us!"

The potter's daughter
  a big girl, a kind girl
  with Aissa in the dust
  long, long ago,
  making circles of flowers
  in a ring of stones.
The potter's daughter
  a big girl, a kind girl
  but not as big
  as the girls that spat,
  "Stay away from us

with the curses you've caught
from the bad-luck brat!"
The potter's daughter
a big girl, a wild girl
pinching Aissa,
scratching, kicking,
slapping hard
till the bigger girls laughed
and said she could play.
The potter's daughter
gone last year on the Bull King's ship
is dead now.

The ship's captain and his warriors are marching up the road. Islanders draggle after them, a safe twenty paces behind.

"Welcome," says the chief, as if he had a choice.

The guards fling the gates open, and the men enter. They crowd the market square more than any nine men should; their weapons and mission fill the air. Strangest of all, an animal has followed them. It looks like Milli-Cat except that its fur is black and its ears twitch as if it can hear.

Milli-Cat comes from a land where cats are worshipped. She was a gift to the Lady from a trader two springs ago, and is the only one on the island. Now everyone's wondering if this new beast will stay small like her or grow into a lion—it's hard to imagine that anything good could come with the bull ship. Aissa isn't the only one trying to be invisible against a wall.

The Lady, says the chief, is serving the goddess and can't be disturbed. The tall guard translates into the Bull King's harsh tongue.

He's lying! Aissa thinks. She'd seen the Lady rush through the Hall to her private chambers when everyone else was running to the gate.

Then the Lady appears, and Aissa understands.

Sometimes the best way to serve is to look magnificent. The Lady's face is powdered white and her eyes painted dark. Her black curls are piled into an eagle feather headdress; a gold snake belts her red robe, and two twine up each arm. Power shimmers around her like her rose perfume.

The Bull King's men shrink a little closer to human size.

"You will feast with us today," the Lady announces, "and leave in the morning with those who are honored to serve."

Why doesn't she make them leave right away? Aissa thinks. *We don't want them around stinking out our town!*

They do stink, too. Stale sweat mostly, but also a whiff of fear. Only nine of them, after all, enclosed in this courtyard with a hundred people wishing them dead. Their shipmates would avenge them, sure as a rock smashing an egg, but it would be too late to bring these warriors back to life.

"We wouldn't wish to dishonor your gods with a hasty choice of tribute" the Lady is saying.

Another lie! The two new bull dancers have lived in the Hall for the past year, training and preparing. It would be easier to prepare if there were bulls on the island, but the rocky soil is too harsh for cattle, and the calves so carefully, expensively brought in by boat have always sickened and died. It would also be easier if they knew exactly what they were training for, but no one on the island has seen the dances that the Bull King loves so much.

In fact the only thing they know for sure is the promise: if a dancer survives the year, they will be free to return home, and their island will be free of tribute forever.

And, of course, the other fact—that so far no one's ever survived the year.

Then, as if the Lady has put the thought straight into her mind, Aissa understands. Her mouth twitches into an almost-smile, and Milli-Cat purrs at her feet as if she's understood too.

Though the tribute is a heavy load for this poor, rocky island, they'd pay four times that to keep their children safe at home. They don't have that choice. All they have is the small secret of knowing that the new bull dancers, gone now for one last day with their families, have been given the best chance possible.

Aissa understands small, silent victories. Things like knowing that a rat is nesting in the corner of the kitchen where Half-One and Half-Two sleep, even if it never bites those wasp-tongued twins...she knows how that is.

But she's never thought of how the bull dancers feel, or that they could be afraid. Even though they're only a year older than she is, and have been living just a wall away from the servants' kitchen, they're as distant as the eagles soaring over the mountain crags. The differences are so complete she can't even be jealous. Except for one thing: *No one spits at the sight of them.* If the gods gave her one wish, that would be it: to have a day when no one spat at her. One full day. She sees it like a smooth pebble to hold in her hand, a jewel that would make the rest of her life bearable.

Suddenly, like a chasm opening beneath her feet, a thought cracks her world.

The dancers will leave tomorrow morning. Eight days after that, next year's dancers will be chosen. Every twelve year old on the island has a chance.

Even me, she thinks. The voice in her head, that no one else has ever heard, is full of doubt and wonder, almost awe. *Even me.*

Bull King's men are tall
    strong
    big in every way.
    They eat like giants
    leaving little for servants;
    nothing for Aissa.
Dreams of hunger
    crying to Mama
    for soft white cheese
    salty dried fish

crunchy hot crickets.
Waking to no Mama
no soft white cheese
no salty dried fish
but her sleeping pallet
black with crickets.
Aissa is a quick cricket-catcher
hungry enough to eat them raw.
"No!" says a voice,
loud in her head.
"They've come to the call!"
A voice she doesn't know.
Words like the oracle.
Oracles don't speak through a No-Name child;
gods don't talk to bad-luck girls.
But hungry Aissa
leaves the crickets alone.
Maybe that's why
the gods let her see
what no one else does:
Milli-Cat and the ship beast
dancing in the dawn,
rubbing heads and yowling.
Aissa is glad
that Milli-Cat has a friend
and wonders
what that would be like.

Aissa doesn't go to her spying place that morning. Already the world is busy and awake; she can see the captain and his men through the open door of the Hall. They're yawning and stretching just like normal people. One of them passes on his way to the privy. Aissa shrinks against the wall, waiting for the first-sight-of-the-day spit to keep her evil luck away from him.

He doesn't spit. His eyes glance over and ignore her, as if she was any other servant girl.

The crack in Aissa's world opens wider.

She should be cleaning; she should have already swept out the Great Room where the Bull King's men slept, and hauled buckets from the well for scrubbing tables. But she hasn't even started. She's back in her nook against the wall, watching the Lady call the sun to rise.

Everyone on the island seems to be there: townsfolk packed tight in the square, children in front, toddlers on shoulders; fishers, herders, and farmers crowded outside the gate, where Fox Lady left Aissa so long ago. Maybe she's there now; Aissa doesn't know. And tells herself she doesn't care.

Even the Bull King's men, watchful as wolves, shiver when they hear the Lady's strange, high notes and see the snake coiling up to her neck. Gold streaks appear in the sky behind the mountain, blinding the watchers. The singing Lady, the sanctuary and the mountain behind it, all disappear in the sun's slanting rays.

But the instant that the sun appears and the song stops, the captain strides impatiently to the gate.

The olive oil, wine, grain, dried fish, and cloth have

been stored for weeks now, ready for this day. Now twelve goat kids are led in through the garden gate, bleating for their mothers.

Goats can cry, but people can't. The only chance of the bull god being merciful is to trick him into thinking that the island is happy to send tribute. When the two dancers come out from the Hall, their faces as white as their fresh new tunics, they're greeted by a cheer of a thousand voices.

Even Aissa opens her mouth, though no sound comes out.

The Lady kisses the dancers' foreheads. "Given freely," she chants, and the people echo.

"Given with joy,
to honor the gods.
Accept our offering,
given freely,
sent with joy."

The gates swing open, and the two dancers fall in behind the captain to lead the long procession of bearers and tributes down the road. People throng around them, touching their arms, tossing flowers and gifts of dried figs or honey cakes for the voyage. The black cat weaves between their legs, his tail high.

The ship's warriors bring up the rear, their eyes darting anxiously and spears at the ready. The chief marches beside the captain, but the Lady stays at the sanctuary, because she's wearing such tall shoes that she can't walk.

Aissa follows the crowd. They're mostly so busy trying to trick the gods that they forget to spit at her. But she knows how fast the mood can change; she stops at the first bend, where she can look down at the cove.

"So lucky to serve the gods!" she hears, as she watches the sailors haul the tribute up onto their black-decked ship. The goat kids' bleating carries over the noise of the crowd.

The two youths are hoisted aboard. Aissa can see the fear on their faces from here.

"What joy, to go across the sea!"

Aissa doesn't have to worry about lying to the gods. If they can hear her thoughts, they know that she'd trade places with the dancers in the blink of an eye.

3

THE FIREFLIES OF REBIRTH

Pretending to be happy only lasts while the ship is in sight. When not even the sharpest eye can see a smudge on the waves, the weeping begins.

The last quarter of the late spring moon has always been the time of mourning—the farewell for all the souls who have died during the year. Now, if two families are crying for the new bull dancers, who are still alive, not even the gods need to know.

Grieving is the only way to make sure that the dead don't come back to haunt the living. They need a lot of tears, a lot of wailing, and the people they've left behind need it too. Families tear their hair and rip their clothes because that's better than feeling as if their souls have been ripped from their bodies. The potter takes her pots, one by one, and smashes them in front of the sanctuary. Sharp shards litter the square and bare feet bleed, but the potter still can't stop crying.

Aissa thinks of the dead she knows: the bull dancers,

the old gardener who just didn't wake up one morning, the tanner's little girl who fell into the pits with the hides, the guard who broke his leg on a mountain trail and died painfully as it rotted. *I could cry for the tanner's daughter*, Aissa thinks. *She was too young to know that I was cursed.*

It doesn't work: her tears are as blocked as her throat.

But now seven days and seven nights have passed, and the moon is full. Tonight is Firefly Night, when the dead souls fly free, ready to be reborn. Today is a time of cleansing and new clothes, to make everything fresh for the rebirth. Servants are given their freshly washed, handed-down tunics for the next year. Aissa's is neatly folded in a corner of the kitchen; she's not going to put it on till she's finished her chores, but her mind keeps going back to it: clean and almost white, with all the tears mended.

The sun is sinking low into the western sea. The square is starting to hum with excitement: farmers and fishers are arriving, hunters are swaggering in their finest skins, and townfolk are parading their finery.

Aissa is scrubbing the servants' privy.

She'd filled two buckets at the well before this morning's dawn ceremony, and she hasn't stopped sweeping, scrubbing, and hauling soil and water ever since. Even this privy, which is really just a shelter around a hole behind the vegetable garden, needs to be spotless by sunset.

It stinks. All the privies stink.

So does Aissa—which is why she'll never see the celebration.

There's a roar from the square. The Lady and her family have appeared.

The first year
Aissa still new
cursed but clean,
Kelya holding tight
when the chief called the names
for Dada, Gaggie, and Poppa.
Kelya howling
waggling her tongue,
"Like this! Like this."
Aissa's tongue waggling
—like this, like this—
with no howl coming;
her throat staying quiet
still as stone.
And the same today,
eight years older
still as silent:
her tongue can wag
but her throat won't wail.
"Honor your dead!"
calls the Lady to the crowd
and they *lululu* back,
fishers and farmers,
hunters and town,
a thousand tongues trilling,

a thousand throats howling
the *lululu* of grief
that Aissa keeps in her heart.
Then the Lady and the chief,
Fila and three small brothers
start out the gate
and the crowd parts
like a river for a rock
to stream up the mountain.
"Honor Melos the guard!" calls the chief
and guards and potters,
bakers and tailors,
toddlers on shoulders,
gaggies with sticks,
and lowly servants
wail for Melos.
The names will be called
all the way up the mountain
and all as one
the island will wail
for each of the dead.
Only Aissa is too impure
to follow the crowd.
Only Aissa won't see
the fireflies of rebirth.

This time I'm not going to miss it!

It won't take long to finish here. If she rushes into the servants' washhouse the instant everyone else is done, she can scrub herself clean enough for that fresh new tunic—

"Did you check the privy hole before you threw new earth in?"

Aissa jumps. Standing behind her, laughing, are the sharp-tongued kitchen twins, Half-One and Half-Two.

It's never good when the twins are laughing.

"Your new tunic didn't stink the way you like it."

"So we threw it down the hole this morning. You can get it out now." Giggling gleefully, they run hand in hand to the washhouse.

The world blackens. For an instant Aissa can't see or hear. Then the blackness turns red and rage fills her, even deeper and stronger than the despair.

Before she can think twice, she hurls her filthy rag down the hole and marches back out into the sunlight. She knows exactly what she smells like. But for once, it's not going to stop her.

As the last of the Hall folk turn onto the road, the crowd surges behind them. They've come from every house in the town and every outlying farm. Old men and women walk with sticks; babies and children ride on their parents' backs. The servants, once they're finally clean, will trail at the end of the long, long line.

Aissa quickly breaks a few twigs off the birch tree beside the privy, and twists them into a new brush. She refills her empty buckets at the well.

Half-One and Half-Two are still waiting outside the servants' washhouse.

They turn when they see her, and like girls in a mirror, each spit over their shoulder.

"You better not come in here till we're finished!" Half-One shouts. "We don't want to be polluted!"

"You better not follow the procession: your stink will kill the fireflies!"

The curse hits Aissa like a slap. The fireflies are the souls of the dead—kill them, and there'll be no rebirth.

But what if Half-Two's right?

It's too late to stop. Her plan is clear now, and she has to follow it.

Something Aissa's never felt before surges through her, up from the soles of her feet and out through the top of her head. Excitement. It's hard to make herself hide it and slump dejectedly, as if their words have wounded her.

"Scrub well!" Half-Two mocks.

I will, says the voice in Aissa's head, and she steps into the Hall folk's washhouse.

She blocks the door shut with her buckets.

There are benches on the two side walls and a door at each end, with a long stone tub in the middle of the room. Hot water runs through it, straight from the bubbling hot springs, and drains away at the other end. Aissa has been in this washhouse every day since she was old enough to scrub. She'd been in it only this morning. But this time is different.

Fear floods over her. What she's planning is even more blasphemous than a joke about dead fireflies.

Not that anyone has ever said, "You mustn't use any washhouse or privy except the one for your class."

No one's ever ordered, "Keep out of here except when you're cleaning."

They don't need to. It's too powerful a law to need saying.

She can't break it. She can't believe that she'd thought of it, even for a moment. No-Name is the lowest of the low, the filthiest of the filth—how could she even think of polluting the Hall folk's washing place?

And what if a woman from the Hall is slow, is late, is coming in even now? She doesn't dare imagine what will happen if she's caught. She has to get out before it's too late.

Aissa grabs her buckets. She shoves her shoulder against the door.

Her stink hits her. The twins' voices ring again in her head.

She turns around and rushes back through the long washroom to the door at the other end. She's never seen through it to the room beyond, but she knows for sure that the only people who use it have already gone. The Lady and her family are at the very head of the procession.

The Lady's bathroom is a smaller version of the outer one, though the bath is just as long, and the fountain that pours into it is richer, taller, and bubblier. On one side of the bath there's a table with oils, combs, and a bronze mirror, and on the other a carved wooden bench. Something is lying under the bench. Automatically, Aissa crosses to pick it up.

It's a cream-colored tunic, shredded under the left arm along an already mended seam. She pictures Fila pulling it off, rumpling it into a ball, and tossing it away in disgust. It needs to be taken to the washer girls, who'll clean it and take it to the tailors for mending, and then it'll be given to a servant the right size. One year, when it can't be mended any more, it may even go to Aissa. If she can keep it away from the twins.

She lays the tunic out on the edge of the fountain and lets it catch the steam.

For a long moment, she feels herself teetering on the edge of the chasm that's opened in her world. It's not too late to change her mind; she could still make some sort of excuse if she were caught.

She takes a deep breath. Then she slips out of her filthy rags and into the tub.

Aissa has felt warm water on the back of her hands when she's scrubbed the Hall folk's bath, but she's never so much as cupped her palms into it to splash her grimy face. Never dipped her tough, blackened toes below its surface.

Servants wash in cold water, squatting in a bowl with someone else pouring the water over their hair. The Hall folk must do it in the same way, except with more comfort and warmth, because there are four seats in their stone tub.

But this bath is long and smooth, with no seats, and as Aissa steps into it she slips and falls.

Sliding into the water, the Lady's pool,
    slippery rock splashing her down
    hot water bubbling
    over her face,
    over her mouth,

her eyes, her nose,
No-Name drowning in the Lady's tub.
Bursting through bubbles
water streaming from hair
stinging her eyes
choking her throat.
Struggling up, grabbing the sides
because No-Name doesn't belong
and the pool doesn't want
the bad-luck girl;
will spit her out
like the filth she is.
She needs
to save herself fast.
Slipping again
but now the water holds
and floats her;
its warmth soothing the girl
in the Lady's pool,
rocking to almost-sleep,
her weight lifted from her,
nothing to do but rest,
safe as if
in a mother's arms.
Then it rocks her awake again,
and she opens eyes
to water draining brown,
draining dirt from skin and hair.
Finding the pumice stone
placed in its nook
for maids to rub

the Lady's feet.
"Scrub well!" taunts Half-Two in her head.
Scrubbing hands, scrubbing feet,
scouring arms and neck
till the draining water is almost clear
and the tub releases her
to scramble out,
wet and dripping.
Grabbing her raggy tunic from the floor
and her twig brush
she scrubs
the tub's rock walls
till no trace of No-Name
and her filth remains.
Hair dripping tangles down her neck;
not thinking now,
obeying her eyes
that see the comb on the table,
tugging it through knots,
yanking combfuls of curls—
and tears, in torrents.
Girls learn to plait hair
at their mother's knee,
but it's too long since this girl
had a mother to lean on.
She twists long tangles
into rough ropes—
then turns for the tunic.
Not the bad-luck girl's own rags
filthy and crumpled,

but Fila's discard,
steamed clean.
Fila two years younger
but taller, rounder—
the tunic is roomy,
the belt goes around twice.
Her own sandals
more dirt than leather,
but even the Lady's feet
will carry dust home tonight.
No-Name's hair from the Lady's comb
thrown in the bucket
with tunic-rag and brush;
comb on the table
just as it was;
a last look around
and time to go.
But her hand hovers
over the mirror—
the magic bronze
that shows the Lady her face.
She turns it over,
looks in, and sees
a girl with staring eyes,
tangled ropes of hair,
thin dark face,
twist to the mouth.
But a girl like others.
Around her neck her mama stone,
its deep-carved sign

washed clean and clear:
the dragonfly of her name.
From her mouth comes a sound
she's never heard—
a croak of no toad,
a bark of no dog—
Mama said, "Quiet, still as stone,"
but she's never had to stop
happy noise before.
The name last heard on Mama's lips
forgotten through the long, bleak years
of bad-luck child,
the twice-abandoned,
No-Name girl.
Remembered now with a rush of heat:
her name,
herself.
"Aissa," she hears in her head.
"Aissa."

The square is empty when Aissa slips out of the Hall, though there are sounds of voices from the servants' washhouse. Half-One and Half-Two must be in there. Any minute now they'll be rushing out, through the front gate, and up the wide road to join the servants ahead of them. That's the way the procession has gone from the beginning of time.

But ever since the Bull King's man didn't spit at her, Aissa's known that things don't have to go the same way forever. Dumping her buckets behind the privy, she races through the kitchen gardens and out the small north gate.

There are a few houses along the narrow lane from the gate to the goat meadow. Aissa runs down it as quickly and silently as she can; there's always a chance that someone too frail to walk is watching at a window. She mustn't be seen.

Her heart's thumping by the time she ducks behind the mulberry tree at the edge of the field. On the other side, she can see the long line of people winding their way slowly up the mountain track.

Aissa turns away, toward the singing path.

It's not really called the singing path. It's not wide enough to have a name, except maybe the little-path-around-the-high-side-of-the-goat-meadow. But for Aissa it's the path Kelya used to take her on when she was searching for the wise-women's herbs. And everywhere she walked, Kelya sang. She sang the herbs, she sang the flowers, she sang the lizards and the eagles. She sang for the child that had no voice.

The child never answered, but she can still hear the notes in her mind.

These days Kelya's too blind to walk through the mountains, and the younger wise-women don't want the privy-cleaner touching their herbs. They go themselves, or send Half-One and Half-Two for the easy ones that anyone could spot: thyme growing through the rocks, or the new asparagus poking skinny spears toward the sun.

No one knows that the twins are so terrified of the mountain snakes that they send Aissa instead.

Aissa knows what snakes can do, and wolves and wild boars as well, but she'd rather spend the day with them than Half-One and Half-Two. Her sharp eyes find the herbs quickly. Then she steals time, like a honey cake from the kitchen. Except that an hour of wandering free in the hills, running fleet as a deer, far from spit and curses, is better than any honey cake. She takes as long as she can before hiding the basket of herbs in the crook of the mulberry tree for the twins to claim.

And when she steps back inside the town walls, her head carefully bowed to hide the purple of any stolen mulberries, she feels a secret thrill like a bright ribbon through her darkness: *Half-One and Half-Two would be so angry if they knew how much I love this!*

But now she's here without being sent, and that's the strongest magic of all. As her feet hit the path, her whole body remembers Kelya's songs; it hums and throbs, singing silently through her hands and feet and belly, as if there's music inside her struggling to escape.

She hurries faster up the hill to where the path forks. The left-hand trail will take her to the procession at exactly the right place and time, but her feet turn the other way, and suddenly she is looking down at the white cave and deep blue water of the Source.

Aissa is sure she's never been here before: it's too holy a place for servants and No-Names. But it calls to her, and something in her recognizes it. She slides down the white pebbles to the edge of the steaming water.

There's a flash of deeper blue. A dragonfly skims over the rock, a breath past her face, and disappears across the pool.

My name! Aissa thinks. *It's my name that was calling*

me. She cups her hand into the pool, splashes the sacred water onto her face, and turns back to the trail.

It leads her into the forest, dark and shadowy, whispering with mysterious noises. Aissa is too full of dragonfly-wonder to be afraid. She comes out again onto a rocky hillside, catching her arm on a wild rose bramble and sucking the blood off quickly, before it can stain her new tunic. She doesn't even notice the blood on her foot, where a stick has speared between her toes.

The hill rolls down to a smaller meadow where the billy goats are sometimes kept away from the herd. Aissa skids cautiously down the hill, skirting the edges of the field. She's so close now, she's not going to be stopped by a charging goat. But if any billies are lurking in the shadows, they don't care enough to charge. She reaches the end of the meadow.

The procession stretches in front of her on the broad mountain path. She doesn't recognize anyone; the people passing now are mostly herders and woodsmen. But farther down, the tail end is in sight: the Hall servants are nearly here. If she's going to join in, she has to do it now.

As the sky purples into twilight, Aissa scrambles over the rock fence, crouches behind bushes—and slides into the middle of the procession. She smooths her tunic as if she'd just ducked behind a shrub to pee.

No one notices. Eyes flick over her and return to friends. She's just another young girl who's strayed up in the crowd from the servants, or back from the craftsfolk. For this one night, she's invisible—and free.

4

THE LIGHT OF THE FIREFLIES

Aissa free in the darkness,
    slipping through the crowd
    as if she were one of them.
    Turning away from familiar faces
    or curious
    or kind—
    but still with them.
Up the hill to the cliff
    high over the marsh,
    the people crowding in—
    the Lady and the chief above
    on a dais of rock.
From the rock to the ground
    the Lady pours wine
    for the goddess to drink,
    scatters poppy cakes
    for her to eat,
    and cries her plea aloud,

"Feed our dead,
and set their souls free."
The people are waiting
anxious in the dark
for that first light,
the brave soul riding on a firefly back,
toward rebirth.
Always-spying Aissa
sees it first:
a light in the sky,
the dancing spirit
of a soul set free.
Now the crowd sighs,
a thousand voices
of *Ah!* relief
and tears of joy.
And the fireflies come,
a cloud more than Aissa can count
till the dark sky flickers
with dancing stars.
And the potter,
the potter's husband,
the dead guard's wife,
the gardener's son,
all who have lost,
sing their last goodbye
to the souls they've loved.
Aissa watching
the firefly souls,
the singing mourners,

the Lady and her family
on their high flat stone,
the guard below
handing an unlit torch to the chief.
The chief passes his hand
over the torch
and presents it to the Lady—
who twirls it gently,
high in the darkness
till a freeflying soul,
seen by none,
lights it with its firefly flame.
Aissa feels the magic,
hears the sighs,
but she has seen too
the red glow of coals
dropped from the chief's leather pouch
to the waiting torch.

The Lady glows like the moon itself. Torch flames dance off the gold of her headdress and necklace, from her gold-laced waist and arms, and the crowd is hushed by her majesty.

Now she passes the sacred light from her torch to the chief's, and then to Fila and the maid walking with the little boys. They step down from the dais and the crowd surges around them.

"Lady!" people shout, thrusting their unlit torches toward their rulers. "Hey, Chief!" and even "Fila, over here!"

It's worth shouting and shoving. The earlier your torch is lit, the higher-born the person who passes the flame to you, the luckier your season will be. So the Lady and her circle light the torches of those around them, and then they light the torches of those around them... Flame by flame, the lights spread all the way down to the servants, till the shimmering tablelands drown the stars above and fireflies below.

Finally every torch has been lit. The guards clear a path through the crowd, and the Lady begins to lead the long bright snake back down the mountain. Castes are confused in the flickering darkness; fishermen walk with wise-women; the stone carver's daughter shares a torch with the garden boy Digger. Aissa slips from one group to another, always a step away from the torchlight. It's easy enough to do—only the richest or largest families have more than a torch or two to share. Aissa's not the only child without her own, and not the only one separated from her family on the return.

For a little longer than is wise, she trails a farmer family, breathing in the pungent smell of their goatskin jerkins. The smell wakes memories that she can't quite reach, teasing her with a glimmer of happiness. *Maybe,* she thinks, *maybe they knew my family. Before I was a bad-luck girl; when I was Aissa.*

The oldest boy is watching her just as curiously. The torchlight falls on his face, and suddenly Aissa recognizes him. He'd come to the town a moon ago to offer the year's firstborn kid to the sanctuary. Now he's trying to figure out where he's seen her before.

Aissa waves wildly, as if to a searching mother, and charges like an angry ram. People slap and shout but Aissa's fast: she ducks and weaves, and is quickly out of reach.

When she dares lift her eyes again, the first woman she sees is the Lady. She's far ahead, but for just that instant, the crowd thins, so that Aissa can clearly see the back of her head and shoulders, and the glinting of the gold ring in her hair.

If the farmers weren't so far behind they might have thought she was claiming the Lady as her mother.

Aissa breathes deep, and slips through the crowd more quietly. Head down, elbows tucked, her thin frame sidles between adults and around children, past craftsfolk and traders, till, as the procession nears the town, the privy-girl is right behind the Lady's people and guards.

I must be crazy! she thinks. *But not crazy enough to go through the main gate.*

No one notices when she steps aside to retie her sandal, and slips silently down the dark path to the garden. A moment later, she's in the servants' kitchen.

Suddenly she feels as drained as an empty waterbag. Too tired to worry whether anyone will notice her new, clean tunic in the morning, she finds her ragged cloak in her sleeping place against the wall. Luckily the twins are too afraid of her pollution to take something she's already worn. She curls up in the cloak on the furthest corner of the stone floor. Long before any of the other servants have stumbled in, Aissa is truly, deeply asleep.

She dreams of fireflies. Dreams that the stale air of the kitchen is full of tiny golden stars dancing above her, lighting her space while the rest of the room is left in gloom and shadows. The free-flying souls light up the lowliest, least sacred place on the island. Voices cry out, and Aissa wakes in a leap of terror.

The fireflies disappear as if her thoughts have extinguished them.

In the morning the fear is gone, but the golden glow is still dancing inside her: a sign that her life is going to change.

It's the day of the lottery.

Every twelve year old on the island will assemble in the square. They will draw the signs of their names on shards of pottery, carefully and clearly, and drop them into an urn—one for the boys and one for the girls.

Year after year, Aissa has watched the solemn guard tip and swirl the urn, mixing the shards so only the gods can know which one is on top. She's seen the pale, tense faces as the chosen shards are pulled out and the new bull dancers are named.

Now Aissa is twelve. And she has a name to call.

As if a firefly in the night
    has brought rebirth
    to a girl who is not yet dead
    but has barely lived,
    the no-name girl
    has a name
    and a sign,

and a light in her shines
secret bright,
as blue as the dragonfly of her name.
Buzzing
as she shakes her cloak at the door
and shoves it in the hole
at the bottom of the wall—
away from the others,
because no one wants the cursed child's things
to touch their own.
Buzzing fierce
as she hauls water from the well
and fiercest of all
when the chores are done
and she squats in the lane
by the kitchen gardens
where she played long ago
with the potter's daughter,
and with a stick in the dust,
draws her dragonfly name.
She draws what she knows
of the long, slim bodies,
their round, watching eyes,
and fast-beating wings.
She draws the sign she saw
on her mama stone
till knowledge and sign
are one and the same
and all her own.

The potter sees her
    drawing in the dust.
    She shouts a curse
    and spits,
    once, twice, three times,
    because her daughter is dead
    in the Bull King's land
    and the bad-luck girl is here
    and alive.
Now the shards
    of the potter's smashed pots
    will choose the girl
    to dance the bulls
    in her daughter's place.
The potter's hatred,
    cold as winter ice,
    makes Aissa shiver
    and chills the joy
    of her dragonfly name.
The morning's too late
    and the square too busy
    for a girl to slide
    under the sanctuary rock.
    But in the gardens
    behind piles of compost—
    rotting weeds and kitchen waste—
    she finds a place to hide
    safe from hating eyes.
Drawing her sign like a prayer
    till the buzzing grows again

because the bad-luck girl
has found her name
in time to draw it on a shard of clay.
She knows,
as if the gods have spoken,
that by this nightfall
the privy-cleaner will be free,
will be warm,
clean and well-fed,
cherished and honored,
with the chance to free the island
and herself.
It will be worth
dying with the bulls
to be that girl for a year.

By noon, the twelve year olds and their families are in the square. Two days in a row, they're clean and dressed in their best. The children are fidgety and self-conscious; the parents' faces are a mixture of pride and fear. They're all pale and dark-eyed from last night's procession—no one is used to staying awake after sunset.

The watching crowd jostles for places. Whether you're grateful or ashamed that you don't have a child to offer this year, you want to see the chosen ones. You want to touch them right at the start, so that their luck can rub off on you. The excitement is growing—and the louder it gets, the paler and more awkward the twelve year olds and their families become.

The guards bang their spears for silence. The Lady and the chief appear; Aissa sidles out of the garden and across the square. There are eleven boys and eight girls. Eight girls plus Aissa.

Another sign, Aissa decides. *Easier for the gods to choose my name.*

Though she's still not quite ready to join the line; she slips behind it to her nook in the wall.

Even now, no one notices that there are actually nine twelve-year-old girls in the square. No one thinks that a girl with no name would have an age. Aissa wouldn't know it either, if Kelya hadn't told her. This is the first spring that the wise-woman has forgotten to remind her she's another year older—that she's five, then six, on up to eleven.

The chief is speaking.

"Welcome!" he says, looking around at the families in the square so that each of them feels as if he's talking directly to them. Then his voice booms out loud, carrying to the furthest listener.

"The chance of honor falls equally on every family. We do not know who the gods will choose: we know only that the new dancers will be chosen from every girl and youth who reaches twelve summers healthy in mind and body. Let no one stay hidden; let no family shrink from their duty!"

He glares so fiercely that people shuffle their feet and stare around too, as if they might spot a secret stash of twelve year olds—but still no one sees Aissa.

The chief takes one last look, and when he's satisfied that he hasn't missed anything, bows to the Lady.

The Lady begins in her oracle voice. "Dancers have died, but some will live. This year brings change, and a greatness that has not been seen before." She pauses. "The Oracle doesn't say whether the change will come from the dancers who have just left, or the two who will be chosen now."

But if this year's dancers live, we won't need new ones! Aissa thinks. It would be evil to feel disappointed. She doesn't care.

The Lady continues, "All we can do is ask the gods to select whom they will to fulfill this prophecy. To choose those who are destined for greatness and change, however and whenever it comes."

The children and their families look solemn. Aissa is shaking. *I've got to step forward. It's what the gods demand; it's what I must do.*

She stays in her nook.

The tall guard places an urn in front of the chief. Another guard puts down a basket of clay shards.

"We call the boys and their namers," says the chief.

Boys and their mothers shuffle into a raggedy line. Two boys don't have mothers; a grandmother stands with one and a father with the other. The woman at the front of the line looks panicked. But she can't run away now. She salutes with her hand on her heart.

The chief nods at her and she takes a deep breath. "I present to the gods Luki, son of Misha the tenth," she taps her own chest, "daughter of Ina, daughter of

Isha, daughter of Misha the ninth…" She chants on right back to Misha the first, so many daughters-of ago that Aissa loses count.

Have there been Aissas before me?

How can I step up with no one to name me and my line?

It's one of the first things a child is taught: the long chant of who they come from, mother to grandmother and on till the beginning of time. But Aissa knows only Mama and Gaggie. She doesn't know their other names, and she couldn't say them if she did.

But she has her own name. That is infinitely more than she had yesterday morning. It'll have to be enough.

Luki chooses a shard from the basket of smashed pots, and the guard hands him a lump of charcoal. The boy squats in front of the basket. Carefully, he draws his leaping-deer name on his piece of clay, and drops it into the urn.

He and his mother step back into the crowd. The next mother and son begin.

Aissa watching from her nook
  knees trembling
  holding her mama stone
  for comforting strength,
  because the last boy
  is dropping his name
  into the urn.
The guard rolls the urn,
  tumbling smashed-pot pieces

for the gods to choose.
The chief reaches in,
pulls out a shard.
"Luki," he says.
The boy stands
straight and proud.
In the audience
his grandmother faints,
thumping hard to the ground
as if her heart can't hold
the joy and dread
a bull dancer brings.
Aissa feeling nothing
outside her quivering self;
the Lady's calling the girls,
but still Aissa hides—
her legs as useless
as her voice.
A no-name girl
can't be named.
The gods won't choose
a bad-luck child.
So she watches as one by one
the girls step up
with their mothers
or a father or an aunt,
with their neat plaited hair,
and their line of names.
She watches the Lady
stare at their faces
as if searching for a sign.

Too late for Aissa
to step up now,
as the last girl
charcoals her name
on her scrap of clay.
Then Milli-Cat comes,
twining round Aissa's feet,
and as the girl
drops her name in the urn,
Milli-Cat nudges
behind Aissa's knees
with love and purrs,
till Aissa steps out.
She holds her head high,
step by slow step.
The square seems to grow.
She never thought it could be so far—
these twelve paces to the Lady.
"Who names this girl?"
the Lady demands.
Blind Kelya does not see
the child she loves
standing alone.
"It's the girl called No-Name,"
says the tall guard
and in the audience
someone laughs.
"She has no voice," adds the guard.
"She doesn't need a voice to dance,"
says the Lady,

filling Aissa with warmth
as if the sun
is shining on her.
"Has she lived twelve springs?" asks the Lady,
and from the Hall,
Kelya's voice, growly with grief,
calls yes,
so that now the sun
glows right through Aissa.
But the Lady startles
at Kelya's voice.
Just for a moment
she looks into Aissa's eyes—
then shakes her head,
as if she's seen something
that can't be true.
"Make your mark," says the Lady,
so quietly,
it seems her voice doesn't work,
and Aissa knows
that the gods have chosen
and this is the sign.
The guard holds out the basket of shards.
Aissa chooses:
a piece long and thin,
tapering down to a point
like a dragonfly tail.
She takes the charcoal,
draws the sign of her name,
and drops it in.

The guard rolls the urn;
　the Lady's hand dips inside,
　slowly, slowly,
　as if touching and choosing,
　and pulls out a shard.
Aissa feels a light
　burn strong within her,
　and holds her breath to hear
　the no-name girl
　named and claimed
　as the Lady speaks out loud
　the choice of the gods.
"Nasta," says the Lady
　and shows the mark
　of a swimming fish.
Nasta, the eighth girl,
　daughter of fishers,
　chosen by the gods,
　holds herself proud,
　salutes the Lady.
　Her mother wipes a tear;
　Nasta turns
　and spits at Aissa.

5

DRAGONFLY BANISHED

The kitchen garden sprawls between the Hall and the houses of the inner town. Its back wall is the solid rock of the mountain. Nothing grows against it, but it's a good place to dump garbage. Aissa dumped dog droppings onto the pile this morning, and the lottery's name shards will end up there too.

That's where mine belongs! Aissa thinks bitterly. *Buried in filth.*

There are also piles of compost: rotting kitchen scraps, weeds, and manure from the dovecotes. The waste shrinks as it turns into rich soil ready to dig into the garden. The three oldest heaps have shrunk so much there's a gap between them and the cliff—a big enough space for Aissa to crawl through and hide. But she can't hide from the voices in her own mind, and those are even crueller than the jeers and curses of the audience.

How did I dare?

I wish I'd never learned my name.

It's a punishment for trespassing into the Lady's bathroom.

Milli-Cat pushed me out there as if she knew. Is she laughing too?

She can't bear to think of her only friend betraying her. It's nearly as bad as wondering what's going to happen next. Because she knows that Half-One and Half-Two, and every other servant right up to old Squint-Eye, will punish her for standing up as if she were a twelve-year-old girl like any other. She just doesn't know what the punishment will be.

She waits till dark before she creeps into the servants' kitchen. The floor is already covered with sleeping bodies, and she's not brave enough to pick her way across them to find her cloak. She curls up on the bare stones just inside the door, where she can get out before anyone sees her.

But her stubborn name whispers around her head as she sleeps, and she dreams of dragonflies.

She wakes to the hiss of whispers. Swift as an eagle plummeting onto a rabbit, Aissa crashes from her dream into her body.

The kitchen is gray with the first light of dawn. The whispers get louder, like a venom-filled hiss. She huddles on the floor while the poisonous words flood over her.

"She's worse than cursed—she's a demon!"

"It's the gods' answer for letting her attempt the lottery."

"She should have been thrown out for the wolves when the raiders left her at the gates."

"The raiders didn't leave her at the gates, idiot."

"Someone did. And they should have left her for the wolves."

"It's not too late. We'll go to the Lady, tell her we can't spend another night with her here."

"Who knows what she'll call in on us next?"

Aissa gives up trying to pretend she's asleep. She opens her eyes.

A cloud of dragonflies is hovering over her.

She flees to the garden, and the dragonflies follow. When they disappear she feels more alone than she's ever been.

Aissa's always hated being small, but today she wishes she were smaller. Even more, she wishes she could have turned into a dragonfly and flown away with the cloud.

"Keep away from us, insect demon!" Half-One snarls when Aissa tries to snatch a barley cake from the kitchen waste.

"Go and eat gnats!" Half-Two adds.

"We should tell Kelya that she's a demon."

"And when Kelya tells the Lady, No-Name will be thrown off the cliffs."

"Or left out to feed the wolves," Half-One finishes. She licks her lips, which makes her look even more wolfish than she means to.

They turn together to Squint-Eye. Squint-Eye is so old she spends most of her life in the kitchens now, organizing the others—with her stick if she needs to. She's older even than Kelya, and the girls know that she is the only one who could approach the wise-woman.

"Stupid girls!" Squint-Eye snaps. "You don't know anything!"

"But..."

The long walking stick slashes at twin legs. "Anyone who talks to Kelya will feel this stick across their back."

Half-Two squeals. Aissa almost smiles to see the red welt across her enemy's calves.

"I'll decide what to do with No-Name," says Squint-Eye.

All that day Aissa sweeps and scrubs, grinds barley in the heavy stone querns, and even hauls extra water, because if she does everything as perfectly as she can, maybe Squint-Eye will forget that for two nights in a row, she's filled the room with insects.

Maybe.

It's nearly time to fill her bucket again and sponge the tables clean for the Hall folk's dinner. Her stomach rumbles emptily; she's had nothing since breakfast yesterday—she'll be glad of the barley soup and leftovers when it's her turn to eat.

She leans over the well to haul up her bucket. Someone pinches the back of her neck, so hard that Aissa jumps and nearly falls in.

Half-One. Of course. Half-One with a smug, malicious smile saying, "Squint-Eye wants you. Now."

All the servants are in the kitchen. Every one of them is watching her.

"Here, girl!" Squint-Eye beckons. "In front of me: I need to see that you understand."

There's not a sound. The room seems to be holding its breath.

"No-Name child," Squint-Eye says solemnly, "you brought a curse to this town the day you were abandoned at the gates. The Lady in her goodness allows you to live. But now you've shown yourself for the demon you are, calling up creatures in the night, I cast you out from the fellowship of servants. You will not sleep in the kitchen; you will not eat when we do. You will live as a rat in the night: you are no longer one of us. Now go."

The words hit Aissa like stones, numbing her brain; she can't understand what they mean.

She stares at the mass of hating faces.

"Go!" they shriek. "Get out of here! Go!"

"Go!" they say,
  and Aissa goes
  but her knees are weak,
  her breath is gone
  knocked from her chest
  with the weight of words.
Creeping, broken, to the garden
  to hide behind the heaps of waste,

because Aissa
is garbage too,
discarded like
a sucked-clean bone,
as if the gods hate her;
the earth rejects her.
Squint-Eye's not a god
or Mother Earth,
but she is the keeper
of food and warmth
for Aissa.
She always thought
there was nothing worse
than being No-Name
the bad-luck girl,
but she was wrong.
No-Name was small,
but she was something—
if only to be
beaten and spat at.
Now she has a name
but she is nothing.
Huddled alone
through the night,
hearing the cries
of creatures in the dark
that she's never heard
from the servants' kitchen;
no cloak or roof,
cold teeth chattering,

stomach rumbling
because there'll be no soup,
not for Aissa,
not tonight,
or ever again.
But worse than cold,
worse than hunger,
is being outside:
outside the kitchen,
outside the group,
outside life.
Because Squint-Eye's curse:
cast out,
not one of us,
banished,
are just other words
for death.

Aissa wakes up colder, hungrier, and more confused than she's ever been.

Squint-Eye will beat me if I don't do my chores.

She'll beat me if I'm found.

I'll die if I don't find something to eat.

I'll die if they see me.

So she's still hiding behind the furthest compost heaps when Half-One and Half-Two come to empty the slops onto the freshest pile. They're talking so hard they don't see her cowering there.

"It can't be true."

"But remember how Kelya used to feed her treats?"

"She never did that for us."

"Tried to get her to talk."

"Ha! That was a waste of time!"

"Did you see the Lady's face?"

"Horrified!"

"Disgusted."

"Not—"

"No, not that."

"Can you imagine?"

"The gods wouldn't be so cruel. No-Name in the Hall?"

"The bulls would have died of fright."

"We'd have had to serve her for a year first."

Their faces twist into identical expressions of horror and they burst out laughing.

"But I still don't understand. The firstborn daughter died."

"Squint-Eye says she didn't."

"Squint-Eye told you that?"

"She told Wormbreath and Wormbreath told Yogo."

"And Yogo told you. Of course he did: darling Yogo."

Aissa hears a soft slap, and a giggle.

"So if she didn't die, what happened?"

"Squint-Eye saw Kelya leave the Hall in the middle of the night with something under her cloak."

"When the first chief died?"

"Twelve springs ago."

"Kelya took her to the farm that was raided?"

"We always knew she was cursed."

"But still...how could No-Name be the Lady's daughter?"

They laugh again. Which is lucky, because they can't hear Aissa gasp.

The Lady's daughter? The Lady's firstborn, the one who died?

It can't be.

They know she's there. The twins would do anything to hurt her, that's one thing she knows for sure. The other thing she knows is that Mama is her mother, and Mama loves her, wherever she is. That's what mothers do. They don't let other people steal them away in the night. They don't look at them and not see them.

Her head is spinning so fast it might come right off her shoulders. The only thing to do is run.

Words like arrows
  chasing her through the garden
  out the gate and up the lane,
  sobbing, panting,
  on the path to the hills,
  past the Source
  with its dragonflies
  mocking her name.
Beyond the path
  to the wild hills,
  far from town

with its spit and jeers
and the kitchen
no longer her home.
Running fleet as a hunted hare
she can't outrun
what's in her mind,
the hating eyes,
Squint-Eye's words,
the twins' story.
A story that can't be true,
a story against nature,
against the gods
because the Lady is everything
and Aissa is nothing.
"Aissa called fireflies,"
says a whisper in her mind,
"and the dragonflies of her name
like the Lady calling snakes."
But the Lady calls snakes
when she wants to,
singing in her big voice
borrowed from the gods.
Aissa doesn't know
why the fireflies came to her
or the crickets
or dragonflies either
when she didn't mean to call.
She doesn't know how they heard
the tiny voice of her dreams.
All she knows

is that the question is too big
and she is too small
to even ask.
But now she's heard it
she can't stop.
If the Lady is her mother
then Mama is not.
But Mama is love,
and the Lady is not.
To have a mother
who is not a mother,
a sister
who doesn't know her,
a father
dead like Papa—
both dead by her curse—
these are more fearful thoughts
than being cast out
from the life she knows.
Aissa runs
till she hears nothing
but the blood in her ears
her heart leaping
as if it would jump from her chest
and run on alone.
Foot hitting a stone,
the stone skidding,
ankle turning;
legs limp as dead octopus,
crumple and fold.

Aissa crashing down
face-first through
a sharp-scented gray-green bush.
The world is black,
quiet and still,
a moment with no seeing,
no hearing or feeling
thinking or knowing.
Then her breath returns,
gasping, rasping
through her scratchy throat.
Salt blood in her mouth,
bitten tongue tender,
pain jolting from her ankle,
smarting hands, and knees,
skinned and bloody.
Dust in her nose—
ribs hurt with the sneeze,
hurt more when she cries.
Aissa never cries,
not for eight years.
Has sniffled with loneliness,
had pain tears on her cheeks,
but not like this,
gulping and choking,
chest heaving,
throat raw,
curled like a hedgehog
under the bush,
rocking, thumping

forehead to ground,
back on her heels,
thumping again,
till the pain in her head
blots the pain in her mind.
But now she hears
an unearthly cry,
a terrible howling,
and Aissa's alone
and undefended—
the gray-green needles
are not sharp enough
to stop a wolf.
Aissa is empty,
a hollow nothing;
no one will care
if the wolf eats her.
Not even Aissa.
But her body cares
about crunching and tearing,
blood and pain.
It does not want to die.
Sliding out from the bush,
grabbing a rock,
then a bigger one,
another and another:
a heap of stones,
because Aissa can throw
rocks that find their mark
and the wolf won't like it

any more than bullying boys.
She is still alone
but not undefended.
Listening again:
to birds singing,
crickets chirping,
no wolf crying.
No gray shape crouches
in the grass
or stands vigil
on the high rock.
The howling was Aissa,
making noise
all by herself,
even though Mama said,
"Stay quiet,
still as stone till I come back."
But Mama's not coming back,
and maybe Mama's not Mama.
Aissa's alone
and making noise
doesn't betray Mama.
Making noise
could be strength.

Next time the wolf might be real. She doesn't want to go back but she doesn't want to die and there aren't any other choices. Squint-Eye said the Lady allows her to live. She is banned from the Hall but not the town. She will find a place to hide and be safe.

Aissa picks a gray-green twig and salutes the bush

in thanks. Its scent stirs a memory that she can't find.

The rain comes out of nowhere. The gods pour rivers over her, washing her clean. When it stops she feels dazed and even emptier than she did before. The old Aissa has been hollowed out and thrown away.

She's run so far she's not sure where she is. Her ankle is aching and she has to get a stick to lean on. Even when she finds the trail she goes slowly, and it's dark when she reaches the garden gate.

The guards pass; her teeth are chattering so hard that she has to bite her tongue to stop the noise. Luckily the guards never worry about the back gate; they stroll through the garden more to keep themselves awake than to check who might be on the other side. The instant they turn their backs she's through.

From there it's a quick hobble across the square to the sanctuary boulder. She doesn't have to think about it—she's never spending another night behind the compost heaps.

Now it doesn't matter that it's dark: her feet and hands, knees and elbows all know the way. She slithers under, wriggles up, and slides into her hollow by the window.

The dark in the sanctuary is a deeper black than the air around her. There's nothing to see: the Lady and Fila are in their own chambers, in beds with soft fleeces and warm woven covers.

Aissa slides down farther to get her face out of a puddle, and sleeps in her cold rock bed.

6

THE SANCTUARY CAVE

Aissa wakes to the sound of mewing.

Milli-Cat never comes into the kitchens when everyone's sleeping!

But Aissa's not on the kitchen floor with the other servants. It's still dark on the second morning of her outcast life; she's tucked into the hollow by the sanctuary window—and a pink cat nose is rubbing against her cheek.

How did you get here?

As if in answer, Milli-Cat jumps to the top of the boulder, looking back over her shoulder to check that Aissa's following.

Aissa does what she's told—Milli-Cat is so sure and bossy with her *Mrrp!* meow that she has to trust her.

The cat trots down the slope toward the cliff face. Aissa skids down it on her bottom.

The cat disappears into the darkness. Aissa slides after her, right over the edge.

Aissa making noise again:
    mouse-squeak of surprise
    as she hits the ground;
    sigh of relief
    because it wasn't far
    and she didn't land
    on Milli-Cat.
    Though she doesn't know
    how she'll get out again
    and thinks maybe
    she'll soon be a real ghost
    not just the half-ghost
    Squint-Eye ordered.
She's in a cave
    half-filled with rocks
    tumbled down in the boulder's crash;
    a space safe from wind
    or burning sun
    and almost from rain—
    the puddles at the front
    are small.
    And it's tall enough,
    once she ducks inside,
    that Aissa can stand
    without bowing her head.
Milli-Cat purrs,
    twining round her legs
    till Aissa touches
    smooth white fur,
    soft and sleek,

sinewy strong underneath.
Because Milli-Cat
might belong to the Lady
but she has chosen Aissa
for her own—
and no one can see them here.
So Aissa strokes
and Milli-Cat purrs
till Aissa jumps awake
because there's not much time
till the day begins
and for so many years
that's meant
sweeping the square
clean of dog dirt and leaves,
scrubbing out privies,
throwing fresh earth down the holes.
Knowing that she doesn't exist
takes a lot of remembering
but yesterday's rain
and tears
have washed away
the confusion:
if she doesn't exist
she can't do chores.
No one can punish
someone they can't see.
But the square has to be swept
and privies have to be cleaned.
Wormbreath's son Pigeon-Toe

can use a broom
but is still too small
to haul water or earth.
A worm of joy
wriggles through Aissa
because sharp-faced twins
can share cleaning privies
but they will hate it
twice as much.
Aissa will need
to stay hidden from them
because if they have the chance to hurt
they'll forget she doesn't exist.
The cave is night-time safe
but she hasn't eaten
for two long days;
she needs to get out
to find water, food,
a place to spy,
and to use the privy—
the privy that she
won't have to clean.
The gap between boulder and cliff
is easier to fall down
than pull up.
Aissa grabs the edge,
swings from her hands,
but her head misses the gap,
bumps hard,
and her knees slam the cliff.

The cliff wall
    is too smooth to climb
    and so is the sanctuary.
    There's no gap at all
    on the town wall side.
    But her cave floor
    is littered with rocks.
Aissa finds a big one, flat on top,
    too heavy to lift,
    so she sits with her back
    against the pile,
    shoves with her feet
    and hurting ankle
    to roll the rock against the cliff;
    shoves a smaller one tight beside
    to stop its wobble—
    and Aissa has built a step.
Now her head is as high as the gap.
    She pulls up,
    slides onto the boulder
    creeping up the steep slope
    to the window hollow.
    Too early still
    for the Lady and Fila
    though the sky is gray
    instead of black
    and it's time
    to slide like a snake
    down the gap
    and into the square.

No one on the island has seen the bull dances, but they've all heard the stories.

Minstrels describe the excitement, the drama, the emotions of the crowd, the betting. Traders are surer of the details: the first day of spring, in a courtyard of the Bull King's palace. There might be others during the year, but they're not important. The palace is huge, bigger than the Lady's town, but that's not important either. What's important is what happens. What's important is the bulls.

The tall guard who speaks the Bull King's language saw the bulls when he sailed on a trading ship; he says their shoulders are taller than he is, and their hooves as big around as his head. Their bodies are thick and as solidly muscled as wild boars, their horns long and curved, and when they gallop the ground thunders.

It's a long time since the tall guard's been at sea, so maybe the bulls have grown in his memory. Nothing could be as big as he claims.

But little by little, the Lady and the chief have worked out a picture. The dancers are highly skilled.

"They're fast," say the traders.

"Best tumblers I've ever seen."

"And strong."

"Handsprings, somersaults, backflips…"

"All across a bull's back."

"No wonder half of them die while they're training."

"Then we'll start their training here," says the Lady. She tries to convince a troupe of tumblers to stay and teach, but tumblers are used to moving, island to island, audience to audience. They're gone before first light, afraid that the islanders might not take no for an answer.

The Lady and the chief replay the acrobats' act in their minds. The Lady can't discuss it with anyone else in case they realize there are things she doesn't know, but the chief talks it over with the guards. Tigo, the youngest guard, can walk on his hands. He's never managed to do a backflip, but he thinks he can work it out. He's put in charge of training.

Every year something is added to the training; every year Tigo is a little better at teaching it. The year that Nasta and Luki are chosen is the sixth year. The chief, the Lady and the guards are all determined that this time it will make a difference.

Aissa doesn't care. She doesn't want to watch them training for something that she knows in her heart is hers. She doesn't care if the new dancers live out their year in the bullring, or if the island has to pay tribute forever. She can't worry about anything now except how to survive.

Though it turns out that their training is very useful for her survival. Later on, in the heat of summer or chill of winter, no one will be nearly as keen to join in, but in this restless spring weather, runners want to race them and wrestlers want to wrestle. Everyone wants to see how the new dancers perform. The other twelve year olds watch especially jealously, jostling around, showing off their own handstands and roaring with laughter every time Nasta or Luki falls over.

"Shoo!" Tigo shouts, flapping them away like stray dogs.

The families of the dancers who haven't returned are watching just as closely. They desperately want these two to survive, and they just as desperately want them not to be as good as their own children. They can't decide which one they want more, and they can't stop watching.

And while they're watching Nasta and Luki, Aissa's watching their market stalls. She's finally discovered what's worse than the thin end of the servants' gruel: nothing. Even when all that was left of the meat was a hint of its flavor, and the vegetables were a shredded mush, there were still bits of barley to roll on her tongue and suck through her teeth. And it was always there. She misses that twice-a-day stomach-filling warmth.

Aissa is very, very hungry.

Silent as stone,
soft as a ghost,
Aissa slips through the Hall
because the Hall folk don't know
she doesn't exist
and see only a servant girl
clearing scraps from tables,
the remains of platters
laden with food—
barley cakes and honey,
the last dried figs,
soft curds of goat cheese—
taking them back
for the servants' meal.

They don't see that the girl
with her head bowed low,
moves the platters,
but never takes them to the kitchen.
They see her reach under a table,
as a good servant should,
for the dropped fig
and broken barley cake
but don't see her swallow both
before she stands.
But Aissa, gulping hard,
sees a twin head—
the rightful clearer of platters—
approaching the door from the kitchen,
and Aissa steps
behind a pillar
out to the square
as Half-One walks in.
In the square Half-Two,
forgetting she can't see
the one who doesn't exist,
spits hard—
a slimy glob of hate
on Aissa's face.
Aissa wipes with a finger
and flicks it back.
So all these days
the rest of the town
watches bull dancers
and Aissa watches
the rest of the town.

Drifting on the edges
like a shadow,
scurrying through hidey holes
like a rat
chased and despised,
racing the dogs
for a bone
thrown from a feast,
sweeping spilled grains
from the stone grinder in the square,
where lucky people
with barley to crush
smash it from grains to flour.
Because after the first morning
the servants are quicker
to guard their share
from meals from the Hall
and there's nothing left
to feed compost worms
or Aissa.
Half-One and Half-Two
would eat till they sicked it back up
before they left something
that Aissa could eat.
The third day without food
her weakened body sleeps through morning
and she slides out from her cave
while the world rests
in the warmth of noon.
At the door of the sanctuary
the table's been cleared

of morning offerings,
but unseen, underneath,
is a bouquet of pigweed
and twelve dried raisins—
a gift from the goddess
telling Aissa to live.
So sometimes
in the busy market,
an olive stored from autumn,
a chunk of octopus leg,
a roasted snail
slides from the stall
to Aissa's hand
and mouth.
Till the day she sees
thin spears of asparagus
fresh and juicy,
heaped to tempt.
The watching woman
spits, "Get out of here!"
and Aissa flees.
But a voice in her head says,
"You found asparagus
long ago
in the hills with Kelya,
and just last year
for Half-One and Half-Two.
You can find it again
for you."

7

THE HILLS

The world is new and different—or maybe Aissa is. She's only a shadow in town, but when she's out in the hills she's alive. It's as if she's just learned to breathe.

Of course she's not the only one out foraging. It's springtime, and after a long winter of dried food, everyone's hungry for fresh green plants. Fat-leafed pigweed and feathery fennel, nettles that don't sting once they're cooked, the unfurling new leaves of wild grapes, mallow, and thistle, and wispy ram's beard... they're all begging to be picked, and most mornings, someone from nearly every family on the island will be wandering the meadows and forests to do it. Only the Hall folk and their servants wait in town for other people to gather food for them.

Baby animals appear too, as if the sun's warmth has magicked them out of the rocks and shadows. Young hares, rabbits, hedgehogs, deer, and ibex are easy prey for slings or arrows. Trees hold eggs in nests, and there are strange birds that land for only a few days, in spring and again in autumn. Sometimes they crash to the ground in high winds and are too exhausted to escape a hungry hunter.

The only problem is the other hungry hunters. The chief killed the last lion for his cloak when he married the Lady, but there are still bears, boars, lynx, and wolves and now they all have young to feed. They like the same meats that people do, but they don't mind adding humans to their menu.

So nobody walks the hills alone, unless they're a hunter or a goatherd with a good sling for rocks. Half-One and Half-Two, before they thought of making Aissa go, always went with girls from the town. Even the wise-women, if they're going far from other gatherers, take a hunter with them.

But for Aissa, a wild-haired, fur-cloaked hunter is just one more thing to run from.

Aissa doesn't have
    a bow with arrows,
    a spear,
    or even
    a sling like Zufi's
    when he guarded the goats—
    though it didn't save him
    from the raiders.
She could make a sling
    if she only had
    a knife to cut cord,

a spindle to make it,
something to spin—
and a basket to collect it—
but she doesn't know how
to make any of those
because a privy-cleaner
doesn't learn much else—
just knows she needs them
to survive as more
than a hunted rat.
Needs to learn
what the tiniest children know
if they have mamas or dadas,
gaggies or poppas,
or anyone
who loves them.
Like a song,
at the back of her mind
is an almost-memory:
a child warm on her grandmother's knee,
Gaggie's old hands
guiding Aissa's young ones
to whirl the spindle
that spins Spot Goat's hair
into yarn.
If Aissa can learn
to spin again
it means she can learn
to be a little
like everyone else—

but all her memory gives her
is that glimpse of love
and sometimes
it hurts too much
to remember that.
So when she sees
a spindle winding wool,
up the spike in its round clay disc,
that disc might as well be gold
for all the chance
Aissa has to own it.
Because the grieving potter
is still so sure
that Aissa's curse
killed her daughter,
that she would smash
every spindle in town
before she let
Aissa own one.

The morning is hot and windy. Aissa is plucking juicy pigweed leaves, heading farther and farther toward the forest, nibbling as she gathers. She stoops again—and touches a brown and bloody bit of something that might once have been a deer.

Prickles run down her spine. She hears a rustling in the trees and pictures the wolf. Or the bear or boar – whatever it is, it has killing teeth and ripping claws, and it probably doesn't care if its next meal is an ibex or a girl.

Aissa turns and runs. She doesn't stop till she meets the path to the goat meadow, where she can see people, and the wall of the town.

Nothing's following her. Maybe it was just wind rustling the leaves.

But the mountain suddenly seems dark and forbidding. At least when she lived with the servants she was only slapped and spat at. Nobody tried to eat her.

Outcast days are busy
with no cleaning or sweeping
but full of learning,
because now her ankle is healed
and her privy-stink
gone with the rain,
she can creep close
to watch and learn.
Spying a goatherd
dozing in the sun,
his staff in his hand
and beside it his sling—
a rope looped in the middle
to hold a rock—
so simple to make,
impossible for her.
Aissa's hand twitches,
wanting that sling—
not far down the hill
to snatch it and run—

but already his dog,
head up and alert,
has caught her scent.
Softly and quietly,
Aissa slips away.
Gathering food
fills the rest of her days—
evading slaps and kicks
when she passes too close
to a market stall,
but not any lonelier
than when she was part of
the servant tribe.
But outcast nights
are long and empty
though full sometimes
of terror,
fear that's worse
for not knowing why.
Her cave under the rock is safe
but in the night
Aissa doesn't always
feel it,
because it's dark,
cold,
and lonely
with owls screeching
as if they're crying
when Aissa can't.

Dark long before nightfall
and no morning light
till the sun has risen
high over the mountain,
so that Aissa might sleep,
not knowing it's day
and slither out
when the square is busy
with people to see her.
Her cave is cold,
even now in sun-warm spring
of longer days and gentler air,
the rock is chill,
and so is Aissa.
Most of all
her cave is empty,
full of nothing
just like Aissa.
Empty of light,
empty of warmth,
empty of food,
empty of hearth fire
and glowing embers;
empty of pots and platters,
goblets and baskets,
jugs of oil and wine,
empty of sound,
the murmur of voices,
the shushing of Squint-Eye,
sleepy groans and snores,

empty even of smell
of goatskin fleeces for lucky sleepers,
of tired bodies,
and a fug of farts.
But in the mornings, in the dark before dawn,
before the Lady greets her snakes,
Aissa's cave has Milli-Cat
rubbing her nose
against Aissa's cheek,
butting her head
under Aissa's chin,
curling heavy and purring on Aissa's chest—
and Milli-Cat is more
than all the emptiness.

8
THE SEA

The servants miss Aissa, and not just because of her chores. Most of them are hoping Squint-Eye will let her back in. Life is easier when they're all bullying the same person—now they're scrabbling for power, terrified of being the next victim.

Aissa would go back if Squint-Eye called her. Even with Milli-Cat's love, she doesn't know how long she can survive.

But this morning she's been exploring the rubbish heap, and has found the scoop of a broken bowl, and half a long bone needle that will work as a pin. She sidles past the sanctuary to slide her treasures under the gap, but has to duck out of sight while a woman places a bunch of fresh sea lettuce on the offering table.

In those few moments, Squint-Eye has come out to the stone bench outside the kitchen, a bowl of lentils on her knee. Her old fingers move quickly, flicking the rotten ones to the ground.

Aissa will have to walk past her to get out the garden gate.

She's so busy she might not see me…

Squint-Eye's good eye narrows spitefully. For a moment she forgets that she can't beat someone who doesn't exist. She reaches for her stick, but Aissa is already running.

"The cursed child is cast out!" Squint-Eye spits after her. "No-Name is nothing!"

A flood of servants comes running, screaming with joy at their game of hate.

"No-Name!" shriek Half-One and Half-Two.

"Cursed child!" calls Pigeon-Toe, too young to even know what it means.

"Squint-Eye, if you can't keep the servants under control I'll beat them myself!" shouts a guard.

Townfolk stop to stare; some are ready to join in, but there's nothing to see. Squint-Eye lashes about with her stick, and the servants go grumbling back to work.

Aissa is already gone. Out in the lane she hesitates. She's not ready to brave the mountain wolves again, but she's discovered something surprising.

I won't go back to being No-Name—no matter how hard it is!

Because she can't unlearn her name again now that she knows it. *Aissa*, it sings inside her, *Aissa, Aissa*. She pictures the dragonfly as she touches her amulet for strength.

She turns away from the hills, toward the sea.

Aissa has never been to the sea. Halfway down the road, where she stopped to watch the Bull King's ship, is as close as she's been—as close as she's ever wanted to be. The sea is where raiders come from.

The only other thing she knows about the sea is that fish come from it—every day the fishers bring up the catch they owe the Hall, and a few more to trade in the market. They use boats and trident-spears, or nets or lines with hooks, and those are more things Aissa doesn't have. But there are sea greens too, like the bunch left at the sanctuary offering table this morning.

Her stomach rumbles.

She turns onto a narrow trail she's never followed before. She's made up her mind: she's going to touch the sea that took Mama away.

At least I won't be thirsty! Plenty to drink down there.

The houses outside the wall nestle into hollows, clinging to the steep side of the hill. The trail winds past them, skirting the craggy boulders, through a field of yellow and white chamomile daisies. The wise-women often come here to pick them; Aissa looks around, but she's alone. She keeps on going.

She is right at the edge of a cliff.

Her stomach rolls. The sea is far below, where waves crash onto a mass of black rocks.

A gull squawks a warning, and Aissa turns to see two figures coming down the trail. She recognizes the way they move: *Half-One and Half-Two!*

They're bigger than her, there are two of them, and she's on top of a cliff. There's no choice.

Aissa slides over the edge. She'll hold on somehow and hide till they give up.

Her feet touch a narrow ledge. When she inches to its end she can see another bump of rock below her clenched toes. Down from that there's a second ledge – and right below that, steps have been carved into the cliff. It's the start of a trail. Not a trail like the hill paths; more of a rough guide to where people might have climbed before.

She'd really like to know if those people survived.

Cautiously as a fledgling eaglet leaving the nest, Aissa slides backward onto the first step. Five more and another five, and then she loses count. They're about the same distance apart, and quite easy for a girl who's used to crawling over rocks to get to her cave home every night. She doesn't even have to look now, just finds a fingerhold in the cliff and steps down backward to the next one.

Nearly there! she thinks. She's forgotten about Half-One and Half-Two; forgotten about getting back up; her only goal now is to get to the bottom of the cliff.

She does it faster than she wants.

The next step's gone, the cliff is gone, and her clutching fingers aren't nearly enough to save her. She plummets like a stone.

And just has time to think, *Half-One and Half-Two won't even know they've killed me!*

She dreams
    of Squint-Eye beating
    a flapping eaglet,
    and the bird, too young to fly,
    crying its fear
    and pain.
Aissa knows
    the beating is real
    because she feels the thump
    in every bone,
    but only the Lady
    could read the meaning
    of a tumbling eaglet.
Struggling to wake,
    though the sun
    is high in the sky
    and another beating
    will follow for sure.
But her bed is soft
    as a pile of fleece;
    her eyes are heavy
    as if they too
    are weighted with wool.
    So Aissa surrenders;
    sleeps again
    till a bolt of light
    hits her face,
    and opens her eyes to see the sun
    sink red and splendid
    into the sea.

Wide awake now,
 though eyes still heavy
 and body limp,
 she remembers the fall.
 No beating except
 in Squint-Eye's wish;
 the tumbling bird herself
 and the bruises real,
 every one.
 No fleeces here,
 but a bed of seaweed,
 piled high
 against a half-moon cave
 where the waves have washed
 the cliff away.

It's too dark to leave. She'll have to spend the night here.

If only I had fire!

But a fire flint is another thing she doesn't have, so she'll stay awake in case wolves or sea monsters come. Her seaweed bed is comfortable, and it's even more comforting to feel the supply of rocks beneath it. So comforting that, with a stone in each hand, she drops back into a deep sleep and doesn't wake till dawn.

Her stomach is clenching with hunger, her throat cracked with thirst, and her face and lips burned red raw from the sun, but her mind is clear. She scrambles up, shaking off seaweed, because it's over her as well as under, down her tunic and between her toes. It's fluffy and dry, up to her knees when she stands, but heavy and wet at the end of her bed. Hollows in the rocks beyond glisten with water.

The sea has come up to her in the night. It could have floated her away like Mama, if the goddess hadn't stopped it in time.

But the water in the rocks looks fresh and clear, and the sea has retreated enough that she can reach the nearest rock without getting wet. She bends and laps it up like Milli-Cat...and spits and gags. The clear water burns with salt.

Now she knows why people say, "Useless as a cup of sea on a summer's day."

The sea begins
on the other side of the rock.
Aissa knows now
that she can't drink it
and knows that nothing good
ever came from the sea
but she is so close
she'll touch its waves
and maybe that touch
will travel somehow
somewhere
to Mama.
Sliding down,
the rock so slippery and steep
that she splashes in fast,
under the water,

feet and knees and all of her;
cold water over her head,
salt up her nose
and in her mouth.
Kicking and scrabbling,
spluttering up to the air,
Aissa pulls herself
onto a rounder rock,
a kinder rock,
that lets her sit,
heart pounding,
nose dripping,
coughing salt.
Sliding back
farther from the treacherous sea,
turning to safety
just as the sun
rises over the cliff.
Aissa alone to greet the dawn,
no Lady or snakes or singing
to thank for the rising,
so she stands with hand on heart
and thanks the goddess,
her inside voice singing high
because she is chilled and wet,
thirsty and hungry,
but very glad to be alive.
So the morning sun shows her
in a rock pool at her feet,
sea lettuce, soft and green,

fresher than the gatherers bring it
to the kitchen and the Hall.
A clutch of seaweed—
slippery and soft, straight to her mouth,
moist and cool down her parched sore throat—
because she's paid for it,
nearly with her life,
and it is hers.
Hers to pick
and eat as she will,
leaf by leaf
or gulp by gulp.
Shells hide
under the fronds
and in between:
tiny snails and fat black mussels.
Aissa has tasted snails
snatched from the plate before her turn,
but never mussels
because roasted mussels
are Squint-Eye's favorite.
Aissa can't roast them,
but she can pluck one off its rock
smash it hard
and swallow the quivery inside lump,
spitting out the shards of shell.
Tastes a second and then a third,
but it's been so long
since her stomach was full
it's shrunk too small
to eat any more.

There's no way back up the cliffs from here. *I'll stay here forever!* Aissa thinks. *All the mussels and sea lettuce I can eat; no more twins; no more spit.*

The half-moon cave with its soft seaweed bed looks even friendlier in the sunlight. But she still hasn't found water to drink, and she hasn't got a roof or fire to protect her from wolves or bears that want to eat her.

Town is still the safest place. Outcast or not, she'll have to go back.

The north end of the shore is a jagged point where water rushes between the cliff and a pillar of rock. The south point doesn't look much better, but it's closer. Aissa turns that way.

Sometimes she can squeeze between big boulders and sometimes she has to climb over them. She stops at rock pools to nibble more sea lettuce or dark purple dulse. It takes a long time to reach the southern end.

The point is a sheer cliff. Waves crash against it, spraying foam. There is no beach at all.

I can't get around that!

I have to.

Clinging like a dragonfly to a rock, she presses herself against the cliff.

Her legs don't want to move, but the rest of her doesn't want to stay stuck on the point forever. Eventually her legs do what they're told. Slowly, so slowly that she could have run to the barley field and back in the same time, she inches across and steps down to a rocky beach.

Her hands and toes are scratched, and the stones are sharp under her thin sandals, but her mind is singing. *I did it! Aissa is strong and still alive!*

The beach ahead is narrow, and curves to a rounded point at the other end. It's covered with rocks, and the rocks are covered with oysters.

Like the Lady eats!

Just as all the servants know that mussels are Squint-Eye's favorite, everyone from the Hall on down knows that oysters are the Lady's. Servants aren't allowed to eat them, even if they're left over—they're for the rulers and Hall folk only.

Though Aissa once saw a hunter snatch two off a platter before it went into the Hall, tipping the oysters off their shells and straight down his throat. Nobody cares what they do in front of No-Name—who is she going to tell?

Mussels are always cooked, and eaten when their shells open, but the Lady likes oysters raw. Cook opens their shells with a short bronze knife.

"That's what I need!" Aissa thinks.

And then she finds one.

It's not really a knife, and it's not bronze. It's a left-over bit from a flint knife someone else made, so it has a sharp edge, just not as sharp as the blade it had been chipped away from. And it's not very big, but neither is Aissa's hand.

Thank you! Aissa thinks to whoever left it here, whether it was someone from long ago before copper or bronze came to the island, or somebody who can't afford metal now.

If she holds the blade tight between her thumb and forefinger, and finds the slit where the two shells join, she can slide her knife in, wiggle it back and forth till the top shell is cut free, pry it off, and scoop the oyster out with her fingers.

The first one takes a long time, and she's afraid she might break her knife. Maybe she should look for more mussels instead. Then she tastes it: *that's why it's the Lady's favorite!*

The next one is quicker, and Cook herself couldn't have done the seventh any faster. They're all just as delicious as the first. Maybe some good things come from the sea after all.

She can't take oysters with her; she doesn't have a gathering basket to cover them with cool seaweed to keep them fresh, and the day is hot. Spoiled oysters are deadly oysters, that's what Cook said when a gatherer handed over a big basket that had been too long in the sun. Aissa still remembers seeing the beating. The gatherer probably still feels it.

So she leaves the oysters, but picks up three shining shells from between the rocks, for no reason except that they're beautiful. She knots them safely into her rag-pouch with her flint knife.

And once they're in her sanctuary cave, no one can take them away from her. *I'll show them to Milli-Cat and remember when I ate Hall folk's food. The Lady's favorite.*

The sun is high in the sky; her sunburnt face is glowing, but there's no shade to rest in. She passes another oyster-covered rock: some have been chipped off.

A knife did that, thinks Aissa. *People have been here.*

Sure enough, when she clambers over a pile of boulders to round the point, she's on the fishers' pebbled beach. Their houses are built into the hill, close to the road winding up to town from the other end of the cove. The little boats are already in from their morning's fishing, but no one is in sight. It's siesta time.

Aissa can sneak past sleeping people, but not their dogs.

Do fishers have dogs?

So many things she doesn't know.

On this side of the point, the cliff is more of a hill. Aissa scrambles up it to meet the chamomile path she ran down yesterday. She can follow that, around the edges of town to the river, where she can finally cool her hot face and drink…

She detours to the cliff top for one last look at the sea.

Nestled into the hollow of an ancient olive tree is a small stone statue. Carved wooden dolphins are laid out in front of her. This is the fishers' goddess.

Aissa salutes her, hand on her heart in thanks: the sea has given her food and a knife, a day of safety, and freedom.

A salute is not enough.

She picks a bunch of yellow chamomile daisies, and lays them out in a pattern in front of the goddess. It's still not enough. Not till she takes the three shells from her pouch and places them in the middle of the circle.

What are you doing? says the mean voice in her head. *This is the fishers' shrine! You don't belong here!*

Her heart is beating hard.

Don't be angry, she begs the stone figure. *I only wanted to thank you.*

It's too late to take the offering back. The goddess might want to accept it.

Or she might throw you off the cliff instead, says the mean voice.

Aissa shudders and turns to see how close she is to the edge.

Far below, out in the sea, three dolphins are leaping.

9

THE ROCK SLINGER

Returning from the sea
her sanctuary cave is darker,
the rock floor colder,
the town more hate-filled—
but there is shelter
and water to drink
from river or well.
And though the sea goddess
welcomed her once,
when Aissa returns
her flowers and shells
have been scattered and smashed.
Nowhere is safe
but sometimes
she is too tired to run—
and sometimes
she is tired
of always running—

so she hides,
squatting behind
a rock or a tree,
her head tucked tight
between her knees,
her arms shielding
her defenseless neck.
Sitting small,
still as stone,
as invisible
as the nothing she feels.

From one full moon to the next, Aissa stays close to town, wandering in the loop of river, barley field, and olive grove, sheltering under a tree or the stone bridge in the heat of the day, creeping back to her cave at night. The barley is being harvested, threshed, and winnowed, the whole community working as one. Women move down the field in a slow dance of bent backs and small flashing sickles. Children and servants glean behind them to pick up fallen stalks.

Even here, Aissa is chased away. No one wants a curse on the year's grain.

But with everyone else occupied, she can wander more freely, collecting greens from the grove and lush riverside. She explores the washing rocks; the river is clear and doesn't taste of salt. Aissa drinks and washes, steals a rag left drying on a bush, and winds it into a shepherd's headscarf. She's still sunburnt from her day at the sea.

The harvest ends, and the townfolk chase her away from their favorite picking spots again. She'll have to go back to the hills.

Wolves can't be much worse than Squint-Eye, she decides.

The farther she gets from the town, the more she knows that's not true. She's twitchy as a hare as she snatches fennel stalks from between rocks. Their liquorice flavor doesn't taste nearly as good when she's wondering how she might taste to a wolf.

A group of families is collecting greens too. They sing as they pick, with the younger children safe in the middle, acting out the song.

Here comes rabbit, hippity hop
See his ears flap and flop;
Here comes hedgehog, curled up small
Roll him over like a ball;
Here comes deer, fast and fleet,
Give a shout and make him leap.
Here comes wolf, with her pup,
If you don't run she'll eat you up!

Behind the voices
Aissa hears a memory
of hillsides with Mama,
green in her fingers,
of Mama singing
and another voice,
a child's song

as if, once upon a time,
Aissa had a voice.
She doesn't slow
her green-gathering,
sweet-leaf nibbling,
but the song pulls her
toward these children
who still have time to play,
feeling the love that binds
the circle of singing
as it drifts across her
with morning warmth.
Then a mother sees
and screams,
"Go away, you bad-luck child!
Keep your curse
from our precious ones!"
And one of the pretty, laughing girls
hurls a stone.
A small girl,
a small stone,
but its weight is heavy,
and Aissa runs.
Up the mountains to the woods
not stopping,
forgetting even to search
for life-giving greens,
till she hears more voices
and crouches to hide
behind a tree.

A goatherd girl,
two younger boys,
and all around them
the goats they guard.
The smaller boy holds a broken rope,
his shepherd's sling, torn in two.
His sister drops it to the ground:
"Time you learned to make your own,"
pointing up past Aissa's tree,
"Cedar bark is best."
"Stay with the goats,"
she tells the bigger boy
and leads her small brother
into the woods.
As if sent by the gods
to teach hidden Aissa,
she stops at a tree
with a dangling dead branch,
thick around as her arm.
With a knife of sharp flint
the girl slices the bark,
yanks it free:
"What you want is underneath."
Delicately now
she cuts again,
peeling pale inside skin
off the branch in long, clean strands
and takes the bundle
out from the woods
to the brother on his rock.

Aissa follows,
slipping from tree to tree
in time to see the girl
rolling the bark on her goatskinned thigh
till all the cords are rough and frayed.
Then she wraps and twists,
fingers flying so fast
that Aissa can't see,
and neither can the little brother.
"Slow down!" he begs.
His sister laughs,
stops showing off,
and shows him slowly,
loop by patient loop.
Aissa's fingers copy
without the cord,
learning movements
to remember later.
And when the goats roam west
and the goatherds follow,
Aissa returns to the tree,
to the other side
of the long dead branch;
cuts the bark with her flint,
peels the pale strings free,
and carries them away.

10

THE BULL DANCERS

Aissa wakes early. It's the start of summer, the longest day of the year. Tonight goat kids will be sacrificed. Their flesh will be cut small and roasted on skewers over open fires, so the gods can enjoy their fill of smoke, and the people their fill of meat. There will be jugs of wine, platters of the best food, and dancing in the square. There might even be enough chaos that Aissa can eat too.

It's not two full moons since she's been outcast, but already Aissa can hardly remember the moment when she believed that she was going to be a bull dancer. Easier to remember the dream she'd had last night, of being a hare fleeing a fox: she can still feel the frantic animal's heart pounding in her chest. She can't feel anything of the bull-dancer dream.

That's why she doesn't care about the dancers, she tells herself.

It's just that sometimes it's impossible not to.

The young guard Tigo is rounding up a community of youths to race with Nasta and Luki, a long-distance run into the hills before breakfast. "Around the goat meadow to the old oak at the start of the path to the Source. First one back wins a honey cake."

A honey cake! Aissa's mouth waters. A whole honey cake, moist and sweet, after so long of nothing but greens...She edges out from her hollow in the wall.

At the same moment the boy Digger approaches from the kitchen gardens. He's older than Aissa, and strong from his outdoor work.

"Not you, Digger!" Tigo roars. "Do you think the bull dancers are going to get stronger by racing with servants?"

Digger scurries back to the vegetables, his shoulders hunched against the jeers. Aissa shrinks back into her hollow, and Tigo's eyes pass over her without seeing.

But Nasta's don't. "No-Name's looking at me!" she wails.

"Get your bad luck away from the dancers!" Tigo bellows.

Without warning, the mocking laughter against Digger turns to rage against Aissa, the crowd turning with fists raised and spit flying—and Aissa is running, fast as the hunted hare of her dreams, faster than any bull dancer has ever run, out the back gate, and up to the hills.

Which is the trail that Tigo has set, so something changes as she runs. She's not running to hide; she's running because she can. She stops at the old oak; the sensible thing would be to go farther, skirting the edge of the forest to collect food for her day.

Instead she climbs the tree.

Up and up, pulling and scrambling until she reaches a high branch that's thick enough to lie on, and that's what she does, like a lynx waiting for prey. Not that she's going to pounce on the runners, who are coming up the trail now, puffing and panting. She's not even going to spit. But she can imagine it.

She imagines it so clearly that when Nasta is below her she can't stop the juicy gob leaving her mouth, shooting through the leaves onto the dancer's head. The girl jerks as if she's been slapped, and stops to stare at the tree.

Aissa lies still along the branch, hardly daring to breathe.

"Keep running, Nasta!" Tigo shouts. "It's downhill now, back to the Hall."

Luki's a little way behind; he hasn't reached the tree yet. He looks up into the branches as he runs, and for a moment Aissa thinks he's smiling.

He's just panting! she tells herself. *He can't possibly see me.*

He mustn't have, because he doesn't call Tigo.

But as Aissa lies in her perch, waiting till the last stragglers have circled the oak and disappeared back down the track, she remembers something else. Luki has never spat at her.

Watching Nasta,
watching Luki,
nasty Nasta, named for a fish,
stings like a wasp

and watches for Aissa,
just to jeer.
Luki doesn't
watch for Aissa
with hate or spit,
but sometimes it seems
that he sees—
which is the scariest of all.
Nasta glowing
with pride of her place,
walking through crowds,
with her god-luck touch,
as a dancer should.
Luki glows too—
pink and awkward in the crowd,
as if he needs
more room to breathe;
shares his god-luck
as if it hurts
and he'd rather be
anywhere than here,
so that sometimes Aissa thinks
he's as alone as she is.
Then her mind scoffs
because Luki is never
ever
alone.
He always has Tigo
or Nasta
or even the chief,

and always the crowd
wanting to touch.
Luki has a bed of fleece,
the best of food,
as if he were
the Lady's child;
nothing to trouble him
except being a dancer.
Luki is strong,
though not as quick on his feet
or agile as Nasta.
Luki's mother is a farmer,
his father and grandparents too.
They belong to the land
in the island's north—
as far up the mountain
as gardens will grow—
with olives and grapes,
vegetables, figs, and barley.
They come to the market
one day in five,
first mother, then father,
a brother and a sister,
sometimes an aunt,
but the walk is too long
for grandparents
or a toddling brother.
Aissa hears him—
the dancer in his clean white tunic
and neat oiled hair—
asking for news of home,

not just baby and grandparents,
but dogs and goat,
and the fruiting trees.
The family answer
stiff words that say little
as if to a stranger
who doesn't care how
the black dog barks at the wind
or the fig tree leans
over the spring.
Though sometimes
Aissa sees
tears in his mother's eyes,
and in Luki's.
Nasta's family
shed no tears;
her mother glows as bright as Nasta,
so proud, so sure
her daughter will be the one
to save the island.
She comes each day from the fishers' cove
with fish to trade
or pay the Lady,
but mostly so she can say,
"My Nasta, the dancer,"
and touch hands for luck,
as if it were her.
Like her daughter,
she watches for the bad-luck girl,
as if Nasta's glory
has been besmirched
by No-Name's hopes.

She corners Aissa
 against the town wall,
 with spit on her lips,
 hate in her eyes,
 says, "No-Name,
 bad-luck child,
 twice abandoned,
 I know that you
 passed by our shrine,
 cursing our holiest place
 with your stink.
"The goddess that watches
 the fishers at sea
 will toss you off the cliff
 if she finds you there.
 And if she doesn't,
 I will."

Ever since he came to the Hall, Luki has been curious about the girl called No-Name. She's short for her age, as thin and wary as a stray dog, and fast as a hunted hare. Her hair is black, like most people's, but curlier than most, a tangled frizz instead of plaits. She's never with the other servants—in fact, he's never seen her do any chores.

He's almost sure she's the girl he walked with on Firefly Night, except that girl looked free and happy. This girl is freer than he is, but she's the only person in the Hall who's more unhappy.

Maybe that's why he wants to laugh when he sees her spit onto Nasta's head. It's certainly why he doesn't give her away.

Because Luki knows that his fate is tied to Nasta's. Luki's worked with animals all his life, and he knows that surviving the bull dances will need teamwork. All Nasta cares about is beating everyone else—including him.

So that night at the solstice feast, he takes an extra honey cake from the platter. The party is nearly over before he spots the no-name girl skulking around the edges. Luki sidles into the shadows, and leaves the cake behind.

A honey cake
all for Aissa
as if she's won
the race after all.
As sweet in her mouth,
moist in her throat,
warm in her belly
as she's dreamed.
And as she licks
the last sweet crumbs
from every finger,
Aissa wonders how Luki
could leave it there
on a clean rock ledge
and walk away.
If she didn't know
that no one would ever
do something kind for her,
she'd almost think
it was a gift.

11

MILLI-CAT AND THE SNAKE

Foraging farther from town means worrying about wolves again. Aissa goes back to work on her rock-sling, but making rope isn't as easy as the goatherd girl made it look. All she's got from the bark she collected is fingers full of splinters.

The morning after the solstice festival she goes to the cedar trees and strips another bundle. Sitting on a rock till the day warms, sheltering in the forest shade when the sun is so hot that only the cicadas can sing, it takes nearly till sunset to tease out the bark and roll the prickly threads into strands. She tries to splice them in the dark of her cave that night, and ends up with a tangled mess.

Milli-Cat kneads and shreds it even more, making a nest—much cosier than the hard rock floor.

Did you think it was my offering to you? Aissa wonders, as the cat headbutts her in thanks. *Maybe it was.*

No one has ever thanked her before.

But she wants to make a rock-hurling sling, not a cat nest. She works at it every day, her fingers toughening as they get faster, until finally she has a rope. She splices the middle into a flat pouch to hold a stone, and knots one end into a handle.

Aissa's seen herder children practicing in the fields. The loop of rope whirls over their heads; the end flies free and the rock shoots out with it. She places a stone carefully into the pouch.

She whirls…the rope snaps; the rock lands on her toe.

Thank the goddess I chose a small rock! But even as she rubs the sore toe, she's studying the broken rope. *I see what I did wrong!*

Three days later, Milli-Cat's bark nest is big enough for a whole family of cats, and Aissa has a strong rope sling.

It's too big for her pouch, and servants don't have slings. She doesn't know what happens to outcast servants who break the Hall folk's rules, but it won't be good.

So she wears it wrapped three times around her waist, under her tunic. Now, when she goes out to the hills, she doesn't mind being out of sight of other gatherers. As soon as she's on her own, she unwraps the sling from under her tunic, grabs a rock, and starts practicing. Sometimes she even hits the tree she's aiming at.

This hot summer night
  Milli-Cat is restless,
  meowing complaints
  Aissa can't understand,
  rumpling and rustling
  her nest of bark
  as if it's nearly
  but not quite
  right,
  till she flops on her side
  with a yowl of pain.
Aissa's heart clenches
  in its own pain and fear.
  There is something wrong
  with her only friend
  and she can do
  nothing to help.
  She has nothing even
  to offer the goddess
  in a plea for mercy
  for this small being,
  alone like Aissa,
  the only one of her kind.
All she has
  are the chips of stone
  swept to the side
  of her hard floor bed,
  three empty snails,
  a shining mussel shell
  and a raven's feather.

She makes a circle,
a pattern to please the goddess
and with her sharp flint knife
slices her thumb,
hard and fast.
Her gift of blood
splashes the design,
red drops on the rock.
Then Milli-Cat yowls
a different call,
pain and surprise mixed into one,
and Aissa turns
to see the cat
licking a tiny wet bundle
of new life.
Licking hard,
as if she will shape
this squirming form
into a kitten.
And soon, it is.
Hand on heart,
Aissa thanks the goddess,
promising a gift
better than shells and feather,
because Milli-Cat can't do it herself—
she is busy again
birthing a second kitten.
Small as dormice
with blind, shut eyes,
but Milli-Cat knows them

as her own;
curls around them
till they nose to her side
for their first drink.
Too dark to see now
and though Aissa tries
to keep awake,
her eyes close
and she sleeps to the sound
of Milli-Cat's strong mother tongue
licking her babies into life.
Wakes for a yowling—
once, twice,
three, four more times—
each one a heart pang
for her small friend's pain
but the yowl always followed
by that busy licking
that says all is well
in this dark cave this night.
Till the dim light of morning
shows Milli-Cat curled
around six nuzzling kittens.
Two white like Milli,
two black
like the bull ship cat,
one patched both black and white
and the biggest
a strange soft gold.
Milli-Cat lifts her head
for Aissa's hand,

the touch that says,
"How clever you are,
and how beautiful
are your children!"
in the dark of the cave
where no one sees
the mute girl touching
the Lady's deaf pet.
And Aissa's heart swells again
with a different pain,
the strong, sharp ache
of love.

Aissa's home under the sanctuary rock is cold, hard, and cramped. She's grateful for its shelter but never slides into it without a slight shiver of dread, of wondering whether tonight it will fall and crush her. Now, on these long summer days, she can hardly wait for the secrecy of darkness so she can return to Milli-Cat's kittens.

Her only worry is that she has promised the goddess a gift, and she doesn't yet know what it could be. She doesn't have the first fruits of harvest, or the firstborn kid from a flock, or any of the usual offerings. She just hopes that she'll know when she finds it, and that the goddess will be patient till then.

Milli-Cat's babies
have blind, shut eyes,
are squirmy and helpless,

but Milli-Cat cares for them
as if they were jewels,
licking and cleaning,
nuzzling them to her side
so they all get her milk,
though the smallest, white like Milli—
is always the last to drink.
Milli-Cat goes out to hunt
early in the night
when Aissa is settling into sleep
and watching the kittens.
Not touching
in case Milli doesn't want it,
but watching,
learning them,
and watching Milli-Cat love them
she learns to love too.
The runty, white one
is not Milli's favorite
she saves her nuzzling for the strong
who drink hard
and grow fast.
But Aissa wonders
if the unloved kitten
would be just as strong
if it were loved.
She wants to see it grow
and is afraid
when a new guest comes.

Every home
needs a house snake to bless it,
the goddess's pet,
accepting bowls of milk
and family prayers.
Aissa's home is not a house,
just a rock she slithers under
as if she were a snake herself
so she is glad for the blessing
but afraid
because she has no milk to offer.
The snake is thin,
twice as long as the Lady's vipers
but not so deadly.
Aissa brings him
crickets and lizards,
hoping he doesn't
want something bigger.
She wishes that Milli-Cat
would offer a mouse
but the cat doesn't know
they must pay
for the snake's blessing.
The kittens grow, day by day
so every night,
Aissa sees them stronger,
eyes opening,
trying to walk
till her heart beats
with strong proud joy.

Late on a hot, full-moon night
  townfolk and Hall are in the square
  singing sad farewell to dying flowers
  and welcoming
  the fruits to come.
Aissa watching from the shadows;
  there is food to steal
  as the night grows dark
  so it's late when she slithers
  under her rock
  up and across
  and down to her cave
  like every other night.
But this night
  Milli-Cat is gone.
  No purring headbutt greets her
  though she can hear
  the soft breathing of kitten sleep
  and can feel in the darkness
  furry bodies snuggled
  in their nest of bark—
  but only five,
  no matter how she counts them.
The runty kitten
  that Aissa loves
  is gone.
Her heart tightens with pain,
  as if a hugging boa
  is squeezing her chest;

she searches the cave
hoping the runt has tumbled
on staggery legs
away from the others
because every day
the kittens walk a bit more.
Patting dark corners,
searching warm fur,
until she touches
in the furthest gap
where the rock slopes to the ground,
the solid smooth flesh,
cool in the night,
of a sleeping
well-fed snake.
Lifting its head
in a shaft of moonlight
the snake's eyes
look into Aissa's,
straight from the goddess
down to her soul.
The moonlight moves;
the spell is broken.
There's only the pain
that the kitten is gone
and rage
because it never had a chance
at life
simply because
it wasn't loved.

Wanting to choke the snake
make it cough up its kitten dinner—
the snake may be the goddess's pet
but Milli-Cat's runt was hers
and she screams inside,
I hate you, hate you, hate you!
till rage is swallowed by fear
because Milli-Cat is missing too
and what if
she's not out hunting
but inside the snake with her baby?
Heart twisting,
stomach churning,
tears dripping—
not for her,
not like the day she wailed on the mountain
but for the runty kitten
and her Milli-Cat friend
and the other babies
who will die
without their mother's care
because Aissa can love them
but they need milk.
"There's milk in the kitchens,"
says the voice in her head.
"The Lady can order it—
the kittens are hers."
Heart clenching tighter—
maybe some of
the tears were for her—

Aissa makes the picture in her mind:
taking kittens
from cave to Hall
while the Lady is at table
because if soft-hearted Fila
sees the kittens
they will be cared for.
And that's more important
than Aissa being alone
again.
The picture doesn't stop her sobs
but it unwinds her heart
soothing her to sleep,
until she feels
a warm nose against her face,
a head rubbing under her chin—
Milli-Cat home from the hunt,
not eaten up by the snake
just leaving the kittens alone
because Aissa was late.
Milli-Cat doesn't care
that the runt is gone
but cares that Aissa is crying;
she grabs her strong favorite
by his orange scruff,
carries him swinging
from her mouth,
and drops him onto
Aissa's neck.

In the morning
  Aissa remembers the goddess
  staring through the snake's slit eyes,
  thinks that Milli made her offering
  and now the runt's been taken
  the others will be safe.
  But just in case,
  she leaves her gifts
  of lizards and frogs
  at the front of the rock
  near the sanctuary door,
  far from the kittens.
And when the market traders
  see the snake there
  they leave offerings too.

It's the hottest morning of summer when Milli-Cat leads her five kittens proudly out from under the sanctuary rock. Her tail waves like a flag and the kittens march in a trail behind it. The Lady has barely finished singing the sun up when the crowd sees the parade of cats.

The Lady hears the gasps and waits for the chorus of, "Thank you, Mother!"

"Cats!" she hears.

"Little ones!"

"The Lady's pet's had babies!"

Fila forgets the ritual and runs to scoop up the black-and-white kitten. "So sweet!"

The kitten squawks in surprise, but Fila is gentle; after a moment he starts to purr. Milli-Cat meows sharply and marches on to the kitchen, the other kittens following. Fila puts the black-and-white one down and picks up the black one with a white snip on his chest. "Are you the cutest?" she asks, and then changes her mind and cuddles the pure white one.

It doesn't hurt as much as Aissa had thought—not until Fila picks up the orange kitten.

Ever since his mother dropped him onto Aissa's neck, Gold-Cat has claimed her for his own. He yowls when she comes back to the cave, twining around her ankles till she squats to hold him. He sleeps tucked between her chin and shoulder—Aissa doesn't know how she'll sleep again without that soft warmth.

"Ow!" Fila squeaks. The orange kitten scampers away with an indignant meow.

Milli-Cat glances at him, and goes on eating the fish Squint-Eye's offered her. Fila picks up the other black kitten. Gold-Cat hisses every time she comes near.

That evening, Milli-Cat leads her babies back to the cave for the night, and the orange kitten finds his place under Aissa's chin.

But the kittens don't know that this should only be for night-time. They haven't heard of outcasts and they don't know that No-Name doesn't exist. They don't know how hard it is to be invisible with a parade of tail-waving cats behind you.

It's confusing for the servants, too. They can't throw rocks at No-Name anymore, in case they hit one of the Lady's cats. They'd have to chase her out in the fields—only the golden kitten tries to follow her through the gate, and she always makes sure he stays inside. Half-Two even sees her pick up the little cat and put him back when he slips out after her.

The twin forgets the figs she's been sent to pick and races back to Squint-Eye. "No-Name touched the Lady's cat!"

Squint-Eye's stick whacks her across the legs. "Stupid girl! Are you going to tell the Lady that the beast prefers No-Name to her own daughter?"

Half-Two would like to, but another whack tells her that's the wrong answer.

12

THE GOATS AND THE WOLF

Aissa looks for more paths to the sea
for oyster rocks,
mussels, and seaweed
but sometimes
on a cliff
far from the fishers' cove,
she still feels the chill
of Nasta's mother,
waiting to throw her off.
The mountain is not so lonely
with sling in hand—
only hungry.
Slinging a rock at a rabbit
but never hitting it;
she doesn't know if
she could eat one,
raw and bloody,
anyway.

She's never tasted meat
except the shreds
at the bottom of soup
and maybe that's enough
for a girl like her.
In a high meadow
at the edge of the forest,
a goat grazes with her half-grown kid.
Aissa can't see a goatherd—
maybe they're wild,
belonging to no one.
If they belong to no one
they could be hers.
Remembering Spot Goat,
Mama milking,
the smell of whey,
of curds, and cheese
though she can't quite
remember the taste.
But she does remember—
more than she wants—
Spot Goat guarding
on the night of terror
and Aissa drinking
like the goat's lost kid;
remembers warm milk,
and the feel of her mouth
against the belly;
the sad bleat

when Fox Lady took
Aissa away.
Her heart fills with thanks
and hope that Spot Goat
is still grazing a meadow
with a kid at her feet.
Then the goat, not Spot Goat,
but the same *ble-aah* call,
trot-trots toward Aissa,
forgetting her kid,
and never seeing
the wolf crouched behind.
The wolf doesn't trot,
stays low in the grass,
creeping up on the kid,
closer and closer.
Aissa watching in a dream,
not breathing,
still as stone,
but her hand moves,
all by itself,
knowing just how
to reach for a rock
and fit it into the sling
while her eyes watch the wolf—
its tail twitching
mouth grinning
sharp teeth waiting,
ready to spring.

Aissa's arm whirling over her head,
 once, twice,
 no time for more,
 clutching tight to the knot,
 letting the other end
 slip through her fingers
 cracking like a whip
 as it hurls the stone
 hard, fast, and free.
Time slow as a dream;
 the wolf in his leap
 hangs in the air
 and then
 his head meets the rock,
 and they crash
 together to the ground
 and the wolf is just
 as dead as the stone.
The mother goat and kid
 are running, bleating,
 finding each other,
 racing farther in their panic,
 while a goatherd runs closer,
 her sling in one hand,
 staff in the other.
It's the girl who taught
 her brother to splice cord
 and taught Aissa too.
 She stares at Aissa,
 and at the wolf on the ground.

Aissa's heart's still thumping
 and her knees are weak.
 She doesn't know how
 she can run away.
"You killed it!" says the girl,
 with hand on heart
 and tears in her eyes.
"Thank you!
 Our flock thanks you,
 our family thanks you.
 Thank you, thank you!"

The goatherd girl isn't much older than Aissa, but she's a lot bigger. In fact Aissa isn't any taller than the nine-year-old brother. Maybe that's why the girl thinks she needs looking after. She looks anxious when Aissa doesn't speak.

"Sit down, child. I am Lanni, daughter of Panna the goatherd. Please, let us thank you."

Kindness is such a shock that Aissa's knees give way. She drops to the ground.

The goatherd blows two loud, sharp notes on her bone flute.

"Sammo, go see if they're coming," she orders her brother. "Stay up on that rock so I can see you."

"The wolf set all the goats running," she explains. "My other brother and the dog are rounding up the strays—we need to get these two back to the flock."

She takes a deep breath and shouts. "Parsley! Parsley!" She turns and mutters to Aissa, "Don't blame me, Sammo named her."

She picks up her flute again, but this time the notes are long and sweet, curling gently into the sky. Aissa feels a coil of fear begin to unwind, and the goat and her kid slow their frantic running. Lanni plays on until they turn back toward her.

"I can see Onyx!" Sammo calls. "He's got three does and kids."

"Three! What's he doing coming back without the others?"

"Wait, I can see more!"

"Go down to the flock," Lanni orders. "Keep your sling ready. That wolf will have had a mate."

She shakes the spit out of her flute and blows again. The doe and kid are almost calm as they approach. Lanni waits till the mother goat has come right up to her before she moves. Gently, she scratches between its ears.

"Will you come with us?" she asks Aissa. "When you're ready, we can take you back to your people."

She'll turn me over to Squint-Eye, Aissa thinks in panic, *and Squint-Eye will beat me because...well, just because she'll always beat me if she can.*

Lanni thinks Aissa's silence is from shock.

As well as the bone flute, the goatherd has a wooden bowl on another leather thong around her waist. She grips it between her knees as she squats beside the goat, crooning softly, and gently squeezes the udder until the bowl is full.

"Drink," she says, holding it to Aissa's lips.

Aissa drinks. It is the taste of childhood, of safety, love, and warmth. She drinks till her belly is full and her eyes are overflowing.

Lanni plays her flute again, almost the same music that called Parsley and her kid, but deeper, wider. The other goats start to join them. Sammo dances excitedly, shouting the story to his older brother. The dog trots behind the goats, keeping them in a tight group; the boy looks as if he's used up all his energy in the chase.

"When we got there, she'd killed the wolf!" Sammo explains.

"But that's No-Name," Onyx sneers. "The cursed servant!"

"She's the girl who saved Parsley's kid," his sister snaps. "And you'll thank her for it."

"Thank you," the boy mutters.

"The wolf's huge," Sammo adds.

Suddenly Onyx is interested. "I'll take its pelt!"

The skin! Aissa thinks. *A wolf fur would be so warm in winter—why didn't I take it right away?*

Though she could never be sorry for drinking that milk.

"It's not yours," Lanni tells her brother. "It's the girl's."

"Servants can't wear wolf skin. That's for hunters, and..."

"...and herders that earn them," his sister finishes. "So remind me about when you killed a wolf—I seem to have forgotten."

"Onyx has never killed a wolf!" squeals Sammo.

"Exactly. The girl's earned the pelt, and that's the end of the story. Do you have a knife, girl?"

Aissa shows her the little flint.

"It's not very big," Lanni says doubtfully. "Have you ever skinned anything with it?"

Aissa shakes her head.

"Onyx and Sammo, keep the goats away from those woods. I'm going to give the girl a hand."

With her own sharp stone knife, Lanni cuts the pelt at the neck and starts down the shoulder. There's a lot of blood, and the stink makes Aissa want to vomit.

"You haven't done this before, have you?" says Lanni. "It'll be worth it when you've got a fur cloak in the winter."

She hands Aissa the knife and shows her how to peel the skin free of the body.

"I wish you could talk! I guess you wish it too. Anyway, you can hear, so listen: wash the blood off as soon you can, then soak it in sea water—and you need to scrape every bit of fat and meat off the skin, or it'll rot and smell. Your little knife will be fine for that. It'll take you a few days."

They work together in silence.

"Are you safe where you are?" Lanni asks suddenly.

Aissa can't answer. She doesn't know.

"If it's true you belong to the Hall, we can't take you in. Except if you're a servant I don't know why you're up here on your own without so much as a gathering basket, or how you learned to use a sling."

You taught me! Aissa wishes she could say.

"Our home is a day's walk from here, but our summer cave is nearby." She points higher up the mountain. "If you ever need us, remember that we are in your debt."

The goatherd girl guesses
that Aissa hasn't killed before,
except crickets to eat,
mussels and oysters,
or ants as she walks,
but not an animal
with a beating heart,
breathing and living
as she does.
"You must wash," says Lanni,
"not just the fur.
Wash the blood from your body
and the death from your spirit.
Thank the wolf for dying;
thank the goddess
that it was him and not you."
These are simple rules
but in a life
of cleaning privies,
hauling water,
and grinding grain,
there were many things
Aissa couldn't spy.
She doesn't know
what her life is now
only that she needs to learn
all she can to survive.
Thanking the goatherd—
so strange to see
it signed back to her—

"Be well," says Lanni,
watching in worry
Aissa heading down the mountain
toward the town.
But first to a creek
where she does what the goatherd said:
dips the fur in cool running water,
swirls and wrings and dips again.
And when no trace of pink flows on
dips herself
clean from toes to hair.
Her body is clean
but her spirit not cleansed,
so early next morning, before first light
she leaves her cave,
waiting at the garden gate
for the Lady to raise the sun,
and while the world breakfasts
Aissa runs up the lane
all the way
to the Source.
Sliding down the white pebbles
to the steaming water's edge,
dipping a toe to test the heat
and with her tunic folded
on a rock beside,
she slides in where Kelya dipped her
on a long-ago morning—
the newborn daughter
the Lady couldn't keep.

Aissa, not knowing,
feels warm and safe
as if held
by loving hands—
though she knows
that if eyes spy her here
hands will not be loving—
the sacred Source
is not for servants or outcasts.
And she sees
tucked between rocks,
in crevices and cracks,
wooden carvings, or sometimes stone,
of a foot
or hand,
a leg or even
a tiny baby,
the prayers of people
asking for healing.
Aissa does not need healing
for a foot or leg,
one arm or finger
but for her whole self.
That afternoon she finds
an olive branch,
small and twisted,
and begins to carve
the dragonfly of her name.

13

THE BULL DANCER AND THE BOAR

Aissa takes the wolf pelt to the sea, and washes and scrapes it more times than she can count. In some places she rubs so hard she makes holes, but the fur is thick, and Gold-Cat has stopped attacking it now that it doesn't stink. He likes sleeping on it with Aissa. Aissa does too. She likes having something soft to lie on, and that she's done it herself.

There are other things in her cave home that she's done herself. Some she's made and some she's found: the shells, stones, and feathers that she arranges into patterns, her flint knife, the bone pin, and the dragonfly that she's carving.

The cave is cool even now in the middle of summer. When the noon sun empties the square, and the town and Hall doze in their afternoon siestas, Aissa can slide back into her home to escape the heat. She races over the baking top of the rock, hands and feet burning, but underneath is dark and shady. The cooling northerly breezes whisper in through cracks and gaps. She doesn't want to think what that will mean for winter.

Purple figs are ripening in the Hall garden and on wild trees around the island. Birds love them as much as people do—little Pigeon-Toe gets beaten nearly every day for falling asleep under the tree when he's supposed to be scaring birds. Townfolk and servants come back from the hills with baskets of the ripe fruit. Some are eaten but most are strung on cords to dry in the sun.

Aissa finds a tree far out from the town. The figs are fat and dark, splitting with juice; the sticky sap clings to her fingers as she eats them hot from the sun. One after another...she eats so many that she spends the rest of the day squatting behind a rock with painful diarrhea.

After that, she eats only a few at a time, and crams the rest in her pouch to take home and dry on the top of the sanctuary boulder. Birds swoop to steal them.

"Look how the goddess is favoring us, calling the birds from the tree to her roof," she hears Yogo say.

"Pigeon-Toe's finally learned from his beatings," says Squint-Eye.

Watching out for figs
    and other fig-pickers,
    Aissa still has time
    to spy on bull dancers.
She knows
    what she doesn't want to—
    that Nasta is quick,
    light on her feet,

her handsprings sure and free
a joy to watch
if only she wasn't Nasta.
Luki is strong
can pull himself to a branch,
can spring from hands to feet
and back again,
cartwheel along a wall—
but not lightly or surely.
Aissa imagines the feeling
of whirling hands and feet
and would hold her breath
in fear of his falling—
if she cared.
She sees too
that sometimes,
when the world sleeps
in hot siesta lull,
she is not the only one
to steal through the back gate
out to the hills.
Bull dancers don't belong to the Hall
the way servants do,
but they belong to the gods—
their lives are not
theirs to waste.
So even though
they don't have servant rules
or beatings for straying,

everyone knows
they must never go out
without a guard.
But Luki is leaving
sly as a thief
slipping into the garden
keeping in shade
looking left, looking right,
and sidling out to the lane—
not seeing Aissa
waiting behind the fig tree
while Pigeon-Toe sleeps
for her moment to snatch
a ripe, bursting fig
ready to be eaten.
Aissa doesn't let it
wait any longer
but she barely tastes
that sweet red juice
because her hunger now
is to know where Luki goes.
Racing through
the bare barley field
he turns to the mountain,
his route home:
his feet know their way
up the slopes and through the trees.
Aissa rushes not to lose him
but Luki,
sure he's alone,

sings as he goes,
laying a trail with his voice.
The song stops
and Aissa creeps
quietly, closer:
Luki is watchful
but not for her.
The ground is rough,
plants grubbed up;
the stink of pig
rises high.
Across the hill
a swineherd sleeps in front of his hut,
his dog beside him.
Luki reaches a clearing
where a big boar dozes
under an oak;
and forgetting that his life is sacred,
tempts the boar
away from the trees.
The day is hot
the boar is sleepy,
wanting to nap
like everyone else.
But Luki dances
until the beast charges.
Aissa's mind screams,
but Luki stands
until the boar is nearly there,
then leaps
as if he'll somersault

down the boar's back—
but instead crashes
hard to the ground
and lies still.
The boar turns in shock—
the swineherd has never
begged him to charge
or jumped over his back—
and starts to rush
the boy on the ground.
There's no time for Aissa
to get out her sling
or find a rock
or do anything except scream
a silent *No!*
till the boar stops
and wanders back
for his afternoon nap.
But Luki doesn't move.
Aissa doesn't know what to do
or how to help.
Doesn't know if Luki
is alive or dead;
doesn't want to curse him
with her touch.
The fear in her belly
says that her curse
has already followed him here.
Even if he's only stunned
when the boar wakes again
to see a body in its field

it will nose,
and trample,
and eat
until Luki is gone.
But if she goes closer
to see if he breathes
and he wakes in fright
with a spit for No-Name
it will seem
too much to bear.
Fear tells her to run;
if anyone sees her
or Luki wakes and tells,
she will die too,
thrown off the cliffs
for cursing the dancer.
She stays frozen
and in that long moment
sees
an adder
sliding toward the boy on the ground—
fast in the midday heat,
messenger of the gods,
such a small snake
for such a deadly bite—
up to Luki's face.
Aissa sure she can see
the tongue flickering
tasting his scent,
nothing she can do,
no way to run

fast enough to save him,
but she calls to the snake
with her mind,
"Turn away, turn back!"
And from somewhere near
comes the Lady's song,
the song that sings the sun to rise
and sings the snakes
up from their baskets;
the snake lifts its head
and turns.
Luki sits,
wobbly, blinky-eyed.
Aissa stands,
shaky too.
The voice disappears
and so does the snake.
"Thank you, Mother!" says Luki,
hand on heart.
"Praise the snake singer!"
Then stares around, lost,
because there is no Lady,
or even Fila,
but only Aissa.
Aissa searches too
because how could the Lady sing
if she isn't here?
"It was you!" says Luki,
with wonder,
almost with fear.

Aissa waves away
his blasphemous words
but the Lady
is still not there.
Luki stands,
shakes his head,
rubs his back,
"That was stupid," he says,
"but I wanted to know
what it would be like
to leap an animal
instead of a wall.
The boar was the biggest
one I could think of,
and I've known this one
since he was a porker.
You won't tell?"
Then he remembers
that Aissa can't.
"But you sang!
You're the snake singer,
the one to follow the Lady.
People say it's Fila,
but I've heard her voice—
it must be you.
How can you sing
when you can't talk?"
Aissa doesn't know,
though she would like to understand.
Doesn't quite believe

that she was the singer
except that her throat
feels raw and open,
as if something great
has passed through it.
And no one else was there to sing.
There's a lot she doesn't know
and a lot Luki wants to.
"I won't call you No-Name—
you must have a name,
you marked it at the ballot."
Aissa holds out
the mama stone around her neck
to let him read the dragonfly mark.
"Aissa," says Luki,
the first person since Mama
to call her by name,
and she never knew
how perfect it could sound.
"Aissa the snake singer,
who lives under the sanctuary rock—
you're not the only one who watches."

Luki's head hurts, but he is walking straight and tall; it's Aissa who's trembling as they turn into the shelter of the oaks. The world has shaken and changed—and yet leaves flutter, birds hop from branch to branch, and a pair of eagles soar overhead, just like any other day. When they pass the swineherd's hut, the herder and his dog are still asleep. The sun has barely moved in the sky.

"It feels like days since I left," says Luki. "I can't believe we'll be back before the end of siesta."

Aissa shakes her head violently, *No!* The servants will be up and bustling soon. She can't go back to town till dark.

"Where do you go?"

Wherever's safest! Aissa thinks, gesturing widely out to the hills.

"I'm going to tell the Lady what happened, and how you saved me. The worst that can happen to me is a lecture—but she'll have to treat you better!"

A chill runs through Aissa's body. *Tell the Lady that No-Name has sung a snake!* It's like asking for the end of the world.

She feels Luki's eyes on her, and forces herself to meet them. Finally he seems to hear her silent scream.

"I won't tell if it scares you," he says more quietly.

They walk on quickly.

At the stone bridge. Luki makes the thank-you sign again and runs the rest of the way back to town. He's hoping to be back on his bed before anyone knows he's gone.

Aissa huddles under the bridge all afternoon. If it weren't for the cats waiting in the cave, she'd stay there all night.

The fear
    is bigger than Aissa
    and her mind flees.
    She looks down

at her hollow self,
her body as sheer
as a black dragonfly wing
and where her belly
and heart should be,
there is nothing.
"Snake singer, snake singer,"
she hears in her head,
more terrifying
than any other chant
she's heard.
It was easy to lock
the story of the Lady's dead daughter
in a secret box in her mind,
because it was impossible
that it could be her.
Only the Lady can sing snakes,
and only the Lady's daughter,
the Lady-to-come,
can learn.
Yet Aissa has done it—
without learning,
without voice.
And though she could never
be the Lady-to-come
could it be
that she's the daughter
who should have died
and didn't?

Death might have been easier
    than bearing the gods' anger
    for living.
    Only the gods' rage can explain
    why the Lady's daughter
    is hiding alone in a cave
    cast out even
    by the servants.
If she is the Lady's daughter
    then who is Mama?
    And Papa
    and all who loved her—
    she knows they did
    though she remembers
    not much else
    and now she's not even sure
    of that.
Her thoughts spin
    in jagged circles,
    till she feels
    sick and dizzy.
It's impossible
    that the Lady could have borne Aissa—
    Aissa is nothing
    and the Lady is everything.
If she is the Lady's daughter
    why did the Lady want her dead
    and not love her as she loves Fila
    and the little boys

and as Milli-Cat
loves her kittens?
But if she is not
the Lady's daughter
then how
did she sing the snake?
She knows in her heart
that it was her,
that wild, strange music,
high as a flute,
a song with no words
and powerful magic.
She just doesn't know how—
and that's a very big thing
not to know.
"And what about
the fireflies above your bed
when you dreamed them,
the dragonflies
when you learned your name,
and the crickets
the goddess told you not to eat?"
asks the voice in her head
that isn't silent at all.
"Or Parsley the goat
that came to you
when you held Spot Goat
in your mind?"
Hands over ears
can't block the thoughts

till another voice—
a new, small voice—
says, "Maybe I could try."
She doesn't know
what she could try,
but knows that if it's true
the gods will send a sign.
And they do.
The very next day,
foraging wild grapes—
leathery sweetness to pop in her mouth—
she watches a bee
hunting its own sweetness
in fading flowers;
sees it leave the plant,
bumbling no longer,
to fly a straight line
back to its home.
So Aissa follows.
In her spying,
she's watched beekeepers
rob a hive
with smoke and masks.
Farther back,
there's a memory of Kelya,
the old woman holding
tiny Aissa on her knee,
coaxing her tongue
with honey dripping from a spoon,
though failing to make the mute child talk.

"That was kindness!"
Aissa thinks in surprise,
and knows there are more
questions of Kelya,
but now she must think
only of the bee.
It's hard to see as it crosses a rock
and she doesn't want
to lose it now.
Flying to a rocky cliff,
a small outcrop on the mountain's face,
the bee disappears
into a hole—
a buzzing, humming hive.
Aissa stops,
watches,
and thinks.
If she can sing out the bees
and rob their hive,
it could mean
that what Luki says is true—
but if she fails,
is covered with stings
from an angry swarm
she'll never have to
think of this again.
And of course she'll fail,
because when she opens her mouth
she hears Mama say,
"Don't make a sound,
stay quiet,

still as stone, till I come back,"
and no song comes out.
But she can't help
a silent song within her mind
of flowers and nectar,
bees in flight,
and one by one
then in a cloud,
the bees fly past her
till the buzzing hive
is silent.
No choice now but to climb the rock
to the sweet-scented hole
and dip her arm into the darkness,
waiting for the sting
that never comes.
The hive is full
of waxy cells
dripping with honey,
a gift from the gods—
and even though she'd wanted to fail
Aissa is grateful.
She throws the first comb
to the goddess.
And then she tastes
and knows that even the Lady
could never have anything
better than this;
crams her mouth
and the pouch on her belt

with honeycomb to store in her cave
for the hungry winter.
But even sliding to the ground,
chewing the last sweetness
from her ball of wax,
thanking the bees with her mind
as she'd thanked the goddess with the comb,
she wishes she was running
from angry bees.
Easier to be No-Name
and have no mother at all
than be a maybe daughter
to both Mama and the Lady.

Even though she passes the sanctuary window every morning as she leaves the cave, Aissa doesn't spy into it anymore. It's been too frightening since she'd heard the twins' crazy story of who she might be; too painful to watch and wonder.

Now she has to.

She crouches in the hollow in the rock, waiting for the Lady to come. Every cell of her body is alert, as if this morning the Lady will read an oracle just for her, and Aissa will understand. With her sharpest spying eyes, she watches the Lady choose a pot from the snakes' cool cave to carry into the sanctuary.

Watching as Fila
drops a mouse from her basket to the snakes,
seeing that Fila

still wants to cry.
"She could never
kill a wolf," thinks Aissa,
with a thrill of almost-pride,
even though
it's hard to believe
she's done it herself.
The Lady's song begins;
the snake begins to rise—
a hugging snake,
not a deadly biting viper
which is good
because when Fila starts to sing
her voice is still as sharp
as Milli-Cat's claws
and when she leans
over the pot
the snake rears and bites her hand.
Now Fila does cry,
for hurt and shame
as she sucks off the blood
but no real harm.
And Aissa knows—
the Lady knows—
Fila knows—
that if it had been a viper
her tears would be only
the start of her dying.
So the Lady will always choose
the hugging snakes

for Fila to sing
and not think of the day
when her daughter must call
a deadly viper.
The Lady singing again
till the snake is calm
and she can carry it out
to raise the sun.
And all the while,
through the snake song,
through the tears and calming
and the tune for the sun,
Aissa feels her own song
rise in her heart,
swirling, rushing,
flowing through her
like the river
from the Source to the sea—
and her only fear
is that it will burst out
as it did for Luki.
So the Lady doesn't need
to read an oracle
because that inside song
tells Aissa who she is
though it doesn't say why
she doesn't belong.

14

DRAGONFLY AT THE SOURCE

The night-time cave is too dark for Aissa to work on her dragonfly carving, but she keeps it in her pouch to whittle when she can. It takes days to lick off all the honey after she crams the honeycomb in with it.

The olive wood feels good in her pouch, a solid reminder of who she is. Every afternoon she thinks the dragonfly's finished and that she'll offer it to the goddess in the morning, and every morning she sees a reason to work on it another day. If she doesn't stop soon there'll be nothing left.

She'll take it to the Source early in the morning, as soon as the sun is safely risen, like she did the first time she saw the carved offerings.

The mornings are cool again. It's grape-picking time out in the hills; days are warm and bright, but the nights are cold. Aissa and Gold-Cat sleep folded in the wolf fur, warmth over and softness under. She'll need the fur when she gets out of the water at the Source.

Servants don't wear furs. Outcasts definitely don't.

But servants catch cold and sometimes die if they're wet and can't get warm again. Squint-Eye gives them extra hot soup to make them better because she can't boss them if they're dead.

Outcasts never get hot soup. Aissa figures that's why she's never met another one—they die even faster than servants.

She'll wear her wolf cloak. Inside out, so it looks like goatskin, fastened tight at the neck with her bone pin.

Her dragonfly,
carved bit by bit
over long summer days
and cooler autumn,
chipped and scratched,
wings ragged
where she pushed too hard
with her small flint knife,
maybe not much like
a dragonfly at all,
but it's part of her
and she hopes the goddess accepts it
as her gift.
Not safe to let
anyone else see
because if they guess
the dragonfly is hers
they might destroy it
hoping they'll kill
Aissa too.

So she hesitates
    on the slope to the Source,
    steam rising in cool morning air;
    she can't tuck her dragonfly
    under the rocks at the edge
    like the other offerings
    anyone can see.
She strips off her cloak,
    her rope sling and tunic,
    folds them neatly on the rock
    and slides in,
    not where the water's coolest,
    but where she can see
    an islet of rock
    poking through the blue water.
    The water hotter
    than she thinks she can bear
    and deeper;
    but she's in too far
    to turn around.
Toes clinging
    to the end of a ledge
    where the floor drops to nothing,
    the heart of the earth,
    the source of life;
    she stretches to the islet,
    face in the water,
    feeling the dragonfly land,
    letting it go
    with a silent "please"
    not sure exactly

what the please is for—
and throws herself backward,
arms flailing,
hot deep water over her head,
but her feet still touching
as she splashes to the edge,
safe,
her dragonfly prayer safe on the rock,
while a dragonfly,
real and blue,
hovering over her as she drips,
accepts the goddess gift.

The grape harvest is good this year. Luki's mother and brother arrive at the Hall leading two goats with panniers of grapes: one for the Lady and three for the market. The rest will be dried into raisins or stomped into wine. It's a busy time.

"I'll ask the chief if I can go home to help," Luki says. "A few days without training won't make any difference."

"Luki!" His mother looks around furtively. "Your life is in the Hall."

For now, Luki thinks gloomily.

"Why would you even want to work if you don't have to?" asks his brother. "Are you crazy?"

"Don't call the bull dancer crazy!" his mother snaps.

"I don't care," says Luki.

A few months ago he would have punched his brother and they would have wrestled until they were pulled apart. Now he could kiss him for it. His brother is the only one who sometimes remembers that he's still himself.

He can't explain that to his mother. He can't tell anyone how much he misses the farm; how he'd rather be worn out from a day of picking grapes than be pampered in the Hall. Tomorrow is the autumn festival, when night and day are the same length and farmers bring in the baskets of grapes they owe the Lady. They'll pour them into huge tubs, and everyone will have a turn at climbing in to tread them into juice: the Lady and her family, and Luki and Nasta right after them, stamping their god-luck into the wine. He'll feel the juice and the slippery skins squishing between his toes, but he won't do it long enough for his calves to ache, and he won't haul the juice out into barrels to make the wine—and it won't be his family's grapes or his family's wine.

And he won't ever grow up to harvest his own grapes or olives or barley...*But I'm a bull dancer!* he reminds himself. *What an honor!*

Some days he almost believes it. Just not today.

"I need a favor," he says abruptly.

"The god-luck boy needs a favor?" asks his brother.

Luki ignores the sarcasm.

"The girl they call No-Name..."

"You're too holy to spit at her yourself and you want us to do it?"

Luki punches him. It feels good. "No! I want you to help her."

"But she's cursed—and you want us to help her?"

"Why?" asks his mother.

Luki's taken a long time to work out the answer. They won't help unless they know she saved him, but he can't admit he put his life in danger.

"I tripped on a training run..."

His brother snorts.

"I banged my head when I fell."

"Are you hurt?" his mother shrieks, forgetting the bull dancer's honor as she feels his head for lumps.

"I'm fine! I only blacked out for a moment. But I landed by a viper..."

"Where was your guard?"

"He wasn't far ahead!" Luki says desperately, seeing his mother ready to attack. "It didn't matter because the girl called the snake away."

Stunned silence. Luki has never heard his brother be quiet for so long.

"You really did bang your head," his mother says finally. "Because whatever you think you heard, you mustn't say that. Only the Lady can call snakes."

"But she did!"

His mother kisses his forehead, holding his head firmly between her hands. "Luki, even the bull dancer doesn't challenge the Lady. Promise you'll never tell anyone else what you've told us, and we'll help the girl."

Helping her isn't easy, because Aissa's not to be found. In the end they leave Luki with three big bunches of grapes in a goatskin bag. He adds a stolen poppy cake and cheese from the kitchen, and waits to see her.

But if it's not easy to find Aissa, it's even harder for Luki to hide. At dusk the market is gone and the square nearly empty, but people come out of the shadows to be close to a bull dancer—to press his shoulder, touch his hand, soak up his god-luck.

Until finally Luki realizes: the only way to escape his power is to use it.

"I want to be alone," he says, facing the sanctuary with his hand on his heart. No one's going to interrupt a bull dancer while he's praying—and they can't know the only thing going through his head is, *Go away! Get out of here before Aissa comes back!*

They obediently disappear. Luki slips the bag under the boulder, and stands a little longer. It feels good to be alone, and even better to know that he can make it happen. He's so still that Aissa doesn't see him as she sidles along the wall. She jumps in surprise.

Luki feels as proud as if he's snuck up on a wild deer. Aissa glares at him.

"There's a bag under the rock—for you, not the snake."

Aissa's glare turns to suspicion.

"It's not a trick!" Luki says, hurt. "It's from my mother, for saving me."

But he knows that his mother's bag of grapes is not enough. Tomorrow the days will start getting shorter. Winter will come, and Aissa can't survive it under that rock.

15
THE COLD NORTH WIND

Squint-Eye has been watching too. She's afraid she's made a terrible mistake in banning No-Name. Sometimes, seeing the girl slip by with a parade of cats behind her, wearing a cloak that looks suspiciously like fur, it seems that she's actually given the cursed child her freedom.

Squint-Eye has never tasted freedom. She's never longed for it; ruling the other servants is all she wants. What could be better than the power to beat and punish the same way the older servants used to beat her? What's more rewarding than seeing the fear in her fellows' eyes?

But she's old now and slow to move, and last year she'd seen that the other servants weren't as afraid of her as they should be. She'd needed something to show her authority.

She had never hated No-Name. The child was a good worker; not talking back was a bonus—and

Squint-Eye's seen worse things than dragonflies in the kitchen. But the drama of banishment was exactly what she needed. Squint-Eye is feared again.

The problem is that No-Name herself doesn't seem to be as punished as she ought to be. She's hungry and uncomfortable, but she's free of the chores that the other servants complain of; she's got a sort of home and a house snake to bless it. And she's not as alone as she was in the middle of the servants; Squint-Eye can't prove it, but she's sure that someone is helping her. Worst of all, sometimes when she thinks no one can see her, No-Name stands like a free person. That's the reason that Squint-Eye does hate her now.

Without admitting that she was wrong, Squint-Eye needs to regain control over the banned girl. Her allies are the twins—who can follow and spy where she can't—and the winter. She just needs to wait and the weather will do the rest.

But this morning the north wind is blowing cold and sharp, and Squint-Eye is suddenly afraid that she might not survive the winter herself. It would be unbearable if she died before seeing No-Name beg to return.

So she waits on her bench, pretending to doze in spite of the biting wind, until Aissa tries to slip past. Lashing out with her stick, furious when she misses, she shrieks, "No-Name child, you think you can go where you please! But you belong to the Lady the same as those cats—steal what's hers, and it's the cliff for you or anyone who helps you!"

Aissa runs.

"Half-One!" Squint-Eye bellows. "Follow her! Don't come back until you find her."

Half-One shivers. She's never been as brave as her twin.

"I'll go," says Half-Two.

Squint-Eye's so angry now that her lips are frothing. No one is ever going to defy her again. "I called Half-One! And don't think you can try your tricks with me: you'll sit at my feet and not move till she's gone!"

Aissa is faster now
than when she was a privy-girl
and sometimes she wishes
she could race against Nasta
because she might win.
Half-One is strong
but not a runner
and Aissa knows she can beat her.
Sprinting to the sea path
through dry chamomile flowers
Aissa sees
Nasta's mother
waiting at the top of the cliff
like a trap
and Aissa the rabbit
running into it.
So Aissa loops wide
around the town
and across the hills,
but Half-One guesses,

goes straight up the path
and sees Aissa there—
chest heaving, breath puffing—
but Half-One is fresh
and ready to chase
so Aissa keeps running
up to the forest
because surely the twin
will give up there.
But Half-One
has seen Squint-Eye's rage
and that is scarier than the forest,
so she goes on
though her heart is pounding
harder than Aissa's.
Gasping and stumbling,
chasing through trees
to the mountain crags
with their rocks and caves,
until finally Aissa is faster,
so far ahead
she can't hear Half-One follow
and can sink to the ground
to catch her breath.
Then the wind
catches it too—
that cold north air
swelling from breeze to gale,
bringing rain
that stings like ice.

Aissa's tunic
is as drenched as if
she had fallen in the sea
while her fur cloak
waits safe and dry
at home.
The wind howls so strong
she can hardly walk,
the rain lashes so hard
she can hardly see,
but she hears from somewhere
goats bleating,
ble-aah, ble-aahing
and remembers Lanni the goatherd,
"Our summer cave is nearby,
if you need help."
Aissa doesn't know how
to ask for help
but this might be
the time to learn.
She turns into the wind,
pushing against it,
pausing to listen
for the goats to guide her
till she smells the smoke
of a good wood fire
and sees the narrow mouth
of a mountain cave
with a gate of branches
to stop the goats from leaving—

and a barking dog
with Lanni beside him.
"Wolf girl!" calls the goatherd,
pushing the dog back
and the gate open.
"What are you doing?
You'll die out there,
come in to the fire."
"No-Name!" says Onyx.
"We don't want her here."
"Parsley's rescuer," says Lanni.
"If you don't want her, you can go out."
So Onyx is quiet,
while little Sammo
shows Aissa his sling,
"Next time,
I'll get the wolf like you did."
Aissa tries to smile
but hasn't had much practice
or reason
for smiling
and her teeth are chattering too hard
for her lips to move.
Lanni pulls her
close to the fire,
throws a goat fleece on the ground
and wraps another
around trembling shoulders.
"Sit and warm up;
you are our guest."

As she warms,
as her shaking stills,
Aissa sees past the fire
to the shadows of the cave—
not a cave under the lip of a rock
like hers—
but half as big as the Hall,
with room for the flock,
bundles of green branches
for them to eat through the storm,
gates to hold them
back from the fire,
stacks of cheeses,
bags of milk becoming yogurt,
and Lanni in the milking pen
filling her wooden bowl
with warm milk for Aissa.
"Drink," she says, and Aissa does,
then curls like Gold-Cat
in the rug
and sleeps,
even though it's still morning
because it's been a hard one
and just for the moment
she is warm and safe.
When she wakes they feast her
with cheese and grapes
and barley cakes
till Aissa's belly
feels round and full
and a little bit sick.

"You're lucky," says Lanni,
"When the storm stops
we'll be gone,
it's time to take the goats
home for the winter—
a day later,
and all you'd have found
would be a cold
and empty cave.
But I wish I knew
why you were on the mountain alone,
as if you were running
from a lion."
Aissa nods yes,
though Half-One is no lion.
"Everyone chases No-Name," says Onyx.
"We don't," says his sister.
"Because she chases wolves,"
says Sammo.
All the rest of the day,
while wind and rain howl,
Lanni plays her flute,
the brothers sing,
sometimes they dance
around the fire
and after a while
Aissa does too,
feet stamping
in time with theirs,
hands clapping

just like theirs
as if she is one of them.
And she wishes the day
would never end.
Or even the night
as they sleep by the fire
wrapped in fleeces,
with the smell of goats,
stale milk, and smoke—
the safe smell of home
before the raiders.
So Aissa dreams and thinks,
"I could stay here all winter
and no one would know."
But the goats would be gone
and so would the herders;
Gold-Cat would miss her,
and worst of all,
Squint-Eye's threat is real:
a push off the cliff
for anyone who takes her
away from the Hall.

The next morning, the wind is still strong and cold, but the rain is gone.

"Time to go home for the winter," says Lanni.

"Wolf girl could come with us," Sammo suggests.

Lanni and Aissa shake their heads, even before Onyx says, "She belongs to the Lady."

Sammo is too excited about seeing his parents again to argue.

Lanni milks the goats; they all drink as much as they want, and pour the rest into goatskin bags to be jolted into curds on the long walk home. The cheeses are packed into panniers strapped across four billy goats' shoulders; they eat the last of the grapes and a barley cake each.

Aissa folds her fleece to stack with the others but Lanni wraps it around her shoulders again. "It's yours," she says, clasping Aissa's hands between her own strong, warm ones. "Be well."

Little Sammo repeats it, and Onyx gives her a round hard cheese from his pack. It feels like gold in her hands, heavy and hard, and it only just fits into the pouch on her belt. Lanni smiles, but Aissa feels warm tears on her face and doesn't know why.

Then Onyx lifts the gate away from the mouth of the cave, the goats crowd out to graze their way across the mountain, the dog races around in hopes of chasing a stray...the herders are on their way home.

Aissa stands watching them, hand on heart in thanks and goodbye, until they're out of sight and she is chilled right through her new fleece.

Down the mountain,
    sling in hand—
    if Aissa had a voice she would sing
    against the wind.
Through the woods out to the meadow,
    she stops for wild grapes
    smashed and fallen in the storm

and hears a sound like moaning
farther down the hill.
Aissa creeps forward
with a rock in her sling
for whatever threatens,
and finds a body in a puddle
below a rock,
as if it had skidded and fallen
in the pouring rain.
The body is Half-One
and she looks dead
though if she's moaning
she must be alive.
She doesn't hear Aissa
clapping her hands
and when Aissa touches her arm,
the twin's skin is as cold
as the sharp north wind.
Aissa has never touched
Half-One before
though she's felt the slap of the hand
often enough.
Half-One doesn't know
it's Aissa touching—
she turns in trust
as if to her sister.
So Aissa grabs her shoulders,
hauls her out of the puddle,
and rolls her in
the goatherd's fleece,

because Half-One
didn't have time
for a cloak either
when she ran after Aissa.
She is heavy and floppy,
bigger than Aissa,
but Aissa sits her up,
and slides a smashed grape
into her mouth.
The girl's eyes open,
blank and confused;
they don't look
like Half-One's eyes
and when Aissa tries
to pull her to her feet,
Half-One flops down
and starts to cry.
So Aissa pushes
another grape in her mouth,
then runs to the forest
to find a branch for a crutch—
and with that
gets Half-One to her feet.
Stumbling down the mountain
together,
Half-One with a stick in one hand
and Aissa on the other.
Once she looks at Aissa
with a moment's hatred
as if she knows her,

then the light
goes out of her eyes
and she sleepwalks again.
Past the ancient oak,
onto the singing path,
but still a long way to go
and the twin is weakening
step by step,
too weak to use her crutch,
so Aissa is carrying her weight,
pushing, dragging,
with pain in her side,
and her own knees trembling—
when Half-One falls again,
sliding off Aissa's shoulder,
face flat to the ground,
Aissa can't lift her.
Pushing, pulling,
shoving, rolling;
she doesn't know why
she doesn't want Half-One to die,
and the twin is so still,
her head and arms so floppy
when Aissa pulls her
that maybe it's too late.
If Aissa is found
with dead Half-One
they'll say it's her fault
and she'll be thrown off the cliff.

Maybe it is her fault,
    but she only meant to run away.
Then Half-One groans
    and Aissa tries once more
    to lift her
    and can't.
She rolls her to her side
    so Half-One doesn't drown
    in the mud of the path,
    tucks the goat skin around her
    and runs—
    she doesn't know how
    or who she can tell—
    but she must find help
    or Half-One will die,
    for real this time.
Luki! thinks Aissa. *He will trust*
    enough to follow—
    but now she sees Half-Two
    running across the field,
    searching
    and calling her twin.
    So Aissa disappears
    into the woods,
    spying from a tree
    to watch Half-Two
    run to her sister,
    screaming for help
    till more searchers come
    to carry the girl home.

And Aissa knows
    that Squint-Eye and the twins
    will never forgive her
    or believe
    that Half-One would have died
    if Aissa hadn't found her.
    No matter what she does now
    she will never be safe.
Maybe running away
    will be better than staying.

16

THE WISE-WOMEN

The Hall Folk are not as stupid as the servants think. However, it's not a good idea to bother the Lady with petty problems about people who barely count as people—as long as things are running smoothly, it's best to let servants sort things out for themselves.

But No-Name is becoming a problem. Kelya has known that something was wrong since the lottery, but she's still not sure what. *Goddess*, she begs, *what can I do?*

The goddess doesn't answer. The other wise-women don't answer either, because Kelya's never told them her secret. It's not that she doesn't trust them, it's just that she's kept quiet for so long it's hard to even hint at it now.

Lyra and Lena are the other two wise-women; Lyra is the youngest, not much older than Lena's fifteen-year-old daughter, the apprentice Roula. Like the other trades, being a healer is usually passed from mother to daughter, but Kelya never had children, and Lena's other children are all boys. Often a Lady's younger daughters become healers, but this Lady hasn't got any younger daughters. And no matter how much the others remind Lyra it's time for her to choose a husband and have a daughter, she hasn't found a man she wants yet.

"We're fine as we are," she says.

But when the half-dead twin is brought in after the storm, the ruckus is felt all the way up to the Hall.

There's no separate place for sick servants—you couldn't have them sleeping in the sick-room off the wise-women's chamber—so Lyra and Roula check the girl in the kitchen and give Squint-Eye herbs to bring the fever down and her strength up. They can't help but be involved.

"The servants say it's No-Name's fault."

"It could be. Those twins have hounded her often enough."

"The girl's got a sprained ankle and a fever from lying out in the rain—how could No-Name have done that?"

"Squint-Eye set the twin to chase her."

"So Squint-Eye's blaming No-Name to keep her own authority."

"The truth is, that child has been nothing but trouble since she arrived. If the twin dies, sending No-Name to the cliffs might solve—"

"The truth is," Kelya interrupts, "that only the Lady can send someone to the cliffs. And I'm telling you that you do not want the Lady to decide on this one."

There's a short, stunned silence.

"Are you saying that the servants' rumor about the firstborn is true?"

"How did you keep the secret for so long? You could have trusted us!"

"Trust you to giggle and gossip like kitchen maids!" Kelya retorts. She doesn't need eyes to know they're all staring at her. "I'm just saying we need to find a better solution before everything gets out of control. We can start by making sure that twin survives."

Fear now,
    all the time,
    everywhere,
    belly-churning, mind-whirling
    terror,
    even in her cave
    because
    the autumn rains are leaking in
    puddling on the floor—
    she can't stay there much longer.
    But if she runs away
    she must leave Gold-Cat behind—
    he belongs to the Lady.
    So does Aissa—
    but the Lady might want Gold-Cat.
Fear because
    Half-One is still sick,
    even with hot soup
    spooned into her mouth,

drop by warm drop
by her sister;
even though wise-women visit
with healing herbs
and advice for Squint-Eye,
Half-One shivers,
sleeps, and talks nonsense;
doesn't know where she is
or who wrapped her in goat fleece
to keep her warm.
Anger too,
bubbling through fear.
Aissa tried so hard
to save Half-One—
her side still aches
from the twin's weight—
it's not fair if it doesn't work;
and worse
that she gets the blame.
And in case she hasn't heard it,
Half-Two stands outside
the sanctuary rock
to tell the air
that her sister is dying,
that No-Name killed her,
and of how she hopes
to push the murderer
off the cliff herself.
Half-Two
never goes early enough

to see Aissa coming out
or late enough
to catch her going in,
and she's not brave enough
to try sliding
under the rock,
even though she's sure
it's where Aissa goes,
because once when she looked in,
Aissa's house snake looked out.
But even so,
Aissa's cave home
isn't safe anymore.
Luki hears the whispers too,
the talk of the cliffs;
he catches Aissa once,
meeting her at the gate
when he should be eating,
saying, "How can I help?"
and sliding a half-eaten
barley cake
into her hand.
"No one can help,"
Aissa would say if she could
though she eats the cake.
Running away
is dangerous enough,
it's even worse
if someone knows.
But she stores his words

as if they were jewels
or honeycomb,
arranging them with
his family's kindness,
and the goatherds',
tasting their sweetness in the night
when Half-Two's threats
invade her dreams.
So she plans
and hesitates.
She knows that the goat cave
is not a good choice
but it seems the only one.
She gathers acorns to dry,
drags wood for a fire
finds flint to start it,
yet somehow each night
finds herself turning
back to the town
where she's never been safe—
but safer than on the mountain
alone.
Days aren't quite
as bad as nights;
fear is still strong
and more real
but her mind can't whirl so fast
when she's running in the hills.

There are mushrooms growing

on the way to the cave
she has seen the wise-women
picking,
carrying them home
in wide willow baskets.
They're not so wise!
thinks Aissa.
They've missed some,
all along the way.
She pulls them carefully
at the stalk,
not losing any
of the pale brown flesh,
brushing off dirt,
laying them on her outspread cloak
to carry and store
in the goatherds' cave.
Kneeling to reach one more
growing up from under
the root of a tree,
so excited at this sign
that she might survive the winter
she forgets to watch
or listen for danger—
just for a moment,
but that's all it takes.
The thump across her back
knocks her face to the ground,
gasping
as the stick strikes again
and a voice shouts,

"Wicked girl!
Picking the mushrooms
left for the goddess—
how will she grow them
again next year?"
A final thump:
"Get up, girl,
and answer me!"
Aissa wants to run
but the voice is Lyra's,
a wise-woman,
though younger than the rest.
Aissa's not sure what powers
the wise-women have,
but she thinks she'd better
do what she's told.
"No-Name!" says Lyra.
"Now, there's a surprise.
I thought you were a hunter's child
by that cloak.
But I guess I'll never know
how you came by it."
Aissa's heart thumping,
faster still when Lyra says,
"You know there are many
who want you thrown from the cliff—
stealing mushrooms from the goddess
takes you another step
closer to the edge."
Lyra studies the mushrooms
so carefully laid

across the cloak,
and the rope sling
at Aissa's waist.
"Is this how you've lived,
foraging the hills,
since you were cast out
from the servants' kitchen?"
Aissa despairing
at being so wrong,
knows she will never,
ever,
be right.
She nods yes,
though her knees tremble.
"I think there might be
a better plan,"
says Lyra.
"Break up your mushrooms,
throw them back
and thank the goddess
for her bounty—
and for your second chance."
Aissa can't imagine
what a second chance could be,
but scatters pink-frilled pieces
of broken mushrooms
up and down the path
and is happy to thank the goddess
that she's still alive
and not being beaten again.
"Follow me," says Lyra,

setting off down the hill,
never looking back to see
if Aissa is there
because she knows
Aissa has no choice.
At the walls of the town
Lyra passes
the gate to the garden,
taking the road around
to the great front gate,
Aissa so close behind her
she bumps when Lyra stops,
because she's afraid of the wise-woman
but more afraid of the crowd,
as she hears:
"Lyra's bringing in No-Name!"
"Has Half-One died?"
"Is the cursed child finally
going to be thrown from the cliffs?"
Lyra ignores them as if she can't hear;
marches through the crowd,
the busy market,
up to the Hall.
"Stay with me!"
she says,
and leads Aissa through
to the wise-women's chamber.

Kelya is alone, sitting on a stool to sort seeds by feel, when Lyra brings Aissa in. "I've brought you

No-Name," she says. "I have an idea."

Aissa hears a tremor in the young woman's voice. *Kelya's the boss!* she thinks. *Just like Squint-Eye with the servants.*

If a wise-woman is nervous, an outcast servant should be terrified. But as Aissa approaches the old woman, something in her relaxes.

"Little one!" says Kelya. "Come here; sit." She points at the floor in front of her, and Aissa obediently squats at her feet. The wise-woman reaches down, sighing as she runs her hands over Aissa's face.

"Call Lena and Roula," she says to Lyra.

She doesn't speak while Lyra's gone, except to sigh, "Little one!" again, but she goes on stroking Aissa's hair.

The others return, staring in surprise at No-Name squatting by Kelya's feet. Roula shuts the door behind them.

Aissa tries to be invisible, but it's impossible when they're all studying her. All she can do is sit still as stone, forcing her legs not to get up and run away.

"I found her picking the mushrooms left for the goddess," says Lyra.

Lena hisses in shock.

"I beat her!" Lyra assures them.

Roula and her mother nod in approval.

"But she scattered them in appeasement when I told her," Lyra continues. "She did it well—and she'd gathered the mushrooms with respect. For someone raised in the servants' kitchen, she seems to understand the hills and their plants."

Kelya doesn't mention that she used to take Aissa up into the hills for herbs herself, when the girl was tiny. It never hurts to keep a few secrets for when you need them. "She always used to gather the kitchen greens for the twins," she says.

I thought nobody knew that! Aissa thinks. *What else does she know?*

Watching from beneath her lashes, she sees that Lena and Roula are shocked, but Lyra looks a bit more sure of herself.

"So my idea is: what if she became a gatherer for us?"

"But she's a servant!" says Lena.

"She can't be an apprentice!" splutters Roula.

"Not an apprentice," Lyra says quickly, "a servant-gatherer—just for us. To help Roula."

Kelya hides a smile.

"Show them your sling," Lyra orders.

Aissa stands up. She hands Kelya her rope sling, and her cloak as well. Kelya starts in surprise as her fingers sink into the thick wolf fur, and finally she smiles, as if she's made up her mind.

"Just for a moment, let's think of this child as a girl, not a servant. A girl with skills at hunting as well as gathering—she's known what to pick to survive since she was thrown out of the kitchen."

I'm glad they don't know about the figs and the diarrhea! Aissa thinks.

"A girl who will never speak of our secrets," Kelya concludes.

"A girl to keep out of the Lady's way," Lena reminds her.

"We don't need to bother the Lady with servant affairs. We're simply taking one that the kitchen doesn't want."

Aissa squats
at the wise-woman's feet
while the others pull their stools
in a circle around her,
listening
with ears and heart,
mind whirling
but not with fear—
or not so much—
wondering if she can believe
what she hears:
she's going to be safe.
Maybe even
better than safe.
"Stand, child," says Kelya at last,
"this is my decision:
from this time on
you will serve only us,
learning the herbs
and plants we gather
for healing and wisdom.
You will sleep in this chamber
on a fleece by my bed.
Roula will bring you
food when she's eaten,
for you don't belong in the Hall
and aren't safe in the kitchen—

though I shall make it known
that you belong to us
and are not to be harmed.
No-Name is the label of a slave.
A server to wise-women
can't bear a slave's name.
From now on you'll be known
as the wise-women's server.
And in this room,
or alone with us,
you'll be called by your name:
Aissa.
Aissa's never known
there could be tears for joy.
She cries so hard
she has to hide her hot face
on the cold stone floor
and kisses
Kelya's feet.
Because safety is good
but having a name is better.
It's not till dark,
lying by Kelya's bed
on a clean thick fleece
with her wolf fur on top,
her belly full
of hot thick soup,
that other thoughts hit,
hard as Lena's stick:
she will never sleep
with the cats again;

feel Gold-Cat's warmth
under her chin;
hear the murmuring purr
of dozing kittens.
She's happy to leave
her treasures of rock and shell,
goddess-thanks patterned in the dust,
but losing the cats
tears at her heart.
And so does knowing
she will never again lie
in her secret place
to spy on the Lady's magic,
or hear the snake song
as if it were for her.
She chooses safety
but the price is high.
And with that thought,
there's a sound at the door.
Aissa jumps in fear
that Squint-Eye's coming—
the goddess punishing her
for mourning the loss
of her outcast freedom.
But the sound is Gold-Cat,
mewing impatiently
because he's left his mother
and siblings behind
and is waiting to scamper
onto Aissa's mat
to sleep under her chin.

17

THE HERB GATHERER

The wise-women are much more than healers and midwives.

They collect health-giving herbs from all over the island, from beach to mountain top. Each plant tells its own story, as do the spiders spinning their webs, the birds in the trees, and the crabs on the beach. The wise-women listen to them all, so they know better than anyone whether the coming season is going to be hard, hotter or drier or wetter than usual. They keep track of the moon's phases and the sun's warmth, and know if the figs will ripen early, and the best day to plant beans.

It's also their business to know what's going on with the islanders. People tell secrets when they're worried or in pain, and healers hear them. Women gathering greens in the sunshine sometimes forget who they're talking to, and say more than they intend. They gossip about mean-spirited neighbors and loving relatives; about a fisher who's lost his luck or a herder her goats.

The wise-women's real wisdom is that they'll listen to anyone, even the servants. Servants not only spill their masters' secrets—sometimes their own are worth listening to.

Yet the wise-women are also the only people the Lady truly trusts. It's their knowledge that lets her judge exactly what each islander owes the goddess. It's their wisdom that guides her on the dates for sowing and harvesting.

Until twelve years ago, the Lady went out into the fields and hills herself. She observed the birds and took what she saw back to the sanctuary to tell the snakes. She danced in the sacred mountain spaces until she felt the goddess speak.

But the goddess hasn't spoken to the Lady since the night she sent her baby daughter to be killed. She lives in fear of displeasing the gods again, and goes out only for the ceremonies that demand it. And although she still reads the oracle, she always sends for Kelya before she starts. Her maid is sent out, the door is closed, and voices murmur for an hour or two until finally the Lady goes to the snakes' cave to read the future.

Now that Kelya is blind, she relies on the younger wise-women's sightings, and decides not only what is significant enough to be passed on to the Lady, but the best way to describe it. If a hawk carrying a dead dove is attacked by an eagle, is it more important that the hawk has lost its prey, or that it survived the eagle's attack? Or is the significance in the death of the dove? The signs are often so clear to Kelya that she can't help hinting how the oracle might interpret them.

So there are many reasons why Aissa can never become an apprentice. People aren't going to share their news with her, and she certainly can't be a midwife—no woman wants a cursed child delivering her baby. Even her spying skill is useless if she can't pass on what she's learned.

But Aissa's never dreamed of being an apprentice to anyone, let alone the wise-women. A full belly and not being spat at—those had been her dreams. Now she has food at every meal, even if she eats alone. The constant pain in her stomach disappears. Her arms and legs are filling out and she must even be getting taller, because in just one turning of the moon, her tunic has become shorter. Now it's a spare, for when her new one is being washed. She's safe, warm, and fed; she's learning, listening, and not being beaten—and as long as she sticks close to the wise-women, no one dares spit at her.

One cool, cloudy morning, out helping Roula dig up nettle roots for the winter, her hands stinging and her back aching, Aissa is suddenly so full of joy she feels she's going to burst. Roula stops to stretch and groan, but Aissa throws herself into a cartwheel—awkward at first, then whirling free, over and over down the hill.

She can't imagine she could ever ask for more.

Roula is glad
    to have a servant under her
    though she wishes that Aissa
    could eat in the kitchen

and that she, Roula,
wise-women's apprentice,
didn't have to serve food
to her servant.
And sometimes
when she sees Gold-Cat purring
on Aissa's chest
she wonders how a servant
can have a cat
when the cats belong to the Lady
and Roula can't have one.
But Kelya says
to bring the food,
don't ask about the cat,
and Roula knows better
than to disobey.
Not because of fear,
but because Kelya
is usually right—
and besides,
when she brings a meal
Aissa thanks her
with hand on heart and light in her eyes,
as grateful as if Roula
were the Lady herself.
Aissa knows
that Roula doesn't like her,
but she likes that Roula
is kind anyway,
or at least, not unkind.
She feels Lyra and Lena watching

to see what she does wrong
as if they haven't decided yet
what they think of her.
But now that Kelya doesn't care
what the world thinks,
now that Aissa is finally
under her protection
in the wise-women's chamber,
the gentleness of her hands
on Aissa's face
sometimes feels
like the licking of Milli-Cat's tongue
on her precious kittens.
But there's still fear
in the pit of her belly
when she leaves the warm room
to pass the kitchen
or the market square.
She'd thought she'd be glad
to imagine the rage
of the twins or Squint-Eye,
at knowing she's safe—
but when she sees
Half-One pale on a bench
or Half-Two strutting her hate
her body doesn't know it's safe
and shivers.
And now
on her way back from the servants' privy—
the path clear, no one around—
the servants are all

in front of the kitchen
laughing
at Half-Two in a frenzy,
furious because
her sister's still not quite her sister.
She blames Aissa
but can't touch her,
so she's thrashing Pigeon-Toe,
screaming that the floor's not clean,
lashing out with feet and hands.
The little boy's cries
go to Aissa's heart,
and white rage rises
from her belly
to her burning eyes.
No time for fear,
she shoves through the crowd—
servants or townfolk, she doesn't care—
grabbing raging Half-Two
by the shoulders,
so they both fall backward
with the twin on top
and Pigeon-Toe free,
running as fast as he can
away from the fight.
The crowd laughing harder,
shouting and jeering
as Half-Two scrambles up,
sees her attacker,
howls in horror
and jumps with both feet

at Aissa's belly.
Aissa rolls
just in time—
but Half-Two swoops
and yanks her upright
by her hair—
Aissa has grown,
but Half-Two is still bigger.
Time goes slow;
Aissa can hear the whistle
of the twin's raging breath
above the shouts of the crowd,
the barking of dogs;
can see Half-Two's fist
pulling back for power,
flying toward her
like a charging ram,
and knows that at last
Half-Two is triumphant.
Time slower still,
waiting for the pain
that doesn't come
as Roula bellows, "Stop!",
grabbing Half-Two's arm
so the punch never lands
and Aissa's hair is let go,
her head so loose
it might fall off.
The crowd disappears
as if they were never there,
and a guard arrives,

asking Roula
if she needs some help.
Roula doesn't say
he could have come sooner
but looks at him hard
till he stares at the ground,
and she says loud,
"In case you've forgotten,
I am Roula,
daughter of the wise-woman Lena,
apprentice to the wise-women
who care for you
when you're ill—
as your sister is now;
who advise you
in times of trouble—
and I advise you now:
this girl is the server
to the wise-women and me,
under their protection
and mine."
That night
Roula tells the story
and the wise-women smile.
Roula was right
to protect Aissa, they say,
and Aissa was right
to follow her heart
and protect someone smaller.
Aissa hadn't known
she was strong enough

to do it
or that someone could care enough
to do it for her—
or that both those things
could feel so good.
And in the next days
though little Pigeon-Toe
runs from Aissa
and Roula
as well as Half-Two,
Aissa becomes
not so much Roula's servant
but an almost-apprentice
as if Roula is teaching her
all that she can.

Winter comes with its icy winds and running noses, and a frightened young swineherd comes to the Hall.

"My dada fell from a rock yesterday," he tells Lyra. "His leg's broke, and now he's raging as if the gods are after him."

Cold or not, the wise-women still visit anyone who needs them. Lyra packs a basket with herbs and cloths, checking she has everything she might need.

Roula and Lena are out seeing a family of coughing fishers. "You can carry the basket," Lyra says.

It's the first time Aissa's been allowed on a house call. She tries not to grin as they leave the coolroom.

She wonders if the boy's father could be the swineherd whose boar Luki tried to leap, but the boy turns east at the ancient oak and leads them on a rough trail through the hills. It's well past noon when they reach a round stone house with a thatched roof, a sty with a sow and four half-grown piglets, and a stone wall encircling it all.

Dogs erupt into barking, teeth bared at the visitors till the boy calls them off. He lifts the gate and the dogs let them pass, watching balefully, as if they think Lyra and Aissa are just waiting for a chance to steal a piglet.

In the house that smells
of smoke and pig,
the swineherd rages nonsense,
forehead burning,
leg red-swollen,
the fleece he lies on soaked with sweat.
The mother has three small
runny-nosed boys
and a round belly ready
to give birth,
a dozing grandfather,
and a sad-eyed aunt with a lump in her neck
as if she's swallowed an eagle's egg.
The farm remote enough
they don't know that Aissa
is the bad-luck child,
and they're all too ill
or worried
to notice that she doesn't speak.
Lyra has herbs for the fever,

poultice for the leg,
cloths to strap it
straight to a board.
She feels the mother's belly
with encouraging words,
and the aunt's throat
with a promise to return
with herbs for the lump.
The mother offers hot soup:
a bowl for Lyra
and one for Aissa
to drink like anyone else.
The day is darkening
as they leave;
the sad-eyed aunt
pokes a pine branch into the fire
and gives it to Aissa
when it starts to smolder,
in case they are still in the hills
at dark.
The boy goes
to see them on their way,
but he is young—
Lyra sends him back,
and the dogs with him.
Then Lyra turns across the hills,
not the way they came:
"It's a little farther," she says,
"But we'll meet a trail,
then the road from the fishers—

safer in the dark."
The hills are rugged
but there will still be light
for a little longer,
and Aissa,
twirling her branch to keep its fire,
feels a strange sort of joy,
a song inside her
though she can't quite hear the words,
so that Lyra stops in her telling
of herbs and illness
and smiles.
"Happiness in the hills," she says,
"is a gift from the goddess.
Every wise-woman feels it."
Then,
over the next hill,
where sharp-scented bushes
grow gray and thick,
terror strikes—
swooping on Aissa
like a fox on a mouse,
knocking out her breath
like a punch from a twin.
She wants to fall to the ground,
to crawl under
a gray-green bush
but she's frozen,
still as stone.
Lyra staring all around,
grabbing the torch in defiance

of whatever might come—
but nothing is there,
nothing but
a house on the hill,
long deserted,
roof missing
stone walls crumbling.
"Ah," says Lyra, slowly guessing.
"The farm the raiders burned—
and this the place, maybe,
where you lay that night."
She lays the pine torch across a rock,
and hugs Aissa,
tight as a mother.
"I will ask Kelya what to do
to cleanse this place,
and you."
She takes Aissa's hand
and they go on,
making it safely home
before night falls.

In the morning
the wise-women send Aissa
alone
to gather seaweed and mussel shells
for the egg-lump in
the sad aunt's throat.
Aissa has seen
the pile of dried seaweed in the stores
and she knows they want her

out of the way
while they talk about
her terror on the hill.
And if it means
the goddess doesn't want her
even to serve,
then Aissa will be
nothing
again.
Climbing down to the beach—
the far path
where the fishers don't go—
she finds mussel shells first:
"Not the mussels, just the shells,"
said Lyra,
"they don't have to be perfect
to be useful:
we'll crush and burn them
into a powder."
But Aissa chooses the freshest
long-haired kelp
and bright green seaweed,
laying them clean and pure
on top of her shells—
carefully, carefully,
doing everything right
to please the goddess
and the wise-women.
The salt sea air blows through her fears
so when she climbs the cliffs again

Aissa stops at the shrine
to offer the goddess
a bright whorled shell.
Lost in her prayer,
she doesn't hear
Nasta's mother
come up from behind
pushing her hard
toward the edge,
knocking her down,
and spilling her basket.
"Next time,"
Nasta's mother snarls,
"I'll push you right off.
This shrine is for fishers;
you might serve the wise-women
but you're still a slave."
With a final spit
Nasta's mother stomps away,
and Aissa, trembling,
picks herself up,
packs up her basket,
and replaces
her shell on the shrine.
Now she hardly ever
gets spat at,
she hates it more.
That night Kelya gives her
bitter herbs to drink
before she sleeps.
Aissa dreams of her home

with Mama and Dada,
the house on the hill
when it had a roof
and life.
She dreams of the bush—
the sharp-scented, gray-green bush—
where Mama hid her,
saying, "Stay quiet,
still as stone till I come back."
When she wakes,
blind Kelya looks in her eyes
and sees her dream.
"You must go back once more,"
she says.
"It should be me to take you there
as I did before,
but I can't walk so far.
Cut a lock of my hair,
and know I go with you."
Aissa wonders
how she can ever be brave enough
to go alone
and what it is she must do,
but Lyra
and Lena and Roula,
are ready
with baskets of herbs and wine
and the mussel shells
ground and burned for the sad-eyed aunt.
They bathe at the Source,
come steaming out

into the bright cool day,
to follow the creek
across the hills
just as Kelya carried the baby
twelve years ago.
At the ruined house
Lena and Roula
scatter herbs to cleanse.
Lyra pours wine for the goddess
and Aissa offers tears
for dead Dada,
Gaggie, Poppa and Brown Dog,
and for stolen Mama,
Tattie, and Zufi.
Her tears are still flowing
when Lyra leads her
to the fear-soaked bush
for another offering
of herbs and wine,
and Aissa buries
the lock of Kelya's hair,
and a curl of her own,
where she'd lain
that long cruel night.
Then in a circle, joining hands
they dance fast and wild
around the bush
and the wise-women sing
praise and thanks
for lifting the curse.
And then Aissa does too.

No words to her song,
a wild high keening
not the *lu-lu-lu*-ing of grieving mourners
but as if the Lady herself
was singing
the curse to rise
and be gone,
so the others stop
and Aissa sings alone
until she hears it
and sees her own wonder
on their faces—
she'd never quite believed
that it was her
who'd sung the snake
away from Luki,
but this time
she knows.
They lie in the grass,
panting,
wondering,
wrapped in their cloaks,
Aissa's wolf fur like a hunter's,
until Lyra and Roula
turn one way
with the healing herbs for the swineherd family
and Lena takes Aissa
back to Kelya,
who holds Aissa's face in her hands,
saying,

"Tell me."
And just for a moment,
Aissa thinks that she can,
but when she opens her mouth
Mama's voice is still in her head
and no sound comes out.

As the days grow shorter, the wise-women spend more time together in their chamber and storerooms, checking that seeds and herbs aren't going mouldy, grinding and mixing preparations. They sing and tell stories as they work. Some of the stories are about healing and some about history, knowledge passed on from wise-woman to wise-woman through the ages.

One night Kelya tells the tale of a hunter trying to catch the moon. "On a night when the gods were young," she begins solemnly, as if it's sacred lore they need to learn, and goes on to tell the rudest, funniest story Aissa has ever heard.

Lyra and Lena gasp with laughter; Roula actually falls off her stool. Aissa is too shocked to breathe.

"Aren't you listening, little one?" Kelya asks, and tells the whole story again.

This time, when Kelya describes the hunter tumbling off the moon with his tunic around his ears, Aissa sees the whole crazy, ridiculous picture in her head. Warmth bubbles up inside her till it explodes out through her mouth, and she falls off her stool too, rolling on the ground beside Roula, which makes everyone else laugh even harder.

Everyone except Kelya. She is simply beaming, tears

in her blind eyes: Aissa is laughing.

But she still can't make a sound when she tries. And she does try, even against Mama's voice in her head, because the wise-women tried to lift the curse and it's her fault that they failed. She's failed them.

One afternoon when the others are out—winter is a busy season for seeing the sick—Kelya calls Aissa to come and sit by her knee.

"It's time for you to know your story. It's not an easy one, but it's yours. The servants banned you for calling the dragonflies; we've all seen how the cats come to you, and Lena and Lyra have told me of your singing. You must have guessed enough that it's best to know."

She reaches for Aissa's hands and gently rubs the tiny scars on the wrists.

"Sometimes in the Lady's family, a baby is born with an extra thumb. For a boy or younger girl, it's not a problem. But for a firstborn daughter: does it mean that she's not perfect? How can we know what is perfect in the eyes of the gods? If a Lady grows up to have a crooked nose, or walks with a limp, is she still fit to rule?

"No one knows the answers. This time the Lady thought one thing and the chief another. The Lady wanted the chief to be right, you must remember that. So the chief cut off the baby's extra thumbs, thinking to please the goddess—and the sea gods took him the next day. It seemed a sign that the baby must go.

"But the midwife whose job it was couldn't take

the baby to the cliff. What if the gods weren't angry because the chief had tried to trick them—but because he had wounded a child who was perfect as she was?

"So the midwife took the baby to a good woman to raise as her own. That woman had been grieving for a baby; now she was happy, though the Lady grieved so hard for the girl she believed had died that the midwife feared she might die too. But she could never tell her the truth.

"Then the raiders took that family." Kelya strokes Aissa's shoulder, trying to soften the words. "But the goddess spared you—and you ended up back at the Hall. Humans can never outrun the fate the gods have planned.

"I hoped that your voice would return when the curse was lifted from the place of those terrors—but I was wrong. All I know is that the goddess has her reasons. I just hope I live long enough to see them."

Stories aren't only for the wise-women's chamber. The year wheels around to midwinter and the celebration of the shortest day. The Lady offers the goddess wine and a goat to ensure that she'll bring sun and spring again—gods love nothing better than the smoke of barbecued meat. The feasting in the Hall goes late into that long dark night, as people offer their songs or the endless, chanted stories of their ancestors. One of the fishers can make his harp sing as if it were alive. A farmer has such a fine clear voice that no one cares if her songs are clumsy. The oldest guard tells stories as so many different characters it's hard to believe he's only one person. And Kelya adds hers—a wise one and two funny ones, but not the rude one that made Aissa laugh. That's just for them.

They leave the chamber door open so Aissa can share the music and laughter, though she can't hear enough to understand the stories. The smoke from the Hall hearth fire drifts in, and she has a lamp—a small dish of oil with a floating, burning wick—so she's not in the dark.

Roula brings her honey cake and a drink of goat milk mixed with wine. *It must taste better in the Hall*, thinks Aissa. *Maybe nothing tastes as good when you're sitting outside the party.*

Not that I want to be in the Hall with all the Hall folk.

Or in the kitchen with the servants.

Or anywhere but here!

So she sits and spins, because she's finally got her own spindle and has learned to comb wool, and to spin and weave. She doesn't like it as much as she thought she would, but the quiet rhythm is comforting—and she's pleased that she can do it, just the same as everyone else. Gold-Cat likes it too. He bats at the spindle and makes it spin. He claws the wool and tangles it.

Stop it! Aissa thinks at him.

Gold-Cat cocks his head to one side as if he's trying to hear, and taps the spindle again. Aissa laughs.

The sound of her own laughter still surprises her.

Now the days get longer but the nights are colder; the rain comes hard and there's more and more illness for the wise-women to see to. Roula and Aissa are learning fast. When the barley is harvested in the spring, Roula will graduate to be a full wise-woman.

Aissa will never do that, but she likes the learning, and loves traveling around the island to wherever they're needed. She doesn't enter homes in the town, where they know her, but the other islanders don't always recognize the cursed child in the clean young server. Or if they do, they're too sick to care.

One bright, almost-spring day she goes with Lyra to see a fisherman with a terrible, hacking cough. Aissa fetches a jug of water from the river and builds up the fire for Lyra to boil mountain herbs into a tea.

"You're the girl they call No-Name!" the fisherman says, when his coughing has stopped enough to let him speak.

"She's the wise-women's server," Lyra snaps.

"Yes, yes; I'm grateful. It's just—be careful on the cliffs on your own. Nasta's mother...she hasn't been right in the head since her brother died. He was the chief then, you know; she thought that made her quite grand. Then he drowned, and her baby, Nasta, came early with the shock."

Her brother was the chief! Nasta's uncle...the Lady's husband...the baby's father. The baby that was me.

Nasta is my cousin.

Wouldn't she hate to know that!

It's hard not to smile.

"When I'm well," says the sick fisher, "pass by here on your way to the beach. It would be an honor to watch out for you."

18

THE SHIP IN SPRING

Spring comes to the hills
    with its new life and flowers.
    The swallows fly in,
    then the herons and cranes—
    nearly the year's full cycle
    since the Bull King's ship,
    Firefly Night,
    the bull dancer lottery
    and Aissa's exile.
Now,
    gathering greens with the wise-women
    Aissa almost forgets
    she's not one of them,
    and so do they,
    watching her grow
    with big-sister pride.
    Aissa's one of the group
    when Kelya tells them

that the signs are right
for the barley to be cut
and in the morning,
the oracle will say
the harvest is early
and must start that night
at the rise of the moon.
Kelya always knows
what the oracle means
even before the Lady says it.
Sometimes Aissa wonders—
but no;
the Lady's oracle
comes straight from the goddess—
it can't be Kelya.
Next evening
as the full moon rises,
the chief and the guards,
the men of the hunters,
fishers, farmers, and town,
line the path to the barley
with bright flaming torches
lighting the Lady
as she leads Kelya,
Lena, Lyra, and Roula,
then Fila and Nasta—
but not Aissa—
to the shimmering, moonlit
field of barley.

Roula carries a wine jug
    and a basket of barley cakes;
    the Lady pours wine to the ground
    for the goddess to drink,
    scatters the cakes
    for the goddess to eat,
    and sings her request
    for a full-basket harvest
    so they can offer
    the same again next year.
With her curved bronze knife
    like a sickle new moon
    the Lady cuts the first heads
    from the barley stalks;
    hands the knife to Kelya
    then Lena, then Lyra
    and Roula too, for the very first time.
But Aissa
    is not with them
    nor with the women
    from the town and the Hall
    who reap the barley
    in the coming days.
Between two worlds
    belonging to neither,
    watching in darkness—
    careful that no one's polluted
    by her standing close—
    suddenly
    rage burns through her,

darker than the night,
hotter than the torches
the men hold high.
Rage at the Lady,
her mother, not mother
who wanted her dead
and doesn't know she's alive.
Rage at Kelya,
for not dropping the baby
off the cliff as she should have;
rage at herself
for being made wrong;
rage at the goddess
for making her so.
Her rage burns on
against the Lady,
against herself,
and the goddess,
but she can't hold it
against Kelya
because even in her fury
she is glad she's alive.

Luki watches the Lady's barley harvest and wishes he were home. His family's barley is a small field and doesn't take long to reap, because the whole family works together, everyone who's old enough to use a sickle without cutting off their fingers. His mother says men are just as good as women, and if the goddess wants the barley brought in on time she shouldn't care who does it.

Luki's only task this year was to hold a torch while the Lady and the wise-women made the first cuts.

Aissa wasn't with them. He still watches for her, the girl who doesn't speak but can sing snakes like the Lady. She's grown taller now she's the wise-women's server and doesn't live under a rock. Sometimes he tries to catch her eye but she still scurries away as if she's afraid of being spat at or stoned. It hurts that she's forgotten how he tried to help.

He never thinks that she might be avoiding him for his own good.

In the middle of the barley harvest, when all the town girls are helping with the reaping and the boys are busy with the girls' other chores as well as their own, the guard Tigo is looking for someone to race the bull dancers. Luki sees Aissa at the back gate, her gathering basket on her arm.

He points imperiously. "That girl! Call her."

"Girl at the gate!" Tigo bellows, because he can't figure out what to call her now—but what Luki wants, Luki should get.

Aissa turns. Her face lights up so that for an instant anyone can read it: *I'm going to race the bull dancers!*

"Tigo!" Nasta wails. "Can't you see—that's No-Name!"

"She's the wise-women's server," Tigo mutters.

No one hears him. Nasta is shrieking as if she's walked into a hornet's nest. "We're the bull dancers! Are you trying to bring us bad luck? Don't you know she's cursed?"

On and on—she's still going when Aissa slips out the gate.

"Are you afraid she would beat us?" Luki asks, which makes Nasta even louder—but Luki's curious, because he's seen Aissa run and he thinks she's faster than him, maybe even faster than Nasta. Of course he wants his fellow bull dancer to be quick and agile to give them both a chance of staying alive. He'd just like to see her lose once.

But soon we'll be gone and Aissa can race with the new bull dancers.

He stops feeling sorry for her. Maybe she's still a servant and some people spit at her, but when he leaves for the Bull King's land, Aissa will stay safely at home. Sometimes he feels his life is dripping away from him, one spring day at a time. But the ship is late this year, and each day that it doesn't come is another day to wonder if it never will.

Then late one morning, after the full moon, the Bull King's ship returns. Last year's dancers aren't on it. They have disappeared like all the dancers before them.

Luki hadn't known how much he'd been hoping he wouldn't have to go. He's not a coward, but he's a realist: if anyone ever survives the bulls, it will be a natural athlete with balance sure as Milli-Cat's, reflexes fast as a snake's tongue, and light-footed as a goat. Someone like Nasta. Not Luki.

Now there's no more hope.

But I can go home for a day, he thinks. A last night on the farm with his family...it's almost worth facing the Bull King for that.

The running rushing panic
like every other year;
Nasta's father leaving his boat
to run with his wife
up to the Hall
to take their precious daughter
home for a day
and the last visit
to their clan's sacred shrine.
Luki, racing out the back gate,
not wasting time
to run around the walls,
stops
to touch hands with Aissa,
a last thank you
for saving him from the snake.
Aissa, too shocked to refuse,
presses her hand to his
for the first time,
because it's too late
for people to mock him
for kindness to her.
She can only hope
it's also too late
for her curse to taint him
since he needs
all the luck he can get—
though she sees the shock
in Tigo's eyes
at her bad-luck touch—

Tigo, sent to guard the bull dancer
across the hills
and bring him back safe
at dawn.
Feeling the dread
all that long, long day
and anxious night,
like all the other ship days
and not like any other
because she is safe with the wise-women,
but this time she cares
what will become of a dancer.
Dawn comes,
the Lady's song so strong
Aissa feels it
tremble through her body
as if she could rise with the sun—
and as the last notes die
and the praise begins
she almost wishes
she could give up her safety
to hide as she used to
and feel it alone.
Then the trembling grows,
the ground quivers,
birds wheel in the sky,
dogs howl and babies wail,
water shoots from the well,
and the great oil jar at the kitchen door
topples and smashes
with a flood of oil.

The earth swells
like a wave from the sea—
and a booming crash
shakes the world.
A silence follows
louder than sound,
broken by screams
and fisherfolk running
up to the gates.
The goddess of fishers
has taken her cliff
and her shrine,
her image and offerings,
back to the sea,
and Nasta's mother
and Nasta
with them.
Aissa knows it's her fault
for worshipping
the fisherfolk's goddess—
till a voice in her head says,
"It wasn't you she took."
Her heart stops
then beats as surely
as if it had always known
the way things would be.
While the square erupts—
people crying to the gods,
asking why;
weeping women
clutching their children,

servants skidding in oil
and the braver folk rushing
to the cove to help—
stillness
settles on Aissa.
Blind to the world
she sees
Nasta and her mother
destroying the patterns
Aissa left for the goddess.
Deaf to the screams
she hears,
"Your father was a fisher.
It was your shrine
to honor as you did."
She feels the wise-women
close around her
in a ring of protection.
"Little one," says Kelya,
"You've been touched by the goddess."
Aissa wakes from her trance,
feels light pouring through her,
her eyes now
sharp as eagles',
her ears like a wolf's,
and she knows
what she must do.
The Bull King's captain
shaken by the omen—
though he doesn't know
the bull dancer's gone—

tells the Lady
the tide and winds are right—
he'll still sail this morning
and all the tribute
must be on board.
"Your spears
and sharp bronze axes
mean that you
can take our children,"
says the Lady.
"But the gods have spoken—
beware your own king's fate
if he doesn't listen."
The guard who speaks
the Bull King's tongue
is pale with fear
at the captain's reply:
"My king serves the Earthshaker,
the god and bull
who spoke this morning—
and he'll take his tribute."
Now Luki and Tigo
and Luki's family
run in, panting
from the long hike home;
ready for what must be.
They approach the Lady,
and Aissa does too—
wise-women behind her,
like Luki's family
behind him—

the Lady chose Nasta's name
in the lottery
but Nasta is gone
and now the gods
have chosen Aissa.
Through a mist
she hears the Lady,
"These are our dancers,
sent to serve your king
and save our island.
I must give them
the goddess's blessing
one last time
before they go."
The sanctuary is dark:
Roula brings flares,
lights the torches
set around the walls
till shadows flicker
on pale faces:
the Lady and the chief,
Luki with his family,
Aissa with hers.
"This is the girl called No-Name,"
says the Lady to Kelya.
"Until she became our server,"
says Kelya,
her blind eyes staring
straight at the Lady's.
"Her name is Aissa."

And the Lady—
who stood up straight
when the earth trembled,
when the cliff crashed,
and the bull dancer was lost—
crumples at the knees
and starts to fall
like any grieving mother
till the chief catches her.
"Aissa?" she whispers.
"Aissa," says Kelya.
"Twelve years ago I did a great wrong
but now it seems
that it was right.
And if you want
me to go to the cliff,
I'm too old to care."
"The sea's taken enough for one day,"
says the Lady.
"The oracle will tell us
how we must appease the goddess—
but for this, I thank you."
"Thank the child," says Kelya.
"It was she who chose,
or the goddess in her."
The Lady finally
looks at Aissa,
straight in her eyes,
as if she could search
into her soul.
"Thank you," she says,

with hand on heart,
her voice cracking
so when she sings their blessing
she sounds like Fila,
with a voice to scare toads.
Aissa still wishing
the Lady would touch her
with a mother's love
as Luki's mother is hugging him
and his father holding tight to his hand,
but the Lady
is the ruler again;
her voice clears
to sing a last song
and when she kisses Aissa
on the top of the head,
it is just the same way
that she kisses Luki.
The chief does the same,
but Kelya
hugs Aissa so hard
it seems she'll never
let her go.
"It's time," says the Lady.
"Be well,
and return to us next year."
They leave the darkness,
blinking in
the brightness of day,
to the impatient Bull King's men
and Fila, waiting for her mother,

uncertain what to do
in the chaos of the shaken town.
Then Milli-Cat,
tail up and waving,
leads her family
in a loving coil around Aissa's legs,
and Gold-Cat jumps
straight to her shoulders.
Aissa holds him,
feeling her heart
break to leave him,
turns to Fila,
and gives her the cat.
Fila's eyes
open wide with surprise;
she can't put hand on heart
because she's hugging the cat
but she says thank you
not just in her voice
but in her eyes and smile.
And Aissa knows
Gold-Cat will be safe
and even happy.
"Now!" shouts the captain
as the jostling people
race back from the cliff
and grieving cove
to touch the tributes' god-luck hands.
And no one spits
at Aissa.

BOOK TWO

19

THE BULL KING'S SHIP

It's not like the parades of other years. Aissa and Luki follow the chief and the captain, with Luki's family, Lyra, Lena, and Roula close beside them; tribute bearers grunt under the weight of bundled cloth, goats carry panniers of dried fish, jugs of wine or barrels of oil, and the Bull King's men follow them all, eyes wary and spears ready. Kelya stays with the Lady to help prepare for the oracle and discover how to appease the gods.

All the people who should be lining the road to see the dancers on their way are at the cove, searching for any sign of the lost girl and her mother. Sounds of wailing rise from the beach; the goats are skittish and bleating. Fear crackles in the air—the ground feels firm enough now, but no one knows when the Earthshaker will roar again.

They round the curve in the road; the chief walks resolutely on, because he's already seen what isn't there. Aissa hasn't. She gasps.

"No!" Lena exclaims.

"It's really gone!" says Luki.

It's one thing to hear that the cliff has disappeared, and another thing to see it. From the end of the chamomile field there is nothing, just the raw edge of a new cliff, and below it, a mound of rocks and cliff-face reaching to the sea—a greater burial mound than even Nasta's mother would have wished.

The bare, gnarled roots of the shrine tree are sticking out of the top of the mound. Searchers are scrambling up to it.

Nasta and her mother are buried somewhere under that mess of rocks and tree. Aissa shudders. *What if it is my curse after all?*

There's a scream from the searchers. The cry is echoed down the beach: "A miracle!"

And Aissa, still feeling sick at Nasta's horrible death, is shocked to feel herself think, *I'm the bull dancer now, and I'm going to go!*

"The goddess!" the searchers shout. "The Mother of the fishers is safe!"

The stone statue is cradled in the roots of the tree.

The Bull King's ship is pulled up onto the beach. It's as long as the Hall and as wide as the Great Room. It stares at them like a ferocious beast: curved black horns jut from its bow, fierce eyes are painted below, and its long ram looks like a snout.

Two crewmen swing Luki and Aissa up over the side. The tide is coming in and the crew's working fast to load everything before the sea floats the ship off the beach. There's not even time for a last hug goodbye; Luki's mother is still clutching his bundle of new clothes and food for the voyage. Tears run down her cheeks as she tosses it up for Luki to catch.

A man shouts in the Bull King's strange language, as harsh and meaningless as a raven's squawk.

Luki and Aissa look at each other anxiously.

Now Luki can't speak either! Aissa thinks. *And neither of us can hear.*

The crewman shouts louder, gesturing *get down!* as if he's ordering a dog.

This time they understand. They squat at the very front of the ship, behind the horns, legs tucked to their chins and as out of the way as they can possibly be.

"I forgot they don't talk like normal people," Luki whispers to Aissa.

He feels nervous even whispering. They both go back to studying the ship that will carry them to their new lives.

It's like a giant version of the fishers' little boats, except for the decks at the bow and stern, each a few paces wide and two paces long. In between, the ship is open, with rows of benches stretching from side to side. A narrow plank bridge runs down the middle from the front deck to the back. The thick pole of the mast is lying on the bridge.

Aissa counts the benches: twenty-seven, with oars tethered at both sides. She guesses one man for each oar, side by side on the bench—fifty-four men, plus the captain and his warriors. More than the chief and the guards could ever hope to fight. The bull dancers are truly the island's only hope of freedom.

The long line of people and goats carrying the rest of the tributes is moving quickly past the bow; the crew grunt with strain as they haul up heavy jars and baskets, stowing them quickly under the front deck. The last to come are the goat kids. Their feet are tied with rope and they bleat loudly.

Aissa wishes she could hold one— it would be easier to be brave if she was comforting someone else. She's afraid that she might start bawling just like them. "Still as stone," Mama said, but here Aissa is with the raiders, and she's asked for it all by herself without ever making a sound.

Luki's shoulder presses against hers. His family is right below the ship; his little brother is punching the wood and being driven away by the crew. Lyra and Lena stand with the family; Roula has disappeared. *Already?* Aissa thinks, hurt.

"What luck!" a woman sings loudly. "What joy to honor the goddess!"

She sings it to Luki's parents until they join in, pulling Luki's sister and brothers closer around them. Finally even the little brother is singing his own version, "Lucky Luki, lucky Luki is my brother, lucky Luki is going away and it's not fair, not fair, not fair."

The final "not fair!" is just a wail. His father picks him up, pressing the little boy's face against his chest. The chief says something that Luki and Aissa can't hear.

"What JOY!" Luki's father shouts, because he'd do anything to keep the gods happy and his son safe. "What luck!"

Finally, even louder than Luki's father, above the noise of singing and bleating, the captain bellows a command. The last bundles of dried fish are shoved under the deck, the captain grabs one of the horns at the bow, and swings himself on board. He runs down the plank bridge to the ship's stern and lowers the two great steering paddles into the water. More men jump on board and into their rowing places.

A boar-shouldered man pulls a huge pole out from under the benches, pushing the ship out just like the fishers do with their little boats. The crew on the beach wade in deeper, swinging themselves up on deck as the ship floats free. Luki's family follows, the little brother on the father's shoulders, still touching the ship.

"Aissa!" Roula shouts, splashing frantically through the waves with a large bundle over her head. She's nearly at the ship when she stumbles.

Luki's mother reaches out to steady her.

"Catch!" Roula shouts, and throws the bundle up to the bow.

Aissa leans. The captain roars, but Aissa has her bundle of clean tunic and honey cakes, wrapped in love and wolfskin. Tears blur her vision.

The rowers on the left pull hard on their oars till the ship turns around and its fierce eyes are staring out to sea.

The captain bellows again. The mast is hauled upright, the ropes set in place and the square red sail pulled up to fill with wind. The ship lifts and slides over the waves. The people on the beach become a blur and gradually disappear.

They haven't really gone, Aissa tells herself.

"It's horrible what happened to Nasta," Luki whispers. "But I'm glad you're here."

They clutch hands tightly as they sail into the unknown.

The future
    is as strange,
    as impossible to imagine,
    as if the sun
    set in the east
    or the earth turned to sky.
The land Aissa knows
    is out of sight
    and the lives she's lived
    are gone;
    she must start a new one
    again.
And as she sits with Luki,
    feeling the ship
    dipping and rising on the sea,
    hearing the slap of waves
    upon the bow,
    the snap of the sail,
    the splash of dolphins,

seagulls' cries,
and the strange words
of the Bull King's men,
Aissa knows
that wishing to escape her life
by being a dancer
is no more like what will come
than touching a wave on the shore
is like riding the sea.
Even the blueness
is deep turquoise here.

The wind dies near evening. The sail is dropped and the oars come out. The men sing in time with their rowing, a steady rhythm and a crescendo of triumph when a new island appears.

So soon! Aissa thinks. *I'm not ready!*

But she'll be glad to get off the ship. Her stomach is rolling and churning. It's worse than hunger, and she doesn't want to eat. Sometimes Luki looks as if he's actually going to throw up, and that makes her feel as if she might too.

"I thought the Bull King's land would be huge," he says. "This doesn't look much bigger than home."

It's not as mountainous as their island; even from here they can see a wide cove and sandy beach. Soon they can see a town nestled on the slopes. They've never seen so many houses.

"Can you see any bulls?" Luki asks.

Aissa pictures a bull as bigger than a goat, fiercer than a boar, with huge wild eyes like the ones on the ship.

They see the animal at the same moment. They both catch their breath and stare: maybe bulls aren't as big or bad as people say.

A woman is leading it; it's not much taller than a big goat, with long, flopping ears. No horns. It raises its head to look at the ship, and a noise like a sore-throated demon rings out. The crew laugh and one makes a joke. 'Donkey," Aissa and Luki hear.

We were afraid of a joke! Aissa thinks.

Luki grins at her, shame-faced.

The ship touches the sand; the captain strides up the bridge to the bow, ordering Aissa and Luki off the deck. They crouch on the ship's floor with the goat kids while the rowers jump down and haul the ship onto the beach. Crowds of people are running, wailing and shouting, from the beach to the town. The captain and half the crew march up the road with their spears; the rest stay with the ship as if they're guarding it.

Luki and Aissa poke their heads up to peer over the side.

This is like the first time the ship came to the island! Aissa thinks.

"This isn't the Bull King's land!" says Luki. "They're getting more tributes!"

They're right. In the evening, the crew sacrifice four of the goat kids and roast the meat on skewers over a fire. Aissa, Luki and the remaining kids are lifted down. The goats are hobbled so they can graze but not run away. The leader shows Aissa and Luki a rope and points to the last two kids, who are still lying on their sides with their four legs tied together.

"I think he's saying that's what'll happen to us if we try to run away," says Luki. "How are we supposed to answer?"

Aissa puts her hand on her heart in the thank-you sign. Luki copies. It's apparently good enough as a promise, and they're free to squat by the fire and eat what they're offered. But afterwards, when the crew roll themselves in their cloaks to sleep on the soft sand, Luki and Aissa are shoved back onto the ship for the night.

The captain and the rest of the crew return in the morning with an even longer line of tributes, and four more dancers. Their new life settles into a pattern: the sea by day and land at night. The moon goes from full to sickle. Usually they sail, but if there's no wind the men row. On hot, still days the crew puts a shade cloth over the front deck; other days the waves are so high that they splash up from the snout into the ship. Once it's so rough that all the youths and some of the rowers vomit over the sides. They wait on a beach for two days for the storm to clear.

One night they camp on an island with no town nearby, just a spring to refill their water jugs, and another they have to anchor at sea. Those are the only mornings that no tribute is added. All the other nights, the captain and half the crew march up to a town or Hall to demand their payment, and two or four or even twelve youths are hoisted on board to join Aissa and Luki.

By the last day thirty-two thirteen-year-olds are crammed onto the front deck. There's no room to move; the deck stinks of the goat kids or piglets crammed beneath it each morning to feed the crew.

The children all speak different languages. A few can understand each other and a few can understand the crew.

Luki and Aissa don't know many words, but they've learned the commands. They teach the new dancers how to promise not to run away, to scramble under the deck when the captain approaches, and the signs for water and food.

One girl can't stop crying and one boy can't stop vomiting. Most of the rest throw up occasionally and cry at night. There's no privy and no privacy on the ship, but Aissa shows the other girls how to squat on the edge and hope that a shark won't bite their bare bottoms.

They learn that the world is bigger than they'd imagined, and that people are all the same under their different words and clothes. For this little while, it doesn't even matter that Aissa can't speak.

Then late one afternoon, the land that rises up out of the sea goes on so far they can't see where it ends. The sailors' songs have a different rhythm, triumphant and final. There are fishing fleets and ships as big as theirs, more than they can count, sailing in or hauled up on the beach. There are buildings right down to the water's edge.

They've arrived at the Bull King's land.

The road is paved smooth
but everything else
is rough with noise,
crowds, and color:
crews unloading cargo,
bleating goats and squealing piglets;
barrels, jars, and boxes,
people shouting
in different tongues,
wearing different clothes
with skin of different colors—
some are darker
than Aissa and Luki
and many paler
with hair that isn't black and curling
but brown or gold or red.
The huddled thirteen-year-olds
don't feel like bull dancers.
What they feel is
afraid,
but there is nowhere to run
because the road
is packed tight with people,
goats and donkeys,
snorting horses pulling carts,
curtained chairs on stout poles
on the shoulders of slaves—
and where
would they run if they could?

Aissa's always known
that the Bull King's land
was big;
that the men on the ship
weren't all
the men in the land;
that more women and children
waited at home.
But she didn't know
there could be numbers like this,
people swarming
like bees from a hive;
houses and halls
right down to the shore
like mussels on a rock.
She touches fingers with Luki
but a girl from the ship
grabs her hand tight
as if she's drowning
and Aissa can save her.
The whisper goes round,
"Where do we go?
What do we do?"
The words are all different
so some make the shrug—
palms out,
eyebrows arched—
the question mark
that Aissa and Luki made,
so they all understand
but no one has the answer.

A new shout:
a woman and a man
are coming toward them.
The man's left leg
is withered and drags
so he walks with a stick—
but no one would laugh
or call him Flopleg
because he looks as strong
as a mountain goat
with a temper to match.
The woman wears
a short kilt like the man
and looks as strong
but her right arm
is gone.
They shout and gesture
for the dancers to follow.
The man leads;
the woman circles behind
like a dog herding goats
and everything about her says
if they try to run
she'll catch them.
The crowd steps back
to let them through,
though hands shoot out
to touch and pinch,
voices call
and laugh,

and eyes stare,
as if the dancers were lambs
brought to market.
The road is long
and people line it all the way
from the town at the sea
past groves of olives
and fields of new-reaped barley
into another town
that makes the first
look small and plain;
the houses not of stone
or blending into a cliff
as houses should,
but colored bright
in reds and blues
with windows for light
and flat roofs
where people sit
to watch the dancers pass.
Aissa catches
Luki's eye
and they both laugh
to see something so strange.
But they don't laugh
when they see
on the rise of a hill,
lit by the setting sun
the bull god's Hall—
roofs stacked high,

halls on top of halls,
too huge,
too grand,
too rich and bright
to be anything human.
And over the gate ahead,
lit by flares in the dusk
a monster leaps through
a blood red wall
as if he's not made of stone
but alive and charging—
and if that's a bull,
Aissa never wants to meet one.
The limping man leads them
past the guardhouse and painted bull
on the road around the halls
past courtyards
stone steps and pillared rooms
past more gates
that are not for them.
Aissa's head spins to see
so many people,
so many buildings,
so much strangeness,
and she breathes a little stronger
when they turn to a side road,
leaving the palace behind,
past grand houses
to a hall out on its own.
In the central room, lit with lamps,
tables are set

with fruit and cheese,
barley cakes and flatbread,
dried fish,
and jugs of milk with wine.
But first,
the man and the woman
stand at a long bench
with jugs of water
and basins
to wash their hands,
carefully pouring
water over their fingers,
showing the new dancers,
as if they might never have seen
hands washed before.
The man barks an order
and everyone jostles
around the jugs,
because they all want
to do it right.
And they all want to eat.
When the food is gone
down to the last crumb
the man shouts again,
shoving the boys
to a room at one side,
while the one-armed woman
herds the girls to another:
lined with sleeping mats
and shadowed girls within
watching the new ones arrive.

In the morning they roll
their mats and bundles
against the wall,
open the doors to the central room,
and in the daylight
they see
paintings of bulls
with boys and girls leaping
over their backs,
of bulls throwing a girl,
dashing a boy to the ground—
and it doesn't look
like dancing at all.

20

SPRING TRAINING

The man with the dragging leg and the woman with the missing arm are ex-bull dancers. Now they train the new ones, the story of their injuries a constant warning.

Niko had been sold to the Bull King when his parents couldn't pay their taxes. He'd been a strong boy and had worked in the storage rooms, helping much bigger men haul jugs of oil and bags of wheat to store in giant clay pots. But from the first time he saw the bull dances, he practiced handsprings and backflips—and did them whenever there was a chance that someone important could see him. Finally someone did, and Niko was moved from the slave quarters to the training hall. He'd survived the year, till the great spring dances and very nearly through them; freedom had been so close he can still remember the taste of it. Freedom, glory, and wealth: the rewards of a successful dancer. He'd have been mobbed in the streets, a star for life.

But on the last dance, the last bull, his left hand slipped as he grabbed the horns. Instead of leaping into a handstand, he swung one-handed, and the sharp horn ripped through his left leg, shredding the muscles forever.

Mia had come as tribute from one of the farthest lands that the Bull King's navy reached. Niko had been her trainer; he'd pushed her mercilessly because he could see her skill and drive, and knew she had a chance of success.

Like Niko, she lasted until the spring dances, when another dancer, flying broken from the horns of a bull, knocked her to the ground. The bull trampled them both: the other girl died, and Mia's right arm was smashed to a pulp. The healers knew there was only one way to save her life: they cut off the shattered arm. Not many people survive surgery like that, but Mia was lucky.

In fact, they both know how lucky they are. Training the new dancers is the next best thing to freedom; they're respected and honored—especially by the gamblers who come to ask their advice for the coming year. Betting is part of the thrill of the games: from high-society ladies to the poorest workman, nearly everyone has a wager on which dancers will make it through to the end. The real gamblers take it further. They'll bet on every possibility for each stage of the year: who will be left after each dance, who will die, who will turn and run.

But the bullring needs luck as well as skill. No matter how much gold a gambler offers, Mia and Niko never tempt fate by suggesting which of their young athletes will fail. Pointing out a trainee's extraordinary skill or amazing strength is different—and they're quite happy to accept a gold ring or a silver necklace afterwards.

Today is a long way from that. Today is the start of organizing ninety-eight scared children into teams of highly skilled, fearless acrobats.

The first step is to weed out anyone not worth training. There's no time to waste: it's less than two cycles of the moon before these dancers face their first bulls. So, by the end of the day, some of them will be in the slave quarters. They might even be the luckier ones. But as they're woken, sent to the washhouses and breakfast tables, no one suspects they're already being tested.

Neither Mia nor Niko know exactly what they're looking for—they just know it when they see it. The girl who's last out of bed: someone has to be last, but is she always slow? The boy who's still crying; the one everyone seems to shun.

Aissa sees Luki across the dining hall. His face lights up with relief and she feels hers glowing too. They hug like brother and sister, and go together to find the others from their ship, because those shipmates are already like cousins.

In the babble of reunions in a dozen different languages, the trainers don't notice that Aissa doesn't speak.

Breakfast is light, and over quickly. Training is about to begin.

Everyone's still dressed in their native clothing: mostly tunics, in many different styles, though some boys are in kilts. A few girls are wearing long robes and Mia gives them ropes to belt their skirts up out of the way. One starts to cry.

"Send her out now?" calls Niko.

"Let her run," says Mia. "We've been wrong before."

"Not often!"

Mia laughs. It's true. They'll be watching this girl closely, as well as the others they'd noticed earlier.

Dragging his leg behind him, Niko leads the way out the door at the end of the dining hall. Mia does her herd-dog act, rounding up anyone who hasn't guessed that they're supposed to follow, and carefully noting them. Intuition—guessing what someone else is thinking without being told—is as important as running in the bullring.

However, speed is easier to test, and Niko and Mia want to see not just how they run, but how they race: how determined they are to win.

The trainees stop dead as they enter the ring. Across the silver shimmer of olive groves, a distant mountain rises to a peak—but no one's looking at the view. The arena is seventy paces long and thirty wide, enclosed by wooden walls, with tiered seats behind them. The walls are painted with more pictures of bulls and acrobats.

"Just wait till they see the real thing," Niko mutters.

Mia smiles. It's always like this—she doesn't hold it against them. She remembers her own first sight of it: the shock of the vivid paintings in this vast court, and the realization of what she was expected to do. That awe is part of the reason the training ring is so elaborately painted. The other reason is that bulls are sacred. Anything to do with them should be as beautiful as it can be.

Aissa and Luki are standing with the others from their ship, a small known island in a sea of strange faces. The girl who'd cried in her sleep is holding Aissa's hand again.

Mia breaks them apart. A bull dancer is part of a team, but they need to think on their own as well. It's time to break up the friendships and organize new groups.

After some shoving, shouting, and pointing, the ninety-eight youths are divided into eleven groups. Mia sends Aissa to one group with another girl and two boys from the ship and five strangers. The girl who'd held her hand goes to a different group, and Luki to a third.

Aissa studies a painting of a girl grabbing a bull by the horns, and another of a boy doing a handspring down a bull's back.

The bull is enormous, five times the size of the boar Luki had tried to leap. What the acrobats are doing is impossible.

She can see the gate where the bulls will enter…

We're going to die, right now, on the very first day!

Mia lays a straight line of rope across the hard-packed dirt in front of them, and another at the far end of the arena.

Niko shoves Luki's group into a line behind the first rope. Mia comes back and steps into the center spot; the trainees sidle well away from her.

"Go!" Niko bellows. No one in that group understands the word, but when he claps his hands and Mia leaps over the rope into a fast, fluid run, Luki follows. Tigo's training is paying off: Luki mightn't be the fastest runner, but he knows about racing. He runs harder than he's ever run before. He's gasping as he strides over the finish line, his foot touching the ground on the same heartbeat as Mia's. None of the others are close.

If Aissa had a voice, she'd have *lu-lu-lu*-ed for joy. Luki has won the very first race. It's got to be a good omen.

She checks the gate quickly: no sign of bulls yet.

The next group is lined up. Mia doesn't need to run with them this time. Everyone starts when Niko claps his hands—and they all want to win. The race is surprisingly even.

In the third group the hand-holding girl from the ship twists her ankle and tumbles to the ground. Mia beckons; the girl hobbles off to the side and sits out the rest of the morning.

My first friend! Did I give her my bad luck?

A boy who trips his neighbor is sent to join her. The girl who was late for breakfast is just as slow on the racetrack; another boy nearly as far behind flaps his arms like wings. Mia and Niko whisper, and send them to the sidelines.

Those three weren't anything to do with me, Aissa thinks.

But the most important thing now is to get through her own race. She's never run with anyone else—fleeing the twins is not the same as racing. The more she thinks about it the more she worries.

She can tell that the rest of her group are thinking the same thing: *Let us go next! Let's get it over with!*

They're the very last to run. They're all so tense they're ready to explode over the line before Niko has time to clap his hands. One boy actually does.

Niko roars. They don't need to understand the words to know what he's saying: "Get back behind the line! Wait till I clap!"

When the clap finally comes, the boy is so determined not to be wrong again that he starts a moment behind the others.

Aissa never sees him. She runs as if stones are hurtling, as if a wolf is on her heels. She feels the air in her lungs and the spring in her legs. She seems to have barely started when she sees the great gate ahead of her and realizes she's leapt right over the end line. The others are just reaching it now.

Mia's striding up to her.

I didn't stop at the line! I'll be sent off!

But Mia is grinning. She pats Aissa's shoulder and sends her back to her group.

They sleep in the dorms, eat in the dining hall, and train in the arena. The days are hot, hotter than at home; they train before and after breakfast and again in the evening; the afternoon siesta is long. They learn to strap each other's wrists and ankles for strength, and to feel comfortable wearing shorts and a close-fitting top. Life is a haze of shouted commands and pushing their bodies until they ache. When they rest, their minds buzz with new words and their new life.

They learn handstands and handsprings, cartwheels, somersaults and backflips, and how to jump from a standing start. They pull themselves up on a high bar and swing around it.

It's not easy. Shoulders are dislocated; arms are broken and so are ribs; ankles are sprained. Aissa has a bruise spreading like a purple flower on her thigh.

"From the bar?" asks Luki.

With her fingers, Aissa mimes a handspring crashing to the ground.

They'd worked out signs when no one could speak the same language. Now, even though they can understand simple commands, it's still easier to use signs in their mixed dialect groups. For the first time in her life, Aissa can communicate nearly as well as anyone else.

Not only that, she's as good as anyone else. She's small and wiry; years of hard work have made her strong, and a life of hiding has made her quick and agile. She'd turned cartwheels of relief when she joined the wise-women; now she can do them elegantly, and handsprings besides, and that is pure joy.

She points to a red welt across Luki's side. It looks as if he's been beaten, except that they never get beaten here.

"Crashed across the bar," Luki says ruefully. "I was lucky I didn't break a rib."

But soreness only matters if it means more mistakes. Welts and bruises will heal; they're lucky to earn them.

Because it's not just the injured who are sent away—anyone who doesn't learn fast enough gets pointed to the sidelines, and disappears before nightfall.

No one knows where they go. There are whispers of sacrifice. One girl decides they're sent home: the next day she jumps so badly that she disappears too.

A full moon cycle later, only fifty-nine trainees are left. They still haven't seen a bull.

But something is about to happen. Aissa's sure of it. Mia and Niko used to only note trainees who were doing something wrong—now they're discussing her perfect flip. She feels sick with fear for the rest of the day.

The next morning they're divided again. Thirteen boys and five tall girls are told to race circuits around the ring. Luki is one of them. They run for an hour at a time.

Aissa's in a group practicing acrobatics. There's no bar for the next ten days, just handsprings and backflips, leaps and catches: a different routine for each group, over and over. The world whirls; she doesn't know which way is up and which way is down.

But it's nearly the solstice, the first day of summer and the longest day of the year. Aissa guesses that the new dancers are going to be part of the Bull King's celebrations.

The fear in her belly
  is still there—
  part of her

always—
but even it
is not the same
because it's shared
with her companions:
the fear of failing,
of pain
or death by bull,
and though the fear of hate,
of spit, slaps, and stones,
lurks deep inside
it's no longer real.
Reality now
is this new life,
a different world from the one she's known—
though even here
crickets chirp and frogs croak,
larks sing and eagles soar;
there are geckos on the walls,
lizards on the ground,
and the sun still rises in the east—
so it seems that some things
are the same
in every world.
The Bull King's language
is still strange
but every day Aissa learns more,
hearing words
from people on the tiered seats
watching them train.
The words she learns

are bets and guesses
of who will live
and who will die
or be sent to slavery.
Not me, she vows,
and her anger glows bright—
even though servitude
is better than the sacrifice
some had imagined—
Aissa knows
what it is to be a slave
and she's not going back
to that misery again.
She hates to think
that's where Luki is,
despised and trapped—
because Luki and the runners
disappeared
the morning after they were chosen—
and Luki belongs to the hills.
He'd felt trapped
even in the freedom
of the Lady's Hall,
when Aissa envied him.
But one night
Luki and the runners
are back in the dining hall,
and there's time to whisper
before they're sent to the dorms.
"We've been catching bulls:
little ones first—

calves sent back to their mothers
after we'd caught and tied them
with our ropes.
They were tame,
from the Bull King's herd.
But that was just practice.
After that we went to the woods
where the bulls live wild
like the boars at home."
Luki shudders,
and his eyes grow dark.
"We caught the bull
the king's men wanted,
a year old, they said,
not full grown—
like us, they said—
but huge and strong.
He killed a boy,
before we had him tied—
threw him through the air
like your friend Milli-Cat
would throw a mouse,
and the life thrown out of him."
Aissa sees
the sadness in his eyes
and wonders if she was wrong
to think she'd choose death
before slavery;
the dead boy might say
he'd rather be alive.

21
THE DANCE OF SUMMER SOLSTICE

Slaves arrive at dawn to dismantle the bullring fence and stadium seats. Mia and Niko send the runners for a quick jog and watch each group of acrobats go through their routines. Once to warm up and again to perfect it, then they're sent in pairs to the bathrooms with scented oils, scrapers, and combs.

Aissa's guessed right: even the Bull King celebrates the longest day. The dancers need to be clean and perfect to honor the gods.

Aissa is with Zeta, a strong, tall girl who'd been in the runners' group with Luki. They oil their bodies and scrape the dirt off with short leather straps; wash each other's hair and plait it into seven tails, exactly how Niko demonstrated.

Zeta doesn't speak till it's her turn to wash Aissa's hair, but once she starts talking she can't stop. Her eyes carry the same shock and grief as Luki's, and Aissa guesses that the story she's telling is the same, though "bull" and "boy" are the only words she understands.

Mia comes to inspect them. She undoes one of Zeta's plaits and makes Aissa do it again, checks that their hands and short-bitten nails are scrubbed spotless, and gives them their new clothes. Shorts and tops like the ones they've been training in, but bright and new.

New clothes, that no one else has ever worn! For a moment the thrill drowns out the fear bees in Aissa's belly.

"Rest now!" Mia says, when she's satisfied that their blouses are crossed and tucked perfectly, the belt tight enough to hold everything together and loose enough to breathe.

Rest? Aissa thinks. She wants to run and cartwheel, even meet the bull if she has to. The fear will only buzz stronger the longer they wait.

It's the slowest siesta she's ever known. No one sleeps.

Finally Mia and Niko call them. The acrobats and runners are separated again; Aissa presses Zeta's hand as she joins the group following Mia out of the hall that's been their home.

Panic rises in her throat like vomit. *Why are we being separated? I didn't see Luki to say goodbye!*

They follow the road to the palace—another word they've learned—and through a maze of gates to a small room with a basin, where a woman waits for them. Mia stops and salutes.

The Lady! Aissa thinks. The woman has a round, pregnant belly, and is beautifully dressed in a flowing red robe embroidered with birds and flowers. She is holding a jug painted with the sign of the sacred double ax.

"Hold out your hands!" Mia orders, and as each acrobat offers their outstretched hands, the priestess pours water over them, murmuring words none of them know but all understand. They are being cleansed to meet the gods.

The fear in Aissa's belly settles from bumblebee buzzing into a solemn, heavy mass.

Mia leads them through a hallway to a last gate. On the other side is a courtyard, its flat paving stones covered with a layer of sand. The fences and tiered seats from their training arena have been raised around it, in front of the great red pillars and open corridors of the palace.

So the bull can't get into the rooms! Aissa guesses, and shudders. Suddenly the bull is more real than it's ever been—though she still hasn't seen one.

The palace rises above the barricades; people are crowded at windows, on roofs, and in red-painted balcony boxes. A musician is playing a lyre, though it's hard to hear him over the rumble of the crowd; he stands in front of a pair of tall stone horns, looking up at the biggest balcony box.

The Bull King is in the balcony.

His head is a bull, and his body is a man's. Aissa's skin crawls as if she's covered with spiders; her plaits feel as if they're standing on end. The king is more terrifying than her worst nightmare. She can't look away; can't see anything else. It's a long moment before she even notices the woman beside him.

If the priestess who washed their hands was the Lady, this is the Lady of Ladies, the Mother of all— although beside the monstrous king, she looks small and human. Her skirt is layered with red and green flounces, belling out wide from her tight gold belt. More gold glints from necklaces, bracelets, and the tiara around her piled-high hair.

Niko opens the gate. "Go!" he says. "What are you afraid of? There's no bull for you today."

But there are so many faces,
so many watching eyes
Aissa can't move
and neither can
the other dancers.
Mia and Niko order them
but they can't lead
because Mia and Niko
are not perfect
and only the perfect
can dance for the gods.
"Get out there!" they hiss,
"You know what to do:
the tumblers first,
the leapers last.
Don't forget to salute
the king and the Mother."
And in that moment,
Aissa is glad

that she recognized the Mother
and is no longer afraid
because she's lived with enough fear
to know what's real.
She leads her group
onto the court,
the others following
in an anxious huddle—
not dancing as acrobats should—
salutes, hand on heart,
to the balcony box,
though she tries not to see
the bull-headed king.
Then she claps her hands,
stamps her feet
till the others join in
and the first tumblers spring,
roll and tumble
forward and back
over and over in a ring
then join the clappers
and the next begin,
until it's time for Aissa's group,
four of them,
handspringing to the center.
They know they can do it,
they've done it before—
though sometimes
they still get it wrong.
One boy drops to hands and knees;
the first girl flips,

lands on his back
and springs off again.
Aissa sees
their grins of relief
but doesn't have time
to notice
because the second boy's kneeling
and Aissa springs—
leaps from feet to hands,
feels the sand and stone beneath her palms,
pushes hard again,
faster than thought,
flipping up
so her feet land
on the kneeling boy's shoulders;
he grips her ankles tight
and stands—
and so does Aissa, arms spread wide,
then springs from his shoulders,
flying
like a bird set free.
The audience cheers,
and when Mia and Niko open the gate
they are smiling.
Now the acrobats are audience
crowded behind the fence,
and three bull dancers
run in:
two girls and a boy,
survivors from the years before

beautiful and perfect—
like Mia and Niko before they were gored—
stopping to salute
below the Bull King's box
saying words Aissa doesn't know
but the Bull King
and the Mother do;
they nod
and the king answers,
with the deep hollow thunder
of Earthshaker's trumpet,
the sacred conch—
and the crowd roars.
Now Mia and Niko pull a gate across
to make a pen
to keep the acrobats safe
and beside them,
through the corridor
of gates and fences,
comes the bull.
His shoulders are higher
than the tallest man's head;
his horns wide,
long and sharp,
just like Luki and Zeta
and the guard at home said—
but it's bigger when it's real.
Luki and Zeta
and the other runners
run behind him,

flapping capes
as if scaring birds from crops.
The bull prancing and snorting,
the dancers circling;
the bull lowers his head to charge—
a girl dancer
grabs his ripping horns,
which makes the bull
throw up his head,
tossing the girl
into a handspring
just like Aissa did
onto the kneeling boy's shoulders—
except this girl lands
on the back
of a charging bull.
Faster than blinking
the dancer somersaults
off the bull's tail to the ground
where the other girl catches her
and the bull
charges the boy.
Aissa watching,
feeling every move
right through her body,
hearing the crowd roar
as each dancer leaps,
as if they were roaring for her.
The bull wearies of charging
and stumbles to a halt;

the dancers salute the balcony
as the crowd screams their names
throwing flowers
and promises of gold,
till they trot out,
gleaming with sweat
but fresher than the bull,
who is alone in the ring
bellowing
a confused sort of protest.
The runners return
flapping their capes
to make him run again
till his legs are trembling,
mouth frothing,
and nose dripping blood.
They herd him to the center,
Aissa no longer watching—
all she can see
is the three dancers,
proud and perfect
in the seats below
the Bull King's balcony.
"One day I'll be there—
me, the cursed child,
No-Name the privy cleaner,
being cheered and admired—
and it's started today."
A scream
shatters her dreaming;

the crowd gasping
because the bull—
not as tired as he'd seemed—
has charged Zeta's cape,
and his sharp horn
has ripped through her shoulder.
Luki leaps,
daring the bull
with his own flapping cape,
tempting him away
as Zeta falls to the ground,
blood gushing free.
The bull stands,
his head hanging low
his knees shaking
as if he'll fall
while the Bull King and the Mother
leave their balcony—
the king with his bull's head
and his two-headed ax,
the Mother with a bowl and a knife.
They cross the courtyard
to the bull
and while Luki and another boy
roll Zeta gently
onto a cape
and carry her away,
the king chops the bull's neck
with the sharp bronze ax.
The bull drops to its knees
and the king takes the knife

to slice the throat
while the Mother catches
the gushing blood
in the golden bowl.
They cross to the tall stone horns
and the Bull King shouts
in his deep hollow voice
that the god can hear
as the Mother pours
the bull's dark blood
onto the sacred horns—
a drink for the gods
though Zeta's blood
has already been taken.
Aissa weeps
to see her curse strike Zeta.
If she hadn't been dreaming—
if she'd been watching—
maybe she could have
called the bull.
But she didn't even try.
Now the bull is dead
and men with ropes are rushing
to haul the corpse away,
while girls dance down
from the tiered seats
to twirl in the courtyard
in butterfly brightness,
praising the gods
for the sacrifice of blood.

But Aissa stares again at the royal box:
    at a cat,
    white like Milli
    balancing on the balcony's edge,
    and wishes
    she was under her sanctuary rock
    with Milli-Cat and the kittens
    and especially
    Gold-Cat.
She wishes so hard,
    that the cat leaps
    from balcony to seats below
    trots around them
    to above the acrobats' pen
    and jumps down
    to Aissa's shoulder.

22

IN THE MOTHER'S ROOMS

The Mother comes to the arena three days later. She's in a curtained litter chair carried by four men; two young priestesses walk behind twirling their sun parasols, their flounced skirts up over their ankles. The Mother isn't wearing as much gold as she had at the bull dance, but she looks just as much a queen.

Aissa had been right when she'd thought *The Lady of Ladies*. Long ago, in a battle of the gods, the earthshaker bull defeated the earth mother. He destroyed her palaces so that invaders could come from over the sea and build their own kingdom. But only the goddess of the earth can bring new life and the crops in their seasons, so although the bull god's king can make laws and armies, he can't rule this land without the goddess's priestesses.

There are many of them, but this woman is the matriarch of all—which is why she's known as the Mother.

Now the Mother has come to see Aissa.

Her two attendants try to look as if they're not as curious as everyone else when the Mother orders Mia, "I want the girl who called the cat."

Mia pales as she salutes. Aissa is one of her best trainees, and she has a duty to defend her.

"With respect, Mistress," says Mia, "the girl doesn't speak."

The Mother raises an eyebrow, intrigued. "Not at all?"

"Not a sound."

"Interesting. But there's more than one way to call a cat. That's the girl I want."

Mia salutes again and crosses the ring to where Aissa is practicing one-handed handstands. She's fallen over more than she's stood; she's sweaty, dusty, and her hair's frizzing out of its plaits. She's nowhere near fit to present to a priestess.

"I don't know what she wants," Mia murmurs, trying to wipe the worst of the dust off Aissa's nose before leading her back to the Mother's chair. "Remember: you haven't done anything wrong."

Aissa's surprised at Mia's distress. None of the acrobats believed that Mia even had a heart.

But she knows something that Mia doesn't: it's her fault that Zeta was gored. She deserves to be punished. She stands in front of the litter chair, head bowed.

The Mother pulls the curtains back to study her. "Open your mouth—and lift your head, girl...so you *do* have a tongue! You just choose not to use it."

She snaps her fingers imperiously. Mia and Niko

stand to attention.

"I'm taking her. I'll send you a slave as a replacement acrobat."

"But Mistress," Niko dares, "this girl has a real chance as a bull leaper. Would it not be possible to find another slave for your purpose?"

"Slave?" snorts the Mother. "A girl who can call beasts is no slave. She's a priestess."

And just like that, life changes again.

Life whirling
as if it's done so many cartwheels
it doesn't know which way is up.
A last look—
Luki saying words only Aissa can know:
"Snake singer!"
The others shocked to silence
till Mia barks,
"Do you think you'll learn handstands
standing on your feet?"
She sounds like Mia again
and the acrobats leap to their hands.
While Aissa
in her dancer's shorts
follows the girls in their flowing skirts
up the road to the palace
into another new life.

The Mother's wing of the palace is a labyrinth of rooms. They're all joined, leading from one to the other in complicated bends and twists, sometimes through corridors, sometimes up stairs. It takes Aissa weeks to learn her way around. She never does figure out how to reach the Mother's chamber on her own; maybe she's not meant to.

And she's never sure just how many priestesses there are. Their order is as complicated as the rooms. The Mother is the head, with six Sisters under her. Each of the Sisters has assistants, and then there's a cloud of young priestesses and trainees who float to wherever they're needed. Aissa is one of the cloud.

Introducing her that first day, the Mother says, "Aissa doesn't speak, but she'll sing when she's ready. She has a rare gift and the goddess has a use for her that I don't yet know. Welcome her well."

The giggles don't start till the Mother leaves the room.

"How can she not speak?"

"What, never?"

"I'd go crazy if I couldn't talk!"

"We'll go crazy if you don't stop!"

"Why does the Mother say she can sing?"

"What's her gift?"

"Didn't you see the cat go to her yesterday?"

"The Mother's cat? Went to a bull dancer?"

"Very strange."

They find her a cot in a room with three other trainees, and show her how to wear the long skirt with a crossover blouse tucked in at the waist. Her dancer's shorts and top disappear into the palace washing;

her wolf cloak stays in the dancers' dorm. She can't imagine the cloak here. The girls would complain that it stinks. It does stink, just a little bit, but she'd like to smell it again.

Her room is simple by palace standards, and more luxurious than anything in the Lady's Hall. Dolphins leap across the frescoed floor; the walls and ceiling are covered with flowers. There's a soft fleece on the bed and a rug to cover herself with. And there's a mirror, a bronze mirror, just for these four apprentices.

It doesn't take long to work out how important that mirror is. The goddess of this land demands beauty: a priestess doesn't leave her chamber until her face, body, and clothes are all perfect.

"Haven't you ever worn makeup?"

The girls aren't being cruel; they're just curious. They were all born in the palace and have never thought about the very different lives around it, the peasants and slaves who don't have time for beauty. How could Aissa be chosen as a priestess if she hasn't worn makeup?

So Aissa learns
to dip a brush
into a pot of black kohl,
closing one eye
to outline and enhance
without too much smudging;
smearing lashes to make them thick,
not blinking till they're dry.

She powders her face white
and paints her lips as red
as a mulberry thief's—
though she doesn't eat mulberries now
because they stain her fingers
and clean white blouse.
Makeup takes time
but hair is worse:
combing, brushing every morning
and night again;
different plaits on different days,
curls and twists
tied in bunches,
caught by a hair band
or cut in a fringe.
Her roommates
love to try something new,
combing out her thick curls,
but when Aissa combs theirs
her hands tremble—
the last hair she'd combed
was Zeta's,
who was gored by a bull
just hours later—
and if that was Aissa's fault,
she'd rather clean privies
than curse a priestess.
Which isn't saying much
because the palace privies
don't stink or need buckets of earth—

just a servant waiting
outside the closed door
with a jug of water
to flush the pipes clean.
And though Aissa's glad
she's not doing the cleaning
or even the flushing
she squirms inside
at someone else
doing it for her—
until the day
she opens the door
and sees Zeta waiting
with the jug.
Zeta salutes, stiff and formal
but Aissa hugs,
laughing, crying,
till Zeta hugs back.
Aissa questions—
the dancers' shrugging sign
that she can't use
with the priestesses
who share a language
and have enough friends
to chat with
that they don't need her.
"The healers cared for me
till I was well.
I was lucky—
I'd rather clean

than face a bull."
Zeta lifts her blouse
to show the wound,
still a red and angry scar
that Aissa touches
gently
with the love that Kelya
and the wise-women taught.
"Thank you," says Zeta,
kissing Aissa's hand,
not understanding
that Aissa would rather
thank her
for being alive.
In the weeks that follow
she sees other dancers
who've become slaves.
They'd been afraid to meet the eye
of the dancer
becoming a priestess.
Once, going back to the chamber
to return her jacket
as the day warms,
she sees the potter's daughter.
Aissa's stomach clenches,
remembering
spit and hate—
until
the girl comes closer:
not such a big girl,

not a kind girl
or a mean girl,
just a girl
dragging a leg
from her dance with the bull,
sweeping Aissa's floor—
but alive.
Tears welling,
Aissa reaches to hug her
as she had Zeta
but the potter's daughter
jumps back in fear:
she can't see No-Name
in this painted priestess
and waits for a blow
that must come with this trick—
so Aissa smiles
and waves, "Never mind,"
and the potter's daughter decides
she reminds the priestess
of someone else
from long ago
but even so,
there's something
that makes her feel strange,
and after that
she trades her chores
rather than sweep that room again.
But this year's cast-outs
call her "Lucky Aissa"

behind their hands
and are glad to see her,
so that Aissa wishes
Squint-Eye and the twins
and most of all,
the Lady,
could see her being so lucky,
living like a priestess's daughter
with only those two tiny scars
to tell of the journey
that's brought her here.
Maybe the goddess doesn't care
as much about scars
or strange little thumbs
as the Lady thought.

Life as a priestess isn't all hair and makeup. The goddess demands beauty, but it's simply the background to the true rituals. And the true rituals aren't so different from the ones at Aissa's home. The bull god rules in public, but the Mother still talks to the house snake to read the future, and in a room on the top floor, sings the sun to rise each morning.

It's still dark when a servant lights the way from their chamber with a flaming torch. Aissa follows up the stairs with the other apprentice priestesses, and stands at the back of the room. She can just make out the shadowy figure of a woman in front of the windows.

The first morning everything is so strange and

different that when the Mother starts to sing, Aissa still doesn't understand. *How can she call from* inside *the palace?* Then the first rays of sun hit the eastern window. A snake slithers from a pot to the Mother's arms, and the room begins to brighten. Aissa gazes past the dark figure into the pink and gold sunrise, and feels the song thrill through her body. This is one familiar thing.

As the song ends and the room fills with soft morning light, she studies the people around her—she's not going to stop a lifetime of spying just because she's safe for a moment. Apart from a few well-dressed women and children, most are priestesses, but there's a sprinkling of men. One tall man with hair as red as a fox and an aura of kingship stands apart. He speaks to the Mother once the snake is safely back in its pot, and something in the way they stand together reminds Aissa of the Lady and the chief.

"Lord," she hears a younger man say, and finally Aissa understands. This is the Bull King. When he puts on the god's mask and speaks with the god's voice, he's a priest and almost a god; even without it he's the most powerful chief in the world. But he is a man, and needs the sun to rise like any other.

As if to prove it, he sends the younger man—his son, Aissa guesses—to call a servant for breakfast. Small tables appear, fresh cheese and figs, small fried fish and soft breads...and Aissa, who has never eaten in the Hall except to scavenge under the tables for other people's leftovers, is sharing breakfast with the Bull King.

He even notices her once. The Mother points at her,

obviously telling her story, and he looks over and nods. Aissa scrambles to her feet to salute, stumbling in her new long skirt. Her stool tips and clatters on the tiles. The king looks amused and a few girls giggle.

"Sit down!" one of her roommates hisses. "You don't have to do that at breakfast."

One of the others picks up the stool for her.

Aissa blushes and sits.

A perfumed young man says something that makes everyone around him laugh. *Clumsy* and *bull dancer* are the only words Aissa understands—but they're enough.

It's just words, not rocks, she reminds herself, which doesn't help nearly as much as she would have thought a year ago.

But my roommate picked up the stool for me.

That does help.

That first morning
is already a memory
and Aissa now
moves gracefully in flowing skirts,
though she and her friends
are dressed in short shifts
on a hot and moonless night
when a sleepy maid
is sent to wake them—
for the round-bellied priestess
who'd washed the bull dancers' hands
is laboring now

to birth her babe,
and the trainees must watch
and learn
the goddess's work.
The birth room is dark,
like Aissa's cave home
under the rock
where Milli-Cat's
kittens were born;
torches flicker
with just enough light
to see the ring of Sisters
against the walls,
crooning softly
a song without words,
calling the baby
to come out to the love
of this flower-scented room.
The priestess paces like Milli-Cat
and when she stops
to rock on her knees,
her cries are louder
but mean the same
as the cat's.
A wise-woman, old as Kelya
offers sips
of honeyed herbs
to ease her pain,
while the Mother
wipes sweat from her face
with a cooling sponge,

and calls the goddess.
Aissa's friends
join in the singing
and Aissa feels
the song of new life
flow through her heart—
though not her mouth.
The priestess cries loud
and the wise-woman
and the Mother
echo in triumph,
as a small and bloodied,
squalling baby girl
is welcomed to the world.

The Mother is still waiting
for Aissa to find her song
but she is right
that Aissa can dance.
It's a wonderful thing
that the goddess loves
to be worshipped in dance
because Aissa
loves to whirl and stamp,
shake her hair and arms,
spinning wild,
or circling with the others
as she did with the wise-women
in the hills above her home.
So when the bull dance comes
on the autumn day

that light and dark balance
before the nights lengthen
into winter,
Aissa will be
one of the dancers
to praise the goddess
for the bull.
Except
when the day comes
Aissa's belly
begins to cramp
as if she's eaten
unripe berries;
her body
begins to bleed
and she doesn't know why—
and wonders
how much blood
can leak out before she dies.
But her roommates,
seeing her face so pale,
hug her
and give her clean rags
to soak up the blood.
"It happens to all of us,"
they say.
Then wise-women lead her
to the goddess's cave,
dark and silent,
to learn the mysteries
of changing from girl

to woman.

Aissa feels so much older and wiser when she returns after her first period that she can't help hoping she'll regain her voice. She doesn't. The only change is that her roommates have become her friends.

Maybe she's had so many changes in the last year that one more can't make any difference. The only thing that's the same as her life under the sanctuary rock, is the comfort of a cat curled against her in the evenings. And knowing that the Mother's cat, like the Lady's, has chosen her, is a very big comfort.

The day after she returns from the cave, she and the other young priestesses strap on strong sandals, put on divided skirts that let them walk nearly as freely as an acrobat's shorts, and follow a Sister into the hills where the purple autumn crocus blooms. They spend the morning collecting the flowers with orange stamens of sacred saffron, while the sun shines on them and a cool north breeze blows their hair. Aissa is flooded with the joy of the hills, and the peace of knowing she's safe. Suddenly it bursts out of her and she's whirling, spinning in the dance of praise. The Sister smiles.

There are more duties, too, as she goes deeper into the life of a priestess.

She goes to the crypt where the snakes live, and takes her turn at carrying the pot up to the morning room. One full-moon night she hands the bowl to a Sister to collect the blood when the Mother offers a lamb to the goddess. During the day, it's the king who offers sacrifices to his god, but sometimes, at night, the goddess needs her own.

And although the king rules the land of warriors, navies and their taxes, the Mother's scribes in the craftsfolk's wing keep their own records of what is due to the goddess: clay tablets inscribed with details of goods and gold owed.

"But it's always wise," says the Mother, "to remind people that they're working for the gods, not the scribes."

So every half-moon, a Sister takes a trainee down to the scribes to collect the tablets for the Mother to study.

Aissa has never been in this part of the palace. She follows the Sister to room after room of different trades and arts. Rows of weavers sit at looms strung with brightly colored flax or wool, potters spin their wheels to shape wet clay into bowls and vases; sculptors chip stone into statues and carve tiny gemstones that jewellers set into rings or amulets. The metalworkers, dripping with sweat from the heat of their furnaces, form molten gold into the finest jewelry—Aissa sees a bee so real it looks as if the living insect has been simply dipped in gold—or mix copper and tin into bronze for exquisite figurines or sharp-edged swords.

Her head spins with heat, new sights and smells, and with the strangeness of knowing that so many details—everything that has been produced, where the raw materials came from, who's been paid, what is owed—are recorded on these tablets for the Mother and Sisters to see.

All the young priestesses spend time every

afternoon learning to read and write. Aissa knows her own name-sign, but now she learns the symbols for the goddess and the bull, for gold or copper ingots, shells for purple dye, wood for the furnaces, and every other thing that goes in or out of the palace. It's not easy learning to copy each one, and it's even harder to remember them all. But as Aissa scratches the symbols into the soft clay of the practice tablet, she thinks of the words in there, speaking without a voice, for anyone to hear, and knows that the goddess has given her a glimpse of the most powerful magic of all.

The Mother also judges family disputes and women's business. Like the Lady, she listens to the wise-women, but one day in five, the women from palace and country are granted an audience with the Mother herself. The apprentice priestesses sit on benches either side of the throne as the Mother's questions probe and her judgment rings out, clear and strong.

Some of the girls get restless, but Aissa is used to listening. That's why she understands the bull king's language now—and why she hears so many secrets.

"Promise you won't tell..."

How am I going to do that? Aissa thinks, though she doesn't roll her eyes at the stupidity anymore, not since she made a girl cry. Now she nods, looking serious.

So she probably knows more than anyone else about who's got a crush on a young priest or a guard, or even one of the other priestesses, about fears of rejection, of not being beautiful, of becoming ill. Aissa had never known that other people—lucky, perfect people—had so many fears.

Or so much to bicker about.

"My roommate bumped me when Sister was watching me dance," a sow-faced girl whines.

"Cessie won't talk to me because I bumped into her when she was dancing," her roommate whispers.

Tell each other and sort it out! Aissa wants to sign, the way she might have with the acrobats—but they wouldn't come to her for consolation if they thought she'd give advice.

And it's probably just as well that they can't hear her thinking, *Do you really think your friend talking to another girl at dinner is a problem? That the world is going to end because someone laughed when you tripped on the stairs?*

Maybe it's worse because winter's coming; it's not as cold as home, but it's chilly enough for the Mother to keep a brazier of burning coals in her rooms, and for the girls to need an extra fleece on their beds at night.

After ten days of rain keep them inside the palace, not even venturing into the courtyards, it feels as if the whole hive of priestesses is about to explode.

The Mother feels it too. She arrives in the middle of a writing lesson. Everyone scratches harder at their soft clay tablets—Aissa smudges her ox symbol and has to rub it smooth and start again. But the priestess hasn't come to inspect; she is followed by servants carrying goblets and a jug of honeyed wine.

"That's enough writing for a gray afternoon!" she announces, and while the girls drink their wine, the servants open the folding doors to make two rooms into one big one.

"Now move the benches and tables to the side—even the goddess needs to be cheered up on a day like this."

Aissa still has to stop herself from jumping up to help servants move furniture. It's been hard to learn that something as wonderful as dancing is her duty just as much as privy cleaning was No-Name's.

So she plays the rattle, clicking in time as the other girls' voices flood her body; they dance until the goddess is praised and the girls can't think anymore, and dance on till they drop.

Aissa has just finished bleeding for the third time. Tomorrow is the bull dance to celebrate winter's shortest day and the next turning of the seasons. Aissa will be dancing with the priestesses—and she'll see Luki. If he's still alive.

23

THE BULL DANCE IN MIDWINTER

Luki is still alive. It sometimes surprises him. From the confines of the training ring and hall, he's watched the seasons cycle from spring to winter; he's seen the hills go brown in summer and start to green again with the winter rains; he's watched the barley fields being sown, workers on their way to the olive groves for harvest, the grape pickers passing with carts and baskets of purple grapes. He's watched the cranes and swallows migrate south for the winter, and wondered if he'll still be here to see them return in spring.

He tries not to wonder if he'll see his own home again. Maybe he can dare to hope if he survives the dance of the shortest day.

The worst thing about the winter rains is training inside the hall. They're no freer in the arena, but Luki feels that he can breathe. After ten days of being inside he doesn't sleep as well at night; there seems to be more time to think and worry. He wonders about

Aissa, doing whatever a junior priestess does inside that palace. He wonders if she thinks about how they have changed places since he was the god-luck dancer and she was the cursed child. Bull dancers are honored here once they're successful, but the trainees are truly slaves. At least Aissa was able to roam free when she was an outcast.

But on a good day, when the sun is shining and the air is cool, and he does a perfect one-handed vault over a bull-high rail, Luki wishes that Aissa could see it.

Painting her eyes
more carefully than ever before,
offering her face
for friends to inspect—
wiping a smudge and starting again.
Brushing hair,
curling ringlets,
not such a chore today
because
just like the other
chattering girls
Aissa is buzzing inside:
today she will be
one of the elegant priestesses,
seen by the world
for the very first time.
Her skirt,
new
woven fine

flounced red,
yellow, and green;
her blouse fresh and pure.
Looking in the mirror,
she likes what she sees,
which makes her giggle—
which surprises her friends
into giggling more.
So Aissa hides her face
kissing the top
of the white cat's head,
and straightens the hem
of a roommate's skirt,
caught up in a twirl.
The wardrobe Sister
calls to inspect them,
and Sister
is pleased too.
Now in a troop
winding through the maze
the walls painted
with flowers and ferns,
ladies on balconies,
men with gifts,
and Aissa's favorite:
a spotted goat
that she strokes for luck.
The royal box
is for the Bull King and his boys,
the Mother, and Sisters.
The cloud of young priestesses

and apprentices like Aissa
have their own space
in the tiered seats below,
high enough to see the ring
and the crowd;
near the side gate
where they'll go down
to dance at the end.
Aissa's still buzzing
as if a dragonfly
lives in her belly
when the Bull King enters
in the horned mask
that chills Aissa's heart
and turns
her buzzing dragonfly
to stone
because he is not the same
as the red-haired man in the palace
laughing or eating,
playing board games with his sons,
or even
the stern-faced man
talking to warriors
when bad-news whispers
come across the hills.
The rain has stopped
though the sand is damp.
In the ring
three young men wrestle,
their bodies covered

with olive oil
so they slide out
from each other's grip
until one
throws another
hard on the ground
and pins him with his knee,
before the third man
does the same to him.
The crowd's not happy
because most of them
had bet on the first.
Five acrobats take their place—
tumbling, rolling,
a girl flying higher
than Aissa had
half a year ago—
but the crowd is waiting
to see the bull.
It thunders in,
with six runners
flapping their capes—
but none of them is Luki.
Now the bull dancers enter,
the people screaming
just to see them
before they've so much as
started to leap—
the apprentices
and some of the priestesses
scream too

because the dancers are perfect—
as beautiful in their way
as the priestesses themselves.
But this time, behind the three
come the new dancers,
dressed the same,
though without the swagger.
Aissa
doesn't think she knows them
till a boy turns his head
and it's Luki.
She wonders how
she hadn't known him—
and the others too,
now that she sees the person
behind each dancer—
but half a year of training
has changed them all
as it's changed her:
they are athletes now.
Strong and muscled,
they've learned to watch a bull,
while Aissa's learned
how to curl hair
and write lists.
Now the bull is charging,
last year's dancers are leaping,
Luki and his companions
ready to catch and steady
or wave a cape;
the bull forgetting

who's sprung off behind him,
seeing only the next
in front,
until
as he starts to tire—
and the dancers do too—
one of the leapers,
showered with gold outside the ring
but no safer in it,
slips as she springs
over the bull's neck,
and skids down his side.
The bull swings his great head
and spies the girl on the ground
with her leg twisted
and crumpled under.
Luki behind,
waiting to catch her,
rushes to challenge
but the bull
circles the fallen girl,
pawing the ground
with a hoof that's bigger
than her head;
the crowd is standing,
waving, and screaming.
And Aissa is singing,
a full, deep note
she's never heard.
The bull shakes his head
trots toward her,

and Aissa's friends
push her down in her seat,
clapping hands over her mouth
before the Bull King
and the Mother
can hear.
Aissa is shaking—
it's never wise
to defy the gods
and she doesn't know
if that's what her singing has done—
or if the Mother will think so.
Watching, not seeing,
the rest of the dance
enough to know
that no one is injured,
apart from the bull
sacrificed at the end.
As the men with ropes
come to haul him away,
Aissa and her friends
run down from the stands
hand in hand
singing and dancing into the ring
to praise the bull's gift.
Aissa opens her mouth—
but her song has gone.
So she stamps and rattles
her castanets,
twirling with the others,
hoping all will be well

when they return to their rooms
before the feast
of the sacrificed bull.
But the Mother sends for her—
a servant at the chamber door—
the other girls tiptoe
and whisper;
her friends squeeze her hand
but don't want
to walk with her.
The Mother's eyes are shining—
a hard, clear anger,
and her mouth is tight.
"So you found your song?
It wasn't quite
what I'd intended.
A song like yours
comes from the goddess—
but you have used it
to thwart a sacrifice
and defy the gods.
"If you were a priestess,
sworn and blooded,
you would die for this—
and though the omens tell me
to let you live
and learn,
you can never
be a Sister now.
I won't have a slave
knowing goddess secrets—

so how can you
best serve
and atone?"
The Mother studies her
as if Aissa has an answer—
there is only one
that Aissa can see.
Tucking her skirts
into her belt
and hoping she still
remembers how
after six soft-living moons—
she leaps to her hands,
springing over and over
around the room.
The Mother nods.
Her face is hard
and her voice as sharp
as the Bull King's ax.
"So be it.
You'll return to the ring.
But you've made your choice
and if you sing the bull
to save your skin
or that of your fellows,
you will all
be sacrificed with him
in the great spring games."

24

MEETING THE BULLS

"So you think jumping bulls is going to be easier than being a priestess?" Mia demands.

Aissa shakes her head. She hadn't exactly expected a welcome, but—maybe she had. Mia had seemed so sad to see her leave.

"You've got a lot of training to catch up on," says Niko. "Look how soft you are!"

"But your hair's nice," says pretty Sunya. "Can you show us how you did it?"

"Aissa's going to be far too busy getting fit to worry about hair!" Mia snaps, and makes sure that she's right. Aissa has her own program to build up strength while the others are fine-tuning skills.

"Doesn't matter how beautiful your handstand is, if you can't hold it on a bull's horns," says Niko—it's his favorite saying, Aissa thinks; he seems to say it every time she does something well. "And for that, you need a grip that could crush clam shells."

Sometimes Aissa thinks that Mia and Niko can't forgive her for missing half a year of training. On better days she knows that they can't afford to—because the bull won't.

Mia and Niko are too proud to ask exactly why she's come back, as if changing from acrobat to priestess and back again happens all the time, but they're as curious as everyone else.

"You sang the bull!" Luki exclaims. "That's why he pulled away!"

Aissa nods.

The acrobats are desperate for miracles. It had been frightening to see the queen of bull dancers slip and fall. Her leg will never be strong enough to dance again—but they'd all seen the bull turn away from killing her.

Their faces glow with sudden hope. "You can do that! You can save us when we're in the ring!"

Aissa's never felt so cruel. She slowly shakes her head.

"Do you really think the gods would allow that?" Mia demands.

"Don't see why not," someone mutters.

The mood's turning against Aissa—she has to tell the whole truth. It's better than their believing that she doesn't care enough to save them.

She draws a finger across her own throat. Everyone's seen enough sacrifice to know what that means.

"Fair enough."

No, it's not! Aissa thinks. *Not the whole thing*. She trills her fingers out from her mouth.

"If you sing," says Luki.

Aissa draws a circle encompassing all of them, and repeats the throat-cutting sign.

"We'll *all* be killed," several finish.

Standing in the middle of the group, seeing their eyes and hearing them say it is infinitely worse than hearing it from the Mother in her brightly painted chamber. How can all their lives depend on her? There's only one solution. Aissa tilts her head, offering her throat. Better to die now than cause the death of everyone else.

"Don't be ridiculous," says Mia.

"Just don't sing," says Niko. "You don't talk—how hard can it be not to sing?"

No one can guess how hard. Aissa doesn't understand it herself.

The threat makes it even more difficult to slide back into the group. The acrobats aren't just stronger and more skilled than when she left, they're a tight-knit team. Only eleven girls and fourteen boys remain. They know each other's moves and weaknesses, and what they don't know can be discussed, because they've got a language now. Partly the palace language, and partly the bullring's own.

The crowded dorms are now spacious rooms; everyone has a bed, not just a sleeping mat, and a space for their belongings. Aissa's wolf cloak hasn't been moved. She wraps herself in it every night, hoping it will help her reclaim her courage.

Because right now she doesn't feel brave. She doesn't even have the comfort of a cat sleeping under her chin at night—the Mother's white cat seems to know that Aissa's disgraced, and hasn't followed her here.

And in three quick turnings of the moon, it will be the great spring games. She's not as strong as she should be, not as skilled as she should be, and she's sure the others don't quite trust her. Not even Luki.

Aissa's wrong—it's himself that Luki doesn't trust. The reason he's still alive is that he's absolutely determined to free his island from tributes. Every time someone is trampled or gored in the dusty bullring, or sent broken into slavery, Luki sees his younger brothers and sister. *That is not going to happen to them!*

For the six months that Aissa was away being a priestess, it was all his responsibility. Now she's sharing it again, and Luki's afraid that will let him fail. He wants to survive just as badly as everyone else, but it's the island that has given him that extra drive. That extra luck. Every morning before training starts, he stands out in the ring to gaze at the mountain in the distance. It doesn't matter that on these winter days it's often covered by clouds—for those moments, he transforms it to his own island's mountain, and pledges to return and free it.

Spring creeps closer. The moon is full, shrinks to blackness, and grows full again. Frogs sing night-time choruses. The air smells sweeter; the first cranes fly back from their winter homes. And tomorrow the dancers start practicing on Dapple.

Dapple is one of the five bulls from the palace herd that are used for training. They're not quite as big as the wild ones caught in the woods, but Mia and Niko warn that sometimes they're even more dangerous. These bulls have played the game before and know what the dancers are planning.

At the last minute Mia decides that Aissa's still not ready to leap. "Better to stay alive longer and be ready for the real thing," she says. Aissa can be a runner, flapping a cape to line the bull up for the others.

She's terrified that she will sing him away before he can hurt someone. Knowing that she'll have to let him is the heaviest burden she's ever borne. Nightmare bulls haunt her all night, goring and trampling.

So even as she's waving her cape, driving the bull to the center, she makes herself imagine all the terrible things that could happen. Which isn't hard to do, because the bull is even bigger now that she's in the ring with him.

He's going to trample Mia! He'll gore Luki. He'll toss Sunya and break her bones...He's going to turn around and charge me!

Dapple does try to do all those things. Mia leaps out of his way, and so does Luki. Sunya is tossed right across the ring, and two dancers leap to catch her. Aissa flaps her cape like the other runners, and drives the bull away.

She doesn't sing. For the first time, she realizes that she can control it. All she has to do is pay attention.

The only injury for the day is a girl who falls at the bull's feet. Dapple tramples her hand as she lands—Aissa wouldn't have had time to call if she'd wanted to.

Niko and Mia spend the evening going over all the other near misses. Idiocies and clumsinesses, Niko calls them. Aissa thinks he's secretly quite pleased with their performance.

They spend the next two days training in the ring, "So there won't be quite so many idiocies next time," says Niko. Then a rest day, then the bulls again—Brownie this time. That's the pattern, but it still rains often, and they don't work with the bulls when it's raining.

"You lot are clumsy enough without slipping in the wet," says Niko.

Mia tells the girls privately that they don't train with the bulls when they're menstruating. And when Niko tells Aissa that she's ready to try leaping a real bull the next day, Aissa is bleeding.

She finishes her period just in time for the games. She still hasn't leapt a bull.

25

THE GREAT SPRING DANCES

Spring is the most important season; spring determines if enough food will be grown for the rest of the year. And so the spring gods need the most gifts to nourish them: the most sacrifice; the most blood.

The most dances, Aissa thinks, but it's not that simple. Mia and Niko don't tell them the whole truth until the day before. Thinking about it for too long might just drive them crazy.

"The first game," says Mia, "is with the herd bulls."

"Which one?" asks Luki.

"Can't you hear?" Niko snaps. "She said bulls—the five you've trained with."

"You'll all go in together," says Mia, "and so will the bulls."

"Who will run them in?"

"Anyone with the gold to pay for the honor."

So they won't know what they're doing, thinks Aissa. *The bulls will be crazy by the time they get to the ring.*

"You know these bulls; you know their habits," says Niko. "Dapple gores to the left. Brownie shakes his head before he tosses—hold tight or you'll be gone. Moonsnip's plain crazy. Mudface and Bigfoot are pretty straightforward."

"Will they fight each other?"

"Not likely. They've run together since they were calves. But they're bulls and it's a crowded space—nothing's guaranteed."

"Except death," someone mutters.

Three dancers have died in the last days of intensive training; nine more have been injured too badly to heal in time. Twelve are left to distract, leap, and evade five confused, angry bulls.

"Three survived last year," Niko says. "It can be done!"

Three is the best we can hope for?

Niko looks at their faces and gives up on his pep talk.

"The first dance is about survival," he says more grimly. "Remember that the dead can wait."

"Look after the living," Mia corrects, but it's too late. A shiver goes through the dancers. *The dead. Will I be one of the dead left to wait?*

"The second dance is about beauty. If the first dance offers blood, the second offers praise. Being alive at the end is not enough. Every leap needs to be the highest, strongest, most graceful that you can do. The gods demand perfection: only your best will win your freedom."

"And that of our homes," Luki mutters.

"Pray to Earthshaker, god of the bulls," says Mia. "Pray to your own gods. And sleep well tonight so that your skills are sharp."

They all pray, but sleep isn't so easy.

Honey cakes for breakfast—
Aissa can't believe
she could ever close her lips
to honey cakes
or figs and cheese,
but her belly is churning
too hard for hunger,
though Mia and Niko
are fussing like mamas
begging children to eat.
"Just a bite," they say,
"and a sip of milk."
They check that wrists
are strapped tight and strong,
shortening the cords
of mama stones around necks
leaving no room for a horn to catch;
they see that plaits are neat,
eyes painted,
lips rouged
as neatly as a priestess,
because whether the dancers live
or die under the bull,
the goddess wants beauty—
or so say the Mother
and the king—

and Aissa hopes
if the gods see perfection
maybe they won't need
so much blood.
Then Mia and Niko
kiss them each
on the top of their heads
and for the last time lead them
to the palace
and the bullring in the court,
because even if
they're alive tonight
the dorms will no longer
be their homes,
and Mia and Niko
will start to prepare
for next year's dancers
as the seasons cycle.
Still far from the gate
they hear the crowd
roaring like waves
pounding on cliffs,
the tiered seats packed,
people leaning from windows
or perched on roofs—
everyone in the land
who can possibly fit
and pay their way.
The dancers wait
behind the fence
for a troupe of jugglers in the ring

tossing bright balls high—
a cheer for the skill
of a perfect catch,
a hiss for a drop—
and oiled wrestlers
who throw and fall,
win and lose
with no threat of death,
and more men boxing,
the crowd ready now
for blood,
cheering when a hard fist
splits a face
and teeth are spat.
But the jugglers,
wrestlers, and bleeding boxers
are as unimportant
as gnats
to the waiting dancers.
Some pray,
some are frozen,
some twitching,
but all are together:
twelve sisters and brothers,
Aissa finally
a part of a whole—
even though they won't be
whole much longer.
She names them in her head
as if that prayer
could keep them safe:

Luki, Sunya, and Kenzo,
Milos and—
"It's time," says Niko.
Running into the ring
standing together
to salute the balcony,
the rows of young priestesses—
who wave at Aissa—
then the crowd on every side,
and say the words
Aissa understands now
though she can't speak them.
"We offer ourselves
as gift or sacrifice
to please Earthshaker,
bull of the gods."
And to the goddess,
bringer of life, thinks Aissa,
for the earthshaking bull
is no god of hers.
From the balcony box
the king trumpets
the strident roar
of the sacred conch
then pours wine
from the bull-head jug
to the great stone horns
below the box,
splashing red like blood
onto the sand.

"Praise for Earthshaker," says the king.
"Let his dance begin."
In the sudden hush
the dancers look at each other,
make the good-luck sign,
as hooves thunder,
a man screams
and the bulls gallop in
leaving a runner tossed and gored
before the entrance gate,
bleeding out his life.
Aissa wonders
if he still thinks
it was worth the gold.
The gate is locked
the time for thought has passed—
the courtyard is
a chaos of bulls.
Dapple bellows,
collides with Moonsnip,
horns clatter,
and then they both
turn on Milos,
who doesn't have a chance
to leap
or any chance
at all.
Someone tries
to pull the body aside
but Aissa doesn't see who

because Brownie,
snorting rage as he runs,
is charging at her.
The bull comes fast,
time moves slow,
she grabs his horns,
gripping tighter than she knew she could
as he shakes his head
and her with it,
as if he can hardly feel
the girl doing a handstand
on his horns.
He tosses her
into a flip,
and for just that moment,
standing free on the back
of a charging bull,
before springing to land
safe and upright behind him,
she feels the god-power
burning through her.
The energy so strong
she could almost vault
back over the bull again—
but from the corner of her eye
she sees Sunya
flying off Dapple,
as if she hasn't remembered
what Niko promised—
that Dapple always

gores to the left—
she lands off-balance
but Aissa reaches her
with a steadying arm
and they both move on.
Their other partners
do the same,
but not all
are so lucky.
Someone is dashed
against the great stone horns—
a second libation
of blood for the gods—
Aissa doesn't see who
and can't let herself wonder.
She never sees the crowd,
never hears its roar—
she has eyes and ears only
for the bulls
and dancers.
Her fear is gone,
her body alive as never before,
in this wild dance
of life and death.
"Look after the living,"
Mia said,
and now Aissa understands—
but the living are fewer.
Moonsnip waits
to trample dancers

as they leap
from another bull,
and Brownie is goring
the broken body
of someone who used to be
a friend.
As she sees,
Aissa's fire leaves her.
She knows they will never
be free;
but will die in the ring
under these maddened bulls,
or at best be wounded
and saved as slaves—
and even in the midst
of this death and pain,
Aissa doesn't want
to change it for slavery.
Now Mudface is coming,
but his gallop slows
to a lumbering trot,
head swinging
instead of charging—
and she leaps aside
instead of over.
Brownie finishes goring
and stands over his victim
as if he can't see
the living dancers—
the bulls too
have had enough.

One by one,
they weary to a stop,
heads hanging low;
Dapple next,
Moonsnip last.
The conch horn sounds.
The rich young runners
jog in through the gate,
circling wide around the bulls,
flapping capes to drive them—
not so wild as they ran in—
out and back to the herd.
The healers' men
come to carry the wounded
and the dead,
until only
Aissa and Sunya,
the tall boy Kenzo,
and Luki are left.
Grief washes over them
and not just for the fallen,
but they take these moments
to breathe
and touch hands,
trying to rebuild
strength and courage
for this last dance
with the wild king of the bulls.
He gallops in,
piebald brown,
not so much bigger than the rest—

though it's hard to tell
the exact size
of a bull
intent on charging.
But there's something about
the way he swings his horns,
that says this one
is far more ferocious
than his herd-tamed kin.
"I'll go first," says Luki,
and draws the bull to charge him,
with Kenzo standing back
and a girl to each side.
Luki grabs the horns,
but the bull tosses left like Brownie,
and instead of a flip
Luki one-hand cartwheels
down the bull's neck to his tail.
This time Aissa hears the crowd
loving Luki
and his skill.
The bull charges Kenzo
and the dance rushes on;
they leap
one by one—
and though the bull is still fresh
the dancers aren't;
when he charges Sunya,
her flip is neat
but she lands
flat on her back.

As if he knows
his end is near,
the bull wants more,
charging Kenzo again,
who cartwheels along his back
as Luki did at the start.
Now Aissa is in front—
but just as she's ready
to reach for the horns,
the bull sees
Sunya lying still
and veers toward her.
"Sunya!" Aissa screams with her mind,
and Sunya jumps up
so fast that she startles the bull
and he turns back to Aissa—
who's not ready,
not balanced
as she grabs his horns;
she sees Luki and Kenzo
and Sunya, more slowly,
run ready to catch her—
knowing the bull
will throw to the left.
But as Aissa braces
to spring with the toss
the bull shakes his head
and Aissa feels
what her friends can't see—
that this time the bull
is throwing right.

Her body's still poised
 to be thrown to the left
 as her hands
 slip from the horns;
 if she could shout
 her friends could run
 in time to catch
 but Aissa's voice
 is not ready to save her.
Her heart sings goodbye
 to Luki and
 her brother and sister of the dance
 and she catapults
 like the rock from her sling
 that killed the wolf;
 she tries to tuck
 into a roll
 but her arms and legs
 are wrong,
 the ground is nearing,
 and the layer of sand
 will be nothing on stone.
 Aissa closes her eyes
 against coming pain
 and lands
 safe in the arms
 of Kenzo and Sunya
 and Luki—
 while the bull,
 chest heaving, mouth frothing,
 stops, and stares.

"We heard you," says Sunya,
"like a voice in our hearts."
"Now leap!" says Luki,
and as if they've planned it,
he lifts Aissa to his shoulders,
gripping her ankles
so she stands as she did
in the acrobat dance
three seasons ago.
Luki tosses her up—
Aissa flies free,
somersaults in the air—
and lands on the bull,
hands high.
And as she leaps off
the sweat-soaked
quivering bull
folds his knees
and sinks to the ground.
The screaming crowd,
standing, cheering,
throwing gold and flowers
just as they did
for the real bull dancers—
but Aissa and her friends
are too tired to care
too tired to know
that they
are the real dancers now.
They want nothing more
than to hide and rest.

"Stay!" orders the Mother,
as she crosses the courtyard
behind the bull-headed king with his ax
carrying her sharp bronze knife
and golden bowl
to fill with blood.

26

FROM THE GRAY-GREEN BUSH

The sacrifice is made; the bull lies lifeless, and the Mother holds up the bowl of dark blood.

"Come!" orders the king.

The four young dancers approach.

Does the Mother know I called the others? Aissa wonders in sudden panic. *Will we be sacrificed after all?*

Sunya hesitates, her eyes wide with fear.

"Even you," says the king. "That ugly fall could have sent you to slavery—but I have never seen an ending as elegant as that catch and leap. The bull's sign was clear: you are all free."

He steps back as the Mother dips her hand into the bowl of blood and traces the sign of the sacred ax onto their foreheads.

She looks deep into Aissa's eyes.

She does know!

"It seems you've learned to control your gift. You made your choice well."

Whatever else she might have said is lost in the roar of the crowd. The young priestesses dance into the courtyard and the young nobles leap over the fences. Aissa and her friends are still reeling, still trying to comprehend the meaning of "free", still trying to realize that they've survived, but the cheering lifts them high, filling them with life and joy: "We're the bull dancers now," says Kenzo.

"We're free," says Luki. "We can go home."

The men with ropes start hauling the bull's body away, Mia runs out cheering, Niko follows with his dragging leg, and the priestesses whirl around Aissa, touching her face, smearing the blood. They swirl away, faster and faster, as the power in each of them joins the gods in celebration and thanksgiving. Aissa feels the power of their dance swirl in her, the same energy she'd felt leaping from the bull.

Mia and Niko are hugging them, kissing their heads, bandaging cuts they didn't know they had—the blood isn't all from the bull. Aissa has a long gash down her right leg, and grazes on her elbows and knees. She can feel them now that Mia's found and soothed them with healing oil. It doesn't matter. She doesn't know what matters anymore.

Young men fight for the honor of lifting the dancers onto their shoulders and parading them around the courtyard. Aissa doesn't feel real. This seat feels more dangerous than the bull's back.

They are carried through the maze of halls to the open west court.

More people are waiting outside, packed tight as pebbles on a beach, from the steps to the road and into the olive groves on the other side. Aissa didn't know that one land could hold so many people. Because these are not the palace folk; they're not richly dressed with flounced skirts and tight-waisted kilts; no gold glints in their hair. These are the working people, the farmers, herders, and fishers, wharfmen, and sailors, weavers, potters, and craftsmen making things for everyday people. And they're all waiting for her, for Luki, for Sunya, and Kenzo—for the chosen ones who have danced with the bulls and pleased the gods.

The palace guards step in close behind them, and the dancers are deposited carefully on the wide stone steps.

People pushing through the crowd,
fighting to touch them,
holding up children
to catch the dancers' god-luck;
so many hands,
so many arms.
Despite the guards,
they're separated,
swept up in the throng
charging the steps—
Aissa afraid she'll drown
in this sea of adoration;
her skin tender
from so much touching—
she wants to run,
to get away and breathe.

But a woman
holds a baby for her to kiss
and strokes her shoulder
till Aissa looks at her face—
a face worn with trouble,
bronzed from the sun,
much like
the faces around her
but a mole by her mouth
like a dot
that Aissa loves—
and she looks
into dark
remembered eyes.
"Mama!" cries Aissa.
The woman pales,
shrinks back,
then clasps her tight,
the baby squirming between.
"Aissa!" says Mama.
"I always knew," says Aissa,
"you were alive," says Mama.
"And that I'd find you," says Aissa,
hearing her own voice
with its crack of surprise
and the low-pitched music
of a strong young woman—
not the child's voice
that she hasn't heard
since Mama said,

"Don't make a sound
till I come back."
And now Mama is back.
Hugging and crying,
kohl mingling with bull's blood
to run black
down her face;
wailing so loudly
the guards come
to chase Mama away.
"No!" says Aissa.
"This is my mama."
Even with
a bull dancer's power
a voice is useful.
Mama's words rushing
wanting to hear
all that's happened to Aissa
since she hid her
under that gray-green bush—
but it's too much to tell,
too much grief to bear,
Aissa doesn't want
Mama to hear it,
doesn't want to tell it
in her newfound voice
in the midst of the jostling,
buzzing crowd.
But Mama tells her,
between the sobs,

of being sold as a slave
by the raiders
but later bought
and married to a farmer—
she has a new family.
Grown-up Zufi
has worked for his freedom
as a sailor on a ship
trading over the seas.
But Mama has never
seen Tattie again
and mourns her still.
Mama's surprised husband
takes the squirming baby
while they hug:
his wife and a bull dancer
who was once her daughter.
All Aissa wants
is to be that daughter again,
to stay with Mama
now and forever,
close beside her as a baby,
a child
safe at home.
But first
there will be a grand feast
with every good thing to eat
and meat from the bulls,
to honor the dancers,
and Aissa's heart cracks

because Mama
with her farmer's dress
and work-broken nails,
will not be allowed
at the party—
and what if
she never finds her again?
"I'll come in the morning," says Mama,
to take you home."

27

THE BULL KING'S PROMISE

Mia and Niko,
    and last year's dancers,
    as well as older ones
    who no longer dance
    but have saved their gold,
    rich traders and artists,
    owners of villas,
    priests and priestesses,
    the Bull King and the Mother—
    all will be at the feast.
But first,
    Aissa and Sunya
    Kenzo and Luki,
    must be bathed and perfumed,
    wounds re-dressed,
    hair and makeup redone;
    Aissa wishes she could wear
    her fine priestess dress

with everyone else
so beautifully clad,
but people want to see
dancers in their bull-leaping shorts
as if they might do
acrobatics again—
though they're so tired
they can hardly stand.
The great court too
has been cleansed,
swept,
washed;
the fences removed,
the blood smell purified
with the stink
of burning sulphur.
The halls around it,
with folding doors opened,
are set with chairs,
small tables
lamps and flowers,
while servants offer
cups of wine
mixed with honey and water,
platters of food:
poppy cakes and small fried fish,
octopus and oysters,
raisins and cheese,
fresh greens
and the roasted meats
of the bull,

which the dancers must eat
though it sticks
in Aissa's throat.
When they've eaten,
and washed their fingers
in silver bowls,
the Bull King speaks,
without his mask
but with all his power.
He calls the dancers
to his throne.
Aissa shrinks
at the people staring—
but,
"We've faced bulls," says Kenzo—
and instead of death
the crowd brings flowers,
gold and jewelry,
scented oils and perfumes
in crystal vials,
embroidered robes and woolly fleeces—
and offers:
"A room in my home,"
"A suite in my villa,"
because everyone wants
to share in their god-luck
if they go on dancing.
The other-year dancers
make no offers
but explain:

"If you choose
to return to the ring
you can live in luxury
and save your gold—
you can have a house,
slaves of your own,
if you live and are lucky."
But Luki stands tall
salutes the king and the Mother,
and says,
"Great ones, rulers of the land,
we, the dancers,
were told
that to survive the year
would set us free
to return to our homes
and free our lands from tribute.
This is what I ask,
for myself and my friends."
Smiling gravely, the Bull King nods.
"That is the promise.
But you must decide—
do you return
to a poor life, a poor land,
or stay
with all that's offered
for a life of glory?
Your people have already
mourned you—
they'll never know

that you serve the gods here—
and the tribute we ask
is little enough
to protect your homelands
from wandering raiders.
So think and reflect
before you make up your minds."
Luki salutes,
though his choice is made.
And, heads spinning
with fatigue and wine,
the thrill of fame,
confusion of promises
and broken faith—
the bull dancers leave the party,
led by servants
to the great guest chamber
in the palace.

For Aissa,
finding Mama and her voice
is the happiest
bewilderment of all.
It's hard to remember
that she can speak,
her voice so strange and new
she doesn't know
if it will come out loud or soft
or how it will shape
the sound of words
so it's still easier

to stay silent—
and besides,
she knows what she wants:
to live with Mama.
She doesn't want
to live with strangers;
doesn't need more gold—
there's enough in her hands
to buy a goat—
one like Spot Goat, maybe two,
and a dog like Brown Dog
who died with Dada—
to take as gifts
to Mama's small farm.
And no one can say
how much gold is enough
or how many seasons
a dancer needs to survive.
So she listens
as they sit together
in the great guest chamber,
with the finest linen
and the softest fleeces,
and Sunya says,
"My family gave me to the palace
to pay their taxes—
I'll take bulls and glory
rather than go back to them."
Kenzo's story is much the same—
an orphan
with nothing of his own:

"What's there for me if I go back?
The honor of freeing my town
won't give me land."
Luki doesn't care
that he won't own land,
knowing the farm will pass
to his sisters one day,
as long as he can live in the hills he loves.
"We were sent by the gods
to free our island," he says,
and waits for Aissa's sign.
Aissa thinking
that if Luki returns
the island is free—
there's no need for her
and no place either;
servant to the wise-women
is no longer enough
if she's despised by the people.
"I'm staying here," says Aissa.
"With Mama."

Aissa's friends look as shocked as if a bull had spoken. Luki grabs a torch from the wall to shine on her face. "You can talk!"

"Ever since I met Mama," says Aissa, in her strange new voice. "After the dance. I forgot to tell you."

"You forgot!" squeals Sunya.

"I wasn't sure that I could do it again," Aissa admits, but the others are laughing too hard to hear.

"If that was your mama on the steps, how can you sing beasts like the Lady?" Luki asks.

"And you sang us!" adds Sunya.

So Aissa has to explain what she's almost never said in her mind, and never dreamed of saying out loud. "Mama raised me till the raiders came. It was the Lady who bore me—but I wasn't perfect."

"The firstborn daughter," says Luki.

"Seems the gods thought you were perfect enough," says Kenzo.

"You saved me twice over," says Sunya. "Once from the bull, and once from slavery when you called us for that catch."

"I didn't plan the catch," Aissa says honestly. "But when I thought I would die, my heart trusted you, and called your names."

Mama comes in the morning.
Aissa's heart dances
with knowing that Mama's true and real
and they're together again.
A guard follows
because Aissa is free
but precious,
and Mama and Aissa
walk hand in hand
in fresh spring air
an hour down the road
to Mama's new home,
her new family.

The whole world rejoices
with bright spring flowers,
the scent of thyme,
swallows darting,
and the firstborn lambs
suckling in the fields—
as if the goddess herself
is singing for Aissa,
reunited
with her own dear mama.
She thinks the pain
of No-Name's life
will be washed away
as they patch lost years
with threads of love.
Aissa will care
for the baby sister
sleeping now on Mama's back.
She'll pick spring greens,
harvest autumn olives,
dig the soil,
or tend the sheep;
do whatever
there is to be done—
asking only
to be a child again,
safe and loved.
So happy she can hardly hear
the words Mama says,
only the music
of her voice.

Over the years, when Mama's thought of Aissa, she's pictured her still as a four year old, her image frozen in time. It was easier than wondering if the child had died on that terrible night; if wolves had found her before searchers came. It was easier than imagining how her aunt might have cared for her—though she'd never imagined even that evil-tongued woman dumping her at the town gates.

And now, here she is. The baby with the bandaged hands, brought to the farm by a wise-woman in the middle of the night. "A gift from the goddess," Kelya had told them. "You will never tell a soul that she is not the child you bore."

They hadn't. Even in the family, they'd never discussed it. They turned their minds away from the story of the Lady's firstborn daughter who died—Aissa was their own, the child of their hearts. In the years of grieving, Mama has almost forgotten that her little girl hadn't come to her in the normal way.

She remembers it now. There's a thrill of pride that this glowing bull dancer is her own dear Aissa, and a deeper, sadder knowledge. The gods' destiny for this child is much greater than helping to run a small farm in a foreign country.

Mama shows Aissa their land,
their sheep
and what they've made.
Her life is here
and she doesn't want to remember

her life on the island
before the raiders came.
They have a dog already
and she doesn't want a goat
to run with the sheep.
And although she strokes
Aissa's hair,
feeds her the best,
and calls her "Child,"
a sadness lingers
in her eyes.
Aissa feels the emptiness—
it seems that now
she's found her voice
she can't understand
Mama's words;
she cannot believe
Mama is saying
that her heart will always
have room for Aïssa—
but her home
does not.
The world rocks
as if the earthshaker god
has ripped out
the one solid
truth of her life.
"But I've found you!" she wails.
"Stayed silent through the years
just as you told me—

how can you
turn me away now?"
Mama weeps too,
says that the childhood time
of their lives together
is a story of long ago,
wished for and cherished—
but like an outgrown tunic,
it won't fit again.
In this land
the farm belongs to her man,
and though not a slave
Mama is not truly free.
She wants Aissa
to be happy
but her husband's happiness
matters more—
and he can't see
a place for Aissa here.
And Aissa's heart breaks to know
that a bull dancer
can ask for anything
except what she
most wants.
A long hug at sunset—
Aissa still weeping
bittersweet tears
as she leaves Mama's home
for the palace.

But people are waiting
outside, on the road;
the story's been whispered
that a bull dancer's there.
Thronging around her,
they wave and shout,
touch her shoulders,
and give her babies to kiss.
Their fickle love
is for the bull dancer
not the girl who used to be No-Name
and now doesn't know
who she is—
but it fills some
of the emptiness inside her.
She wonders if
like Sunya and Kenzo
she should choose to stay
and dare the bulls
for gold.
Though it's not the life she wants,
flying over a bull
is the greatest thrill
she's ever lived—
she doesn't know
what she'll decide
when the Bull King asks.

The carved bull is still leaping through the wall above the palace gate, just as he was the day Aissa and her shipmates walked up this road. It's hard to imagine that she was ever afraid of him. *I'm a bull dancer now*, she reminds herself. *I don't need to be afraid of anything.*

It doesn't help. She'd happily take back her fear if she could have her hope and dreams again too. Now she's simply too empty to feel.

"The Mother's waiting to see you," says the guard at the gate.

Her stomach tightens—and the nasty voice in her head laughs. *You wanted fear?* it asks. *The Mother knows that you called your friends. Remember what she said would happen if you used your gift in the ring?*

I don't care! Aissa snarls back. *What have I got to live for?*

But she's shaking as she washes the dust from her hands and feet at the font beside the guardhouse, and winds her way through the pillared halls.

The Mother's room is shadowy in the early evening. She's sitting on a low padded chair, the white cat on her lap. The cat ignores Aissa as if it had never slept under her chin, but the Mother studies her quizzically, and laughs.

"You thought you were being called here to be killed—after the gods smiled on you as they did yesterday? I know you used your gift to call your friends, but no more than you could have with a voice."

Aissa's knees go loose with relief. She sinks onto the stool the Mother points at.

"Tell me your story," the Mother says, "now that the goddess has given you back your voice."

Aissa tells it
as best she can:
the imperfect first-born
saved from death
to be given away,
rescued from raiders
by a goat,
only to be
abandoned again.
The spitting and the hate
of being No-Name,
the privy-cleaner;
the outcast living
under the Sanctuary rock;
and then
the goatherds
who'd given her help,
and the wise-women
who treated her as their own
till the earthshaker god killed Nasta
and Aissa
came in her place—
to leap bulls
and find Mama.
The Mother listens,
and hears the bitterness
of what Aissa
doesn't say.
"Finding your foster mama
gave you back your voice

but her home
is no place for you.
If you were any other
I would command,
but you are the Bull Dancer
and the choice is yours:
not only to stay with the bulls
for gold and glory,
or return to the island
where you were despised—
but to serve the goddess here
as the priestess
you were born to be."
Aissa breathes in
the scent of lilies
in this pretty, painted room;
sees the fields and mountain
from the window
and knows she might
be happy here.
But telling her story
has told her too
how much she longs
for Kelya and Roula,
Lanni the goatherd,
and her own wild land.
"I'm going home—
and hope the wise-women
will let me serve them
as before."

28

THE LADY OF THE BULLS

The ship leaping
under its red sail
is not at all like
a butterfly on the waves—
more like a dolphin,
like the ones playing
all around them.
The sailors say
dolphins are good luck,
they've never seen so many,
they say it's Aissa's singing—
even though
she sings so quietly,
still practicing
what her voice can do.
Luki and Aissa see their island
rising from the sea,
bringing tears to Luki's eyes

and Aissa's too
though she didn't know
she loved it:
from cliffs and cove
to snow-capped mountain,
and green hills between.
As if she can sing it
closer, faster
her voice flies free
and from the sky
three eagles come
to circle the ship,
swooping and diving
above the dolphins.
Luki wears his bull-dancing shorts,
for climbing
up and down from the ship;
Aissa too, on the days of voyage,
but now the island
is in sight
she puts on her skirt
flounced in bright colors,
her jacket of embroidered linen,
sandals of the softest leather—
and they both wear
their gifts of gold and jewels
bright on their chests,
their wrists, and hair.
As a parting gift,
Aissa's priestess friends

gave her pots
of kohl and rouge;
and the Mother gave her
a small bronze mirror
and a comb of bone.
So now she paints her eyes and mouth—
offering the paints to Luki
though he says no—
and replaits her hair,
blowing in the salt wind
as the young eagle dives low
and a feather drifts down
to hold firm in the plait.
Luki, impatient
to touch the island,
leaps from the deck
as the sailors splash in
to drag the ship to the shore.
He clutches a handful of sand,
bringing it to
his heart in praise.
The waiting people
already starting to wail their loss,
explode into joy
as they see that it's Luki,
a year older,
taller
and dressed like a stranger—
but safely home.
They can barely believe
that the island is free;

that this year's dancers,
running home from the Hall
for their last precious day,
won't be leaving
to dance and die.
No one even thinks of Aissa,
No-Name,
the bad-luck child,
taking the place of chosen Nasta—
no hope of surviving
and nothing to mourn.
Though they are curious
to see the young woman
leap from the ship
to the sand
in her fine colored skirt,
and a whisper races
from fishers to Hall
that the Lady of the bulls
has come with the ship
to honor victorious Luki.
Part of Aissa longs
to be adored like Luki
with people flocking to touch him,
weeping with joy—
but at least
no one spits.
She remembers when
that was her greatest wish:
now that it's happened,
it's not enough.

"And Aissa," Luki shouts,
    but the people have never
    heard Aissa's name
    and don't understand.
The crowd drifts them up
    toward the Hall,
    dancing, singing,
    all around Luki,
    keeping their distance
    from the captain and crew
    and the elegant priestess.
The Lady and the chief
    stand in the courtyard to greet them
    kissing Luki
    on the top of his head
    before saluting
    the captain and Aissa;
    the captain wonders
    why she's not welcomed like the boy,
    but gives his greetings
    from the Bull King,
    saying the gods have honored him
    with the return of their dancers
    and that from now on
    the island will be free of raiders
    and of tributes.
The Lady is confused:
    the tall guard translates
    "dancers"
    as if there were two.

But she's more surprised
that the Lady of the bulls
leaves the captain to speak.
Calling servants
for food and drink
the Lady leads them to the Hall,
the people still crowding,
cheering, and laughing,
only the potter wailing—
the island's freedom
comes too late for her daughter.
The guards hustle her away
but Aissa crosses,
touches her shoulder:
"Your daughter serves
the bull land's Lady,
alive and well."
The potter drops to her knees
kissing the hem
of Aissa's skirt,
never knowing
it's the child she cursed.
And now
the cats come:
Milli-Cat and her grown-up kittens,
with tails like flags
weaving their way
through to Aissa—
the only ones to see
or welcome her home.

Gold-Cat leaps to her shoulder
and purrs into her ear
while the rest twine around her legs,
and the surprised Lady says,
"Our beasts welcome you, too,"
showing her to a seat
between her own
and Fila's.
Fila pale and ill,
a bruise swelling
across her cheek—
angry red marks
from the bite of a snake.
Then Aissa's belly clenches,
because Half-Two
stands before her
offering a platter
of sweet cakes and fig,
eyes downcast,
not looking like
Half-Two at all.
Aissa takes a fig
just so she'll leave
but the girl stands
as if she's forgotten
what she's doing
till Squint-Eye shouts,
"Half-Dead! Get out
of the Lady's way."
Fila seeing
Aissa watching

says, "She's called Half-Dead
because she and her sister
were one and the same
but her sister died
so now this one's half dead."
Anger like lightning
flashes through Aissa—
though she never knew
her heart had room for the twins.
If I were the Lady
no one would ever
be called No-Name
or Half-Dead.
Even a slave deserves a name!
But it will never matter
what she thinks.
Luki is talking to the guards and the chief;
he points at Aissa,
but the Lady doesn't notice.
"I have never," she says,
"met a priestess from another land.
I would be honored
if you would speak in private
with me and my wise-women
and my daughter,
since it seems
you can speak our tongue."
Aissa, wondering
how to tell the Lady
that she's not a foreign priestess

but the Lady's own
discarded daughter,
follows to the private chambers
that she's never seen,
beyond the private bathroom
where she shouldn't have been.
The chamber
is just a room
not as grand or bright
as the one she'd shared
with her priestess friends—
though the best in this Hall—
and it makes her think
that maybe the Lady
is just a woman
doing the best she can.
The wise-women enter,
Kelya leaning on Roula,
Lyra and Lena behind—
and at their gasps,
Kelya reaches to touch her face.
"Child!" she cries,
delighted tears
leaking from blind eyes
and Aissa wants
to kiss her hands
but is not sure
what she can do or say
with the Lady here.
And the Lady, her mother,
still doesn't understand.

"The oracle is clear,"
she says,
"the dolphins' joy for the dancer's return;
the young eagle marking
this Lady for us—
can it be
that the greatness foretold
is not one of our own
but this priestess
of the bulls?"
"Not one of our own?" says Kelya.
"But Lady,
can you not see?"

The Lady looks, but she still can't see. Does Kelya mean that the Lady of the bulls is the baby she'd sent to die at birth? The scrawny, fear-haunted child who chose her lottery shard with such care? She can feel that long triangular—*dragonfly-shaped!*—shard under her fingers now. But it was impossible that the cringing No-Name could ever be the great one the oracle had predicted—she'd rejected it and chosen another shard: Nasta, who seemed destined for greatness.

And when the gods had laughed and twisted the pattern again, killing Nasta and moving Aissa, the wise-women's server, to take her place, she'd been so sure that Aissa couldn't succeed that she refused to think about her. She'd grieved enough sending her to die the first time. Learning that the baby had not only survived but was living right under her nose, in the most squalid, degrading life possible, was too much to bear. All she could do was try to wipe Kelya's admission from her mind and forget those few short moments of knowing her own daughter before sending her to an almost certain death. The daughter that she doesn't know well enough to recognize face to face.

She's always tried to obey the gods, but they've hidden their plans well.

Goddess! she thinks, *if this is my daughter, send me a sign!*

Aissa wondering—
    under the Lady's stare—
    if it's safe to speak;
    to ask in her new-found voice
    if she can return
    to live and work
    with the wise-women—
    and how much
    of her gifts of gold
    she needs to offer her mother
    for that permission.
The Lady stares on
    till Aissa looks down,
    and spies a small snake,
    a viper,
    coiling under Fila's stool—
    Fila sees it too,
    screams in fear,
    jumps onto her stool

waving her arms
and nearly falling.
The Lady pales
but her voice is stopped—
she's asked for a sign
and cannot prevent
what the goddess wills.
Aissa has not asked for a sign
and she has seen
too much death—
she sings the snake,
her voice high and clear
till the viper slides
under a crack in the wall.
The wise-women and the Lady
freeze with shock,
and Fila
falls off her stool.
"Aissa!" says Kelya.
"You found your voice!"
"Aissa?" says the Lady.
"My imperfect,
firstborn child?"
She takes Aissa's hands,
studying the small white scars
till Aissa's rage burns bright
and her voice comes loud.
"My hands were strong enough
to win with the bulls
and free the island

from the pain of tribute.
The gods of the bull land
cared for what I did
and not my scars."
"The gods of this land too,"
says the Lady,
"but I didn't understand."
"If I'm not firstborn," says Fila,
"no wonder I
could never sing."
"The snakes always knew,"
the Lady says sadly,
"as I knew that you
were too gentle to rule;
it's clear that your gifts
are with herbs and healing."
Anger flares in Aissa again
because Fila
has had everything:
beauty and kindness,
all the love she could want—
now she's going to be
a wise-woman too
and there will be
no room for Aissa.
"I'll return with the ship,"
says Aissa,
"find my place
as a priestess in the palace
or a dancer with the bulls."

"Your place is here," says Kelya—
and how can Aissa say no
to old Kelya who loves her—
but she cannot stay
where she isn't needed.
The Lady lifts
Aissa's hands again
and kisses the scars.
"The goddess's plan
has been harsh but clear—
you are the one
who will sing the snakes
and the sun to rise,
when I am old
and it's time for the firstborn
to rule in her turn."
But in this land
Aissa is No-Name,
the cursed child,
the bad-luck girl
and her fear is greater
than facing the bull—
she doesn't want
to be a slave,
spat at or stoned—
but to be the Lady
is too giant a leap.
Then she remembers her anger
for all the No-Names,
the not-perfect,

unwanted,
those denied a voice;
the boys who can never own land,
no matter how they care for it.
Only a ruler
can sing those changes.
She looks into
the Lady's face
as if she is
just a woman she knows
like Mama
or Kelya
or Mia—
and sees her own tears
reflected in
her mother's eyes.
"I will stay,"
says Aissa,
bowing her head
for her mother's kiss.
The Lady leads her
out to the Hall,
and Luki calls:
"Aissa the dragonfly,
bull dancer,
snake singer,
home at last,
where she belongs."
No words
to say what she feels,
so Aissa sings—

sings of the girl
who lost her fear
and found her voice
when she faced death
on the horns of a bull,
and now is ready
to face her life.
Her voice floats clear
through the square and town,
singing the people
who stop what they're doing
to stand before her
with hands on heart.

About the Author

Wendy Orr was born in Edmonton, Canada, but grew up in various places across Canada, France, and the USA. She studied occupational therapy in the UK, married an Australian farmer, and moved to Australia. She's the author of many award-winning books, including *Nim's Island*, *Nim at Sea*, *Rescue on Nim's Island*, *Raven's Mountain*, and *Peeling the Onion*.

Wendy has always been fascinated by the Aegean Bronze Age. Doodling on a finger-paint app in 2010, she sketched a dark, curly-haired girl with a twisted mouth, and knew that she had to find this unhappy girl's story. The plot and Aissa's fictitious island formed as Wendy researched and read, but the story was sparked to life by serendipitous, seemingly unrelated events, such as finding a piece of chipped flint on a Danish beach, and taking a wrong turn and ending up at the extraordinary deep blue Source de la Sorgue in France. Most mysteriously, every time that she made a significant decision or discovery about the story, Wendy saw a dragonfly the following day…

Also by Wendy Orr

Nim's Island
Nim at Sea
Rescue on Nim's Island
The Rainbow Street Animal Shelter series
Raven's Mountain
Mokie & Bik
Spook's Shack
Peeling the Onion